THE GONDOLA SCAM

'Right, then,' I said. 'Venice.'

He smiled with a gleam in his eye. 'Venice. If you saw a lorry carrying a small parcel containing a Verzelini drinking glass accidentally slewed over the wall of the Chelmer canal, what would you do?'

I thought, sensing a trick. Verzelini was a Murano glassmaker from Venice who made it to Good Queen Bess's London and turned out richly valuable Venetian-style glass in his little City factory until late 1590s. A single glass nowadays would give you enough to retire on. Well, in for a penny . . . 'Okay, I'd try to save it.'

'Now. Supposing that Verzelini glass, in its precarious parcel, was multiplied a million times.'

'Well, yes. But there's less than a dozen Verzelini glasses knocking around. And Venice isn't a parcel on a lorry.'

Grandad smiled then, his face like crumpled kitchen foil. 'All Venice's art can be made into such parcels, Lovejoy. And it is certainly about to fall into water, Lovejoy.'

I thought about that. 'You mean . . .?'

'Piecemeal.'

THE
GONDOLA SCAM

A Lovejoy narrative

Jonathan Gash

CLASSIC CRIME

Hamlyn Paperbacks

A Hamlyn Paperback

Published by Arrow Books Limited
17-21 Conway Street, London W1P 6JD

A division of the Hutchinson Publishing Group

London Melbourne Sydney Auckland
Johannesburg and agencies throughout
the world

First published in Great Britain 1984
by William Collins Sons and Co. Ltd
Hamlyn Paperbacks edition 1985

© Jonathan Gash 1984

Printed and bound in Great Britain by
Anchor Brendon Limited, Tiptree, Essex

ISBN 0 09 936720 3

scam (skam) *n.slang*. A fraudulent scheme, especially
one for making money quickly.

Oxford American Dictionary, Oxford University Press,
Oxford (1980)

CHAPTER 1

Usually people say women come first. Other times it's money, survival, anger, ambition. But deep down it's none of these delectables.

It's antiques.

Antiques are everything. First, last, every single thing. For ever and ever.

Fingers tapped on the table, regular as a metronome. *Dup, dup* they went. And the price rose in tens with each tap from the ring of dealers. *Dup*. Ten. *Dup*. Plus ten. *Dup*. Another ten. And another and another. My face felt white.

Ever been on tenterhooks for nothing? Think of an illegal auction in a seedy upstairs pub room. No public, only a ring of hard grubby antique dealers tapping on the table, watching through the fag smoke with crinkled eyes. Not an antique in sight. Ten blokes and two birds all bidding in utter silence for a painting, with the pub yard and the taproom below heaving like anglers' bait. And me, mouth dry and chest thumping, wishing the whole sordid mess would simply go away. I tell you, this antique game seems quiet and contented—from the outside. Inside, it's horrendous, utterly crazy. I was frightened and fuming.

The genuine auction had ended half an hour ago. The merry old public—that shoal of piranhas—were either celebrating hilariously in the boozer or crawling home in tears according to their degrees of success at today's bidding. Up here, the real business of the day was being done: the closed ring auction of dealers illegally re-auctioning among themselves the items they'd bought a few minutes before.

Dup. My player tapped again, the maniac, though I'd told him no. Five antique dealers had dropped out and now sat sulking. That left seven, including Linda from Tolleshunt. And that lovely ash blonde who seemed so determined. Then there was Sam Wiltshire, he of the merry jokes, supposedly bidding for himself. There was Big Frank from Suffolk, with wives and gelt to spare and antique silver always on his mind—he gets married like other blokes go to the races, meaning to say frequently and never quite sure of the outcome. Then a hoary old dealer from Salford I didn't know but who was taking all this silent bidding in his stride, kippering us all with a dustbin of a pipe. Instead of tapping, his finger nudged a little electronic print-out calculator, a neat way of anticipating the arguments which often happen after the dealers' ring 'knocks down'—stops at the highest bid. He had sense. Jasper Coke (his real name, incidentally) was also keeping in but gradually losing impetus. He's a cheerful square-shaped bloke with a shop somewhere down the sea estuary, supposedly expert in porcelain and Georgian household furniture. That only means he's thick as a plank, because antique dealers always are, though rumour has it Jasper can actually read and write.

That leaves only my player, the goon I was mad at. Mr Malleson was pretty well-known from his 'sweeps' through East Anglia in search of antiques for his London show-room. When he has any doubt, he simply hires somebody like me for a day or so. A sound rule, you might think.

'Call up,' he said at that point. I could have kicked him, almost groaned aloud. 'Five.'

The old Salford geezer thumbed his calculator to increase by fifteens now instead of tens. Malleson tapped the table, and round the morons went, *dup, dup.* Only this time Linda lifted a flat hand, the sign of dropping out. I was glad, because I've a soft spot for Linda. We

once got up to no good together in Norwich after selling a
Gantz watercolour of Madras, genuine early 1820s. (His
paintings in the past three years have soared in value since
the greetings-card people discovered them; if you pass
one up, don't say you weren't warned.) She carefully
avoided my eye (she often does) but must have caught a
vibe of my impotent rage. That luscious blonde sitting
directly opposite my idiotic player was still in there,
tighter lips though and increasingly bitter about something. Pretty as the picture we were bidding for—a
million times more authentic. I'd twice told my player,
the duckegg, that the painting was a fake, but he knew
best like all lunatics. Now he was well on the way to losing
a fortune. Serve the silly sod right.

Sam Wiltshire folded, both palms flat, cracking, 'A
Carpaccio oil sketch just can't be worth nine whole
pence.' He got a wan smile from Jasper Coke, who was
already out of his depth and dropped out next round.
The blonde fingered her pearls (real, a risky baroque
single string) and tapped. Three left.

Malleson, still knowing best, tapped.

The Salford dealer took some snuff, varoomed droplets
over us all and tapped. I was practically screaming inside.

'Call up, five.' The blonde did a complicatedly casual
ritual with powder compact and mirror. It entailed a lot
of lip play, and was watched with fascination by almost
all. Even the morose dealers huddled in the corner
stopped grumbling and admired her. Linda sardonically
lit a fag and walked to the window to show she thought
the blonde was a scheming bitch. You now had to bid on
in twenties. Old Salford disgustedly clicked his calculator
off, raising a palm.

Two left.

'Call up to twenty-five,' Malleson said calmly. My name
would be mud after this lark.

The picture they were after was a clear fraud. Some

mauler had tried to fake that complicated bit of gear from Carpaccio's *Knight In A Landscape* which they guard so carefully in Lugano, with enough grounding to suggest his authentic brushwork. Nice attempt, but done by some soulless cretin, doubtless with a string of diplomas to show how 'expert' he was. Pathetic.

'Call up, five,' the blonde said, which made even the hard drinkers freeze. Bids now in thirties. Disconcertingly, I found the bird's eyes on me. *Stop your man*, her lovely eyes signalled, stop him because he's a fool. I reddened. I don't need birds telling me that, but what could I do? Malleson was big money. I didn't have two pennies to rub together. As usual.

'Call up, five,' said my player, the world's expert knowall. The maniac had raised the bidding to steps of thirty-five quid. I almost fainted. He'd gone bid-happy, that weird state of compulsion in which you'll bid to any level, for any old piece of tat. It happens. I once saw two women go bid-happy, stunning a whole mob of dealers into a dazed silence while they duelled for a Woolworth chair off a junk-heap. It's a very dangerous state to get yourself into, because you just can't — *can't* — stop.

A hand on my shoulder pressed me down. I'd actually reached for Mr Malleson's neck in my blind rage.

'Want a drink, Lovejoy?'

'Eh?' My gaze cleared. Linda had come to stand close, and was smiling calming messages into my face. Some dealer snickered at my name. Some friend interested in his welfare quickly shushed him.

'A drink.' Linda held up her own glass to prove nourishment was available on the premises.

'Er, no, ta.' I jerked my shoulder away to see the blonde spread her palm. It was over. The bird had spotted that Mr Malleson had gone bid-happy, and ducked out.

He turned and glanced at me, proud as a peacock. The London dealer immediately got his tabs out — addressed

IOU blanks. There was a flurry as scribbled IOUs changed hands.

'Hurry up. Next item's Lot Seventy,' Sam Wiltshire said. 'Who got it?'

'I did.' Jasper Coke pulled a face as somebody muttered the price. 'That early monk's chair. Genuine.' Genuine all right, I thought, in a sulk. Only, a wooden armchair which has a rectangular back that hinges over to form a small table resting horizontally on the chair's arms is called a chair-table, or a 'table-chairwise'. We dealers call it a monk's chair (a fairly modern, invented name like 'grandfather clock') to put mediæval flavour into the price-tag. I caught Jasper's eye and he had the grace to give a wry smile.

'Okay,' Sam said, grinning. He always acts as auctioneer. 'Start at ten, up in twos.' He tapped the table and they were off again.

'Cheers,' I said, clearing out.

'Oh, Lovejoy,' warbled my erstwhile player, but I was heading for the bar downstairs. If he didn't want to listen to me, he was beyond hope.

I got my pint after a bayonet charge through the mob of dealers and paid for Tinker's pint to be sent into the taproom. The filthy old devil gave me a gappy grin through the bar hatch but it quickly changed to consternation when I gave him the bent eye. He eeled into the porch.

'What's up, Lovejoy? We in trouble?'

'The goon bought it.'

He goggled, wiped his stubble in a tattered sleeve. 'Christ. An' you let him?'

'What the hell could I do? He's in the ring, not me.'

There are two good things about Tinker. He's the world's best barker—slang for antiques finder—and he stinks to high heaven. The first is great because I'm Tinker's wally, the antique dealer he finds for. The second is great because his pong clears a space in any crowd, so I can pay for more beer. Like now.

'He must be off his friggin' nut, Lovejoy.' He hitched his frayed ex-army greatcoat and shook his head, mystified. 'He know you was a divvie?'

'That's why he hired me, you burke.'

'Here, Lovejoy.' Grinning, he plucked at my arm with his grease-stained mitten. 'I'd like to be there when them London buyers tell him it's a fake.' He fell about at the notion, cackling evilly.

'Everybody'll think I guessed wrong,' I grumbled.

'Nar,' Tinker said scornfully, grabbing another ale. 'Every dealer in East Anglia knows you.'

'Everybody but Malleson. Where is she, Tinker?'

'Your bint? By the fire.' He took the note I slipped him. 'I reckon she's makin' for 'flu, Lovejoy. She only has orange juice.'

Even fuming, I had to laugh at that. The thought of anybody drinking an orange's crushed innards makes him giddy. I told him, 'Be in the boozer eightish. Find out who vans off that Yankee silver salver, and if that Tadolini *Venus and Cupid* changes hands before tonight.'

'Right, mate.'

The rare Edward Winslow salver was a delight, made in Boston about 1695. The illicit ring upstairs would bid for it soon. I had to know who eventually owned it because that's where tomorrow's fakes would come from. It was worth a couple of new cars in anybody's shop window. The Tadolini figure was as beautiful, but only 1845 or so and about a quarter of the price. Rome always did nice stuff, with or without an empire.

Sure enough Connie was there, scrunged up over the pub's log fire. She's always perished, even in the hottest bed.

'Darling. At last.' She reached up to my hand. 'It's so

draughty here. Can we go?'

'Bring my bag.'

We sliced the fug and reached the great beyond where my zoomster waited hub-deep in its flaking rust.

'Why *do* we carry this stupid thing, darling?' Connie indicated the plastic bag. It carried Christie's insignia, 1766, South Kensington.

'To impress customers.'

If her teeth hadn't been chattering from the cold she would have screamed with laughter. She just muttered, 'In this ancient open boat?' and climbed in. Lovely legs.

'You can always walk,' I countered, flipping the switch and going round to crank the handle. It's an old Austin Ruby. People are always trying to nick its candle-powered headlamps and door handles. Connie gets mad because it has no top roof, and the cover doesn't work.

A young bloke nearby laughed, disconcertingly shrill. He was in one of those de Loreans and seemed all fawns and yellows. I shrugged, deciding not to take offence. His lemon leathers could have bought and sold me. I tend not to argue with wealthy dealers because they're the dumbest. Just to prove it, a familiar if irritating voice sounded in my earhole.

'A word, Lovejoy.' Good old knowledgeable wiseacre Mr Malleson had caught us up and stood there in his posh gaberdine. 'Good day, Mrs Lovejoy,' he added, eyeing Connie. I didn't mind that because you can't help looking long and hard at Connie.

'A friend,' I corrected quickly, in case she developed a craving.

'Excuse us, please,' he said with courtesy. I could tell he was frosty. 'Lovejoy. I wanted you for the Flemish marquetry cabinet the northern dealer was putting in the ring. The one with the metallic-paint effect.'

'It's genuine.' I'd told him this a hundred times, but London antique dealers are as thick as those from anywhere else. And, after today's performance, maybe thicker. 'Antwerp, say 1670, 1680. And while we're at it, that metallic paint is chip mother-of-pearl.'

'I failed,' he said, stone-faced. 'The bidding went quite extraordinary after you left—'

'Almost as if the others were ganging up?'

'That's right. I'm not blaming you, Lovejoy—'

'No, Mr Malleson. But *I'm* blaming *you*.' I gave the handle a savage crank and the engine spluttered obediently. If it hadn't I'd have kicked it to bits, the temper I was in.

'Me? Why?' The duckegg was honestly amazed. I ask you.

'You hired me to suss out genuine antiques, right?'

'Of course. You have the reputation of being a divvie. A very valuable gift.'

'Which means I can *feel* genuine antiques, right?'

My car door falls off if you pull the handle, so I stepped over the door and slid behind the wheel.

'Well, yes. That's the supposition, Lovejoy.'

'Not supposition. Truth. I tipped you that painting is modern phoney, and you still bought it.'

'That was your opinion, Lovejoy.'

'Wrong, Mr Malleson.' My frost was at least as cold as his. 'A divvie just *knows*. That's very, very different from a mere opinion.'

'I see. Offended pride.' He gave one of his wintry smiles, clearly the London zillionaire dealer coping with troublesome provincial riff-raff. 'Tell me, Lovejoy. Are you an expert on formalisms in Tiepolo's composition?'

'No.'

'Canvas microscopy? Spectrographic analysis of paint? Chemicals?' He went mercilessly down a formidable list, getting a denial every time. 'It may interest you to know, Lovejoy, that I am an expert on all those topics. And there's one other proof.' He eyed me and my zoomster.

'The fact is you are threadbare, frayed, generally ill-attired and clearly subnourished. Your obsolete car is falling apart. I, on the other hand, have the best from each year's motor show. Three London tailors work very hard to please me. Do I make my point?'

'You'll not be the first expert art dealer I've visited in clink, Mr Malleson,' I said evenly, and gunned my half-pint engine as a hint. 'Sell that fake, and Scotland Yard's fraud squad'll come peering in your window.'

He was examining me curiously. 'You're so sure?'

'There's no question. That gunge was painted this side of Easter.'

He smiled a disbelieving smile and pulled out a bolster-sized wallet. 'We can only agree to disagree, then. Here's half your fee.'

The sight of the notes he held out made my heart fill with longing but to my horror I felt my stupid head shake. My voice said, 'No, thanks, Mr Malleson. I won't help you defraud yourself.'

The engine wheezed and the little Ruby trundled off leaving him standing there. A couple of dealers cheered derisorily and Linda gave me a wave from the saloon bar's window. I saw the ash blonde by that elegant lemon-tinted customed de Lorean. She must have heard every word. As we clattered out on to the main Edmundsbury road Crampie tried flagging me down. His real name's Cramphorn, but with a name like Lovejoy you learn discrimination at an early age.

'Can't stop, Crampie,' I bawled over my engine's din. 'On my way to a deal.'

'Get stuffed, Lovejoy,' he yelled back. 'Thought you were in a Rolls-Royce, not a sewing-machine.'

'Lovejoy!' Connie was scandalized. 'He's your dealer friend! You can't leave him standing in the cold wind.'

Honestly. People are so innocent. Ben Cramphorn's a roadman — that is, he procures lifts pretending he's on his way to buy his poor dying friend's priceless antique. His 'poor dying friend' is fit as a flea because it's his partner Phil Watmore, made up to look ailing. The 'priceless' antique is any old chunk of dross they can't sell. The aim is to get the kindly motorist interested in buying the antique and driving to Phil's auntie's house in Wivenhoe, which is the place they usually work from, seeing she pays the rates, rent and all other costs. Sounds very dicey, doesn't it? Surprising how often it works.

'You're awful, Lovejoy!' Connie was fuming.

'I'll tell Ken you said that.' He's Connie's husband. They own this small chain of shops, shoes or something.

'Where's the heater on this thing, Lovejoy?' That's the best about Connie. Predictability. Her thoughts never leave temperature for long. 'Is there no way we can stop this terrible gale? Take your hand off my knee.'

'I'll stop for a hot-water bottle,' I said.

'Will you, darling?' she said eagerly. 'That's a good idea.'

I glared at her, marvelling. There she sat, hair streaming in the wind, slender throat deep in her mohair, eyes sparkling, luscious lips moist, eyes dazzling. As exciting a picture of beauty as ever a woman can be, and still she takes a sardonic crack as gospel.

She put her arm through mine. 'I hated Mr Malleson. He has no right to speak to you like that. Even if you do look a mess I love you, darling.'

'Er, thanks, love,' I said. Sometimes women baffle me. We pulled in this dark lay-by because I was getting desperate. Only a woman can rub out the toxic anger of a failure such as I'd endured, and Connie regarded sex on the move as vulgarity gone mad.

Which is how we came within a few seconds of seeing the whole terrible thing.

My old crate, wheezing and panting, was waiting to get back on the road—no mean feat, this, because it was uphill at the lay-by's re-entry point — when a limousine cruised out of the darkness behind its great headlights, and I recognized it as Mr Malleson's.

'How lovely!' Connie cried. 'He gave Mr Cramphorn a lift, Lovejoy.'

'Shut up.'

I too had glimpsed two figures in the car. Narked at being reminded yet again of my stupendous failure at the ring auction, I trundled us out clattering into the slipstream. So Crampie was working his antiques scam on Mr Malleson. I wished him luck. The rate my old Ruby trundles, it would be a good hour before I reached my cottage, where Connie would raise me to paradise and send the memory of this catastrophic day into an oblivion it richly deserved.

It was to be a lot longer.

CHAPTER 2

'Stop, Lovejoy! Please!'

'What for?'

'It's Mr Malleson's car! With the police!'

East Anglia becomes a desert of country darkness after dusk. Those roadside cafés are oases of light in the pitch night, because we lack those natty road lamps which make towns so wonderful.

'No.'

'Please! You *must*, Lovejoy! Your friends are in trouble.'

Nothing's so poisonous as a woman bent on Doing Good. These days nobody in their right mind stops at these lonely road noshbars. And you especially don't when those irritable blue lamps are blinking ghoulishly from ambulances and police cars. I tried explaining that yobbos had probably nicked some dealer's antiques from his car—par for the course, really—but Connie turned ugly.

'No love, then, Lovejoy.'

She didn't really mean it, couldn't in fact, and she knew it. But what she did know was that her threat would make me dispirited. I tend to lose heart easily. Teachers at school used to call me spineless but never taught me out of it. I applied the brake—note that singular—and my Ruby contemplated itself to a dawdling stop, drifting sideways as its one block persuasively caressed its feeble motive power into clattering idleness.

'Come *on!*' Connie was already out and trotting back towards the lights. Miserably I followed, cursing. My instincts were drive on with every erg my rusty old zoomster could generate.

Two ambulances hurtled out in tandem, nearly flattening Connie and me. Several bored police constables were hanging about. A few lorry-drivers chatted and exchanged cigarettes, eyeing Connie as we entered the ring of lights on the forecourt.

It was a typical roadside caff. Low hut, depleted neon sign, a few multicoloured bulbs on trailed flex, dark trees crowding in beyond. A few parked lorries, one or two ordinary cars. Mr Malleson's car was prominently agape nearby. Connie, with all the tact of a Stuka, rushed into the fray squealing questions. By the time I came up the whole world knew that Mr Malleson and Crampie had been rushed to hospital. Connie has a habit of repeating in a shrill cry any answers she gets.

'Before you start, Mr Ledger,' I said to the older of the two CID men, 'I must caution you that anything you say will be taken down and flatly contradicted by my alibi.'

'Lovejoy.' He's not a bad old nerk, as cretins go, but we've never got on. Not because he has this unshakable belief that I'm a villain, but because I have this unshakable belief that he's a bigger one. 'Where were you?'

I walked on past while Connie squealed yet more questions. The lorry-drivers, six or seven, were being questioned in turn by a constable with a tape-recorder. The space age. I selected a squat, canny little bloke who'd obviously got fed up and was sitting on his lorry's running-board.

'One of them was my mate,' I said, sitting by him.

'Oh, aye?' Rossendale accent, clean-shaven, tidy. A family man keen on simply polishing off his congealed egg-and-chips and roaring off northwards.

'See much?'

'Not really. There were four or so. Three heavies and a girlish bloke in a bright suit. Sports car, but I didn't see it. Only heard it go beyond the hedge. Stocking masks. A little van.' He spat expertly. 'They drove it across the frigging intersection.'

Smart, that. It was illegal, so nobody could legally give chase.

'Were they bad?'

'Sorry, mate.' He shook his head. 'They both looked poorly, especially the scruff who came in to phone.' He meant Crampie, doing his road trick. 'The city gent was waiting in the car. We heard the hullabaloo. Me and my mate come running and chucked stones, but the buggers were gone. Yon bobby says they pinched a picture.'

'A painting?'

'God knows.' He looked at me, offering a cigarette. I lit up as politeness, though I don't smoke them. I'm in enough trouble. 'Here, lad. If you're going after them I'd watch yon pansy bloke. He clobbered both your mates after his mob had emptied the car. A wrench.'

'Ta, mate.' I rose. 'Regards to the Duchy.'

His face lit in a smile. 'Go careful.'

More common sense in two minutes than you'd get in a

thousand years at university. If only I'd listened to the man.

'Come on, love,' I said to Connie, not pausing. ' 'Night, Ledger.'

'Lovejoy. Where were you when—?'

Connie trotted after, holding her coat round herself as tightly as she could in the night wind. 'That was very rude of you, Lovejoy.'

'Darlin',' I said. 'It's very rude of Ledger to let Crampie and Mr Malleson get done in a crash-wallop. So criticize me second, not first.'

'Some men stole all Mr Malleson's things! Did you hear? And Inspector Ledger's police cars are already searching for the culprits!' She was in raptures at how wonderful our police were.

'Cheapest way of getting antiques,' I said cruelly. 'And the safest. Get in.'

We got to the hospital in Black Notley a few minutes too late, though I don't suppose Crampie would have been able to tell us anything. He was unconscious for his last moments. When I came out after seeing the house surgeon Connie said the police cars had just pulled away.

Connie pulled her overcoat tight round her lovely knees. 'It's freezing. Did you see Crampie?'

'Crampie just died, love. Mr Malleson was dead when they got here.'

'Darling. I'm so sorry. That little man we didn't even give a lift . . . ?' Tears filled her and she wept.

It wasn't any use explaining that Crampie'd not even have accepted a lift from me even if I'd offered him one. Anyway, I was becoming exhausted explaining every little problem to hangers-on. I sat listening to her sniffing, watching the nurses and sisters move beyond the Casualty glass and the tired young house surgeon slumping over the desk writing up case-notes. All their training, all their

labour over Mr Malleson and Crampie, had been a
gigantic waste.

'Help me, Connie, love.'

My voice must have given something away. She blotted
herself dry and nodded.

'Ready.'

Connie may have cold blood, but she sees things I
don't. I drove us back to my cottage, talking all the while
and explaining my slight problem. Why would certain
dealers bid themselves almost into poverty for a fake, and
antique thieves pull a raid for that same fake? Worse, at
least one of them had found a sadistic glee in needlessly
making murder.

Hours later we were still going over the lorry-driver's
story, the pansified bloke in the lemon-tinted suit, the
events at the auction.

Getting on for seven we were lying in bed at my
cottage.

To feed us, Connie had knocked up a soup thing in my
little kitchen alcove, and did something called goulash. It
had been good, but I was narked with her for throwing
my last pasty out. She claimed it wasn't fresh, bloody
cheek. Apart from these visits from enthusiasts like
Connie, pasties are my staple fare and seeing my last
pasty get the sailor's elbow was disheartening. It was a
sign that my days of wine and roses were over. Locusts
would soon settle on the land of Lovejoy Antiques, Inc. I
was about to be spring-cleaned.

'You should have taken Mr Malleson's money.' Connie
was propped on one elbow, her lovely skin glowing and
her smooth breast cool against my face. 'You earned it.'

'Accepting payment means I'd be responsible for him,
the goon.'

'You shouldn't speak ill of the . . .' She shivered and
caped the bedclothes round her shoulders. She hadn't

understood the mysticism of the secret auction ring of the antique dealers, so I had to explain.

Auctions have been around a long time but have changed very little. Oh, we don't any longer do like in Ancient Rome—stick a spear, the famous *hasta publica*, upright in the market square to show one's about to begin—but we do more or less the same as in Pliny the Elder's day. But be careful. There are different kinds.

Everybody knows the common or 'English' auction where the bidders' prices start off low and simply go up a notch with each bid. However there's also a 'Dutch' auction, where the auctioneer starts at a high price, and then calls out ever-lower prices, until a bidder stutters out that he's willing to pay that much. And there's the so-called market auction, where you bid merrily, English-style, but for *one* representative sample of a particular lot, and where you needn't accept more than that one at the price you've successfully bid. Market-style auctions are pretty rare in antiques, except where there's a whole batch of stuff which the auctioneer's willing to split, say a load of old desks, plates, chairs, cutlery and so on. Then there's a 'time' auction, where you get a length of time to *complete* (not start, note) your bidding. The most famous example of this is that French wine auction business, where anybody can carry on bidding anything—for as long as the auctioneer's candle-stub stays lit. It's a real cliff-hanger, because the bidding ends the exact instant the guttering candle snuffs. And there's the famous 'paper' auction, where the auctioneer announces a price below which he won't go, and bidders have numbered or named cards. You simply write down your bid, and the slips are collected by minions. Antique dealers hate this, because it calls for frankness and honesty, probably why it's going out of fashion.

Yes, it pays to suss out the rules governing the particular auction you wish to attend. It might prevent you going broke. But auction risks don't end there. There's the new-fangled cheque trick (bid high, pay the 10% deposit immediately by cheque, try to sell the item for a fast profit that day—and, if you can't, just stop the cheque claiming all sorts of false catalogue description). There's the 'knock-out', where antique dealers resort to any trick to impede or con the public out of bids. There's even evil in some auctioneers themselves (Lord save us!), their assistants, vannies, valuers, clerks, experts and, last and most, the public. We don't have state-owned auction-rooms like the Dorotheum in Vienna, and I'm quite glad about that. 'At least in our system roguery is predictable and perennial,' I told Connie. 'I'd hate it to be legal too.'

Connie thought the ring auction a lot of pointless trouble. 'Why auction among yourselves if you've just already bought them?'

'The dealers all agree not to bid at the public auction. Only one dealer bids. So the price is lower, right? Then the dealers gather in a pub and have their private little auction. The difference in Gimbert's price and the ring's price is the profit, and is shared out. See?'

Connie was outraged. 'But that's not fair!' she cried.

I pulled her down and inevitably her perishing cold feet climbed inchwise up my legs.

'I know that. But the first-ever successful prosecution for an illicit auction ring was in 1981. It's hopeless.'

She forgot the draughts long enough to raise her head off my chest and peer at me. 'But why were you there, darling?'

'I was made to go,' I lied, putting on my noble face. 'Wanted to buy you a present.'

Her eyes filled with tears. 'Darling,' she said, all misty. 'And you risked being caught, put in prison for *life*, just for me?' Even I felt quite moved by my story, and I'd just made it up.

'Well, love,' I said brokenly. 'I don't give you much. And this cottage isn't much of a place to bring you . . .'

'It's absolutely beautiful!' she cried defiantly. 'I just love the village and your lovely little home!'

If she'd agreed it was crummy I'd have thumped her there and then. Hastily I told her how wonderful she was, with inevitable consequences. Also inevitably, she briefly halted the romance for meteorological reasons.

'Darling, couldn't we make love the other way round, then we can stay under the bedclothes?'

'For you, anything,' I said. She said I was so sweet, which is true, though when I came to afterwards I was still narked with her about my last pasty. A single pasty can keep you going a whole day sometimes, which is more than can be said for almost anything else you can think of.

I saw Connie off about ten to eight. She helped me to fold the bed away (it's really a divan thing) and lent me some money for tomorrow's grub. She also sprang a present on me, a pair of shoes obviously nicked from one of husband Ken's shops.

'They're expensive, darling,' she said. 'Real handmade leather.'

'Thanks, love.'

'They look marvellous.' She was thrilled because they fitted. Two days before she had measured me with a complicated sextant-looking gadget. I could tell she was worried in case she got the width wrong. 'Now *wear* them. Don't let me find them in a cupboard weeks from now. Cross your heart?'

'Let me cross yours instead.'

'Oh, you,' she said.

We went to the porch arm in arm. The porch light doesn't work. I'll mend it when I get a minute, but for the moment it was usefully dark. Still, nobody could see us because the people across the lane are always out sailing or racing motors round Silverstone and that, and our lane leads nowhere in particular.

'Got your car keys, love?'

'Yes, darling. See you soon. I'll come early.'

I groaned inwardly. A morning tryst meant she had designs on my dust. She usually brings a vacuum cleaner and blizzards through the cottage till I'm demented.

' 'Night, love.'

She clung shivering for a minute to show the cold night breeze that she knew it was out there, then ran with a squeal of hatred into the pitch dark. She leaves her grand coupé on my gravel path so customers won't spot her car parked in some leafy lay-by and go prattling gossip.

'Go in, darling!' she cried back. 'You'll catch your death!'

'Right, love.' I didn't move. It was quite mild, really, but I've noticed women talk themselves into a shiver. Connie's headlights washed over my garden, shrinking it and fetching the trees comfortably closer. They struck a gleam off something beyond the hedge. I wondered idly what it was. Maybe I'd have a look when I could get round to it.

Connie revved, ambitiously stirring the gears and frightening my garden voles by showering the countryside with flying gravel as she backed and veered. I counted her turns. Three, four, five, six. The horn pipped a triumphant pip and she was off, her rear reds flickering as she zoomed past the hawthorns. That was good, I thought approvingly. She usually takes seven goes to negotiate the gateway.

Nothing can gleam down in our lane except glow-worms and a parked car. I felt daft just standing there so I walked out. No engines roared, no yobbos bawled.

'Good evening, Lovejoy. Caterina Norman.' The ash-blonde bird showed faintly in the greenish dashboard illumination. 'Your phone is disconnected.'

'Er, a slight misunderstanding about the bill.'

'You're to come with me,' she said, dead cool. 'Tomorrow. My grandfather wants to speak to you.'

That's all I wanted, another bird giving me orders. 'I'm busy tomorrow.'

'Surely you can stop . . . *work* for a moment or two.' Her tone was dry. She'd obviously seen more than she wanted when Connie departed. 'It's not far.'

'Well, look. Can't we leave it?' I was knackered. What with the whole day in the auction aggro, the failure with Mr Malleson, and Connie, I needed a restful day reading about beautiful antiques.

'He's an antiques collector, Lovejoy. And he has a task for you.'

That did it. Maybe grandad was a potential buyer. Never mind that I hadn't a single antique in the place. Potential money's only heading one way, right? And that word: task. Not 'job', not 'some work'. Task. There's something indelibly mediæval about it, isn't there? Beowulf and the Arthurian knights did tasks. Profitable things, tasks—or so I thought.

CHAPTER 3

Next morning I was up as usual about seven, frying tomatoes. The robin came flicking along the hedge to the wall where it plays hell till I shut it up with diced cheese. Blue tits were tapping the side window and the sparrows and blackbirds were all in round my feet. A right lorryload of chisellers. And soon the bloody hedgehog would be awake and come snuffling its saucer for pobs, greedy little swine. How Snow White kept so bloody cheerful with this menagerie I'll never know. I tell you I'm the easiest touch in East Anglia.

It wasn't raining for once so I took my breakfast out — it's only bread-and-dip really — and sat on a low wall I've nearly finished. I set my trannie to a trillion decibels to frighten off scrounging wildlife, but the robin only came and nonchalantly cleaned its feet on it with such pointed indifference that I had to share the brown bread.

The robin cackled angrily and flew off, though I'd been stuffing it with grub. Somebody must be coming. Sure enough, Tinker came shuffling up the path, muttering and grumbling.

' 'Morning, Tinker. Get a ride on Jacko's wagon?'

'Aye, thieving old bleeder. Charged me a quid.'

Jacko's a senile villager who runs a van (summer) and a horse wagon (winter) between our village and the nearby town. The van's an elderly reject from the town market. The wagon's a superannuated coal cart pulled by Terence. Jacko sings to entertain his passengers, which is one way of lessening the load.

'You didn't pay him?' I asked, alarmed.

'Nar. Gave him your IOU.'

I sighed in relief. Great. One more debtor. Tinker absently took a chunk of bread in his filthy mittens and dipped in. Like I said, the easiest touch in East Anglia. Still, no good postponing the bad news.

'Crampie and Mr Malleson got done, Tinker.'

'Yeah. Rotten, eh?' I wasn't surprised that he knew. 'That's what I came about, Lovejoy. Patrick see'd last night's rumble.'

I knew better than to doubt his mental radar. 'Patrick? Actually witnessed it? Anybody else?'

'No. But some of the wallies was askin' at the hospital, like you.'

'Who?'

'Patrick. Helen. Margaret Dainty. Linda who was in the ring. That Manchester bloke who comes after antique lacework and Queen Anne clothes. Big Frank from Suffolk.'

He knew this was disturbing. Even if my old Ruby can hardly raise a gallop, I had happened along pretty smartish, and yet Crampie and Mr Malleson had died.

'Margaret's out,' I said. She's the only one of us who's respectable. Tell you about her if I get a minute. Helen's beautiful but hardly a gang leader. Linda was my old flame from the ring. The Manchester bloke was a regular and had his own turf. Big Frank was only interested in marriage, divorce, and antique silver—in reverse order. No suspects among that lot, but a witness is a witness. Jacko's wagon would be starting for town in half an hour.

'Tell Jacko to wait, Tinker. I'll catch you up.'

'The Three Cups opens in an hour, Lovejoy.' He ambled off—his idea of speed—cackling with enthusiasm.

We trundled into town just as the pubs opened, with me still thinking. Something's not quite right, my imbecilic mind guessed. If they gave a Nobel Prize for indecision I'd win it hands down.

I gave Jacko another scribbled IOU and told him the fare was scandalous.

'That why you never pay me, Lovejoy?' he bawled after but I pretended not to hear. I'm sick of scroungers.

We stopped at the corner of Lion Walk, The Three Cups obviously pulling at Tinker's heartstrings. 'Okay,' I surrendered, giving him his note. 'Where's Patrick?'

He thought hard. No mean feat this, when sober. His rheumy old eyes creaked open after a minute. 'Patrick's with Elsie. They're in the Arcade.'

My heart sank. 'Don't you mean Patrick and Lily? I thought—'

'Nar, Lovejoy. He gave Lily the push last night over him seeing that sailor.'

'Ah,' I said as if I understood.

He shot into the boozer with my last groat. I plodded down the town's expensive new shopping precinct—think of redbrick cubes filled with litter—into the Arcade. This is a glass-covered alley. To either side is a series of tiny antique shops, only alcoves really, with antique dealers moaning how grim life is and how broke they are. Tinker was right. Someone emitted a screech.

'Ooooh.'

I followed the shrill groans—the only known groans higher than top G. Today Patrick was in magenta, with purple wedge heels and an ultramarine sequined cape. As if that wasn't enough, he was being restored by Elsie who was frantically patting some pungent toilet water across his cheeks. Margaret Dainty was looking harassed because Patrick had carefully selected her little shop to swoon in, slumping elegantly across a 1765 Chippendale Gothic chair in mahogany. I didn't even know she had one of these rarities.

Awed shoppers were milling about. Understandable, really, because Patrick standing still's a ghastly enough spectacle. Doing Hamlet's death scene he's beyond belief.

I decided not to ask Elsie about Lily. I'm no fool.

'Ooooh,' Patrick moaned, false eyelashes fluttering.

I crouched down, avoiding Elsie's cascade of eau de Cologne. 'One thing worries me, Pat. Why is it you always get bad news before anybody else?'

His stare gimleted me in sudden recovery. 'Patrick!' he screamed, giving me a mouthful of invective. 'Pat's so . . . uncouth.' He instantly reverted to a swoon. 'Ooooh!'

Elsie wailed, 'Please don't upset him, Lovejoy!'

'Mr Malleson and Crampie,' I prompted the reclining figure. 'Who, when and why, mate?'

Patrick sobbed dramatically, beating his breast in anguish. 'Poor Mr Malleson! How many more catastrophes can I be expected to bear?' His voice went suddenly normal. 'Mind my handbag, dear. It's handmade crocodile.' And immediately went back to showbiz. 'Oh, woe! Oh, heartbreak! Oh—'

I looked across at the distraught Margaret. She's a lovable friend, if you can imagine such a thing, though she's a mite oldish and limps a bit. Still, you can't pass up someone who loves you and has looks and compassion. Saints get beatified for less. Look at Czar Nicholas. 'You tell me, love.'

'We haven't been able to get a word out of him—'

'Right.'

I tipped Patrick off the chair with a crash. He screamed, which is hard to understand because the Chippendale antique wasn't even scratched. 'You perfect *beast*, Lovejoy! And *you* can stop *drenching* me in *stink*, you silly cow!'

I'm sure Patrick only does all this to get an audience. God knows what he does when he's alone, probably just goes into suspended animation.

'Sorry, dearest,' Elsie sobbed. 'Now see what you've done, Lovejoy!'

A bobby was pausing outside in the High Street to inspect the swelling crowd in the Arcade. Things looked like getting distinctly out of hand. I put a knee on Patrick's chest.

'Tell, or I'll crumple your cravat. You were there, weren't you?'

He wheezed as I pressed harder. 'Yes. Three great *bruisers* out of a lorry did it. Wrenches and things. They hit poor Mr Malleson.' His eyes welled with tears as he sniffed out the rest of the story. 'Crampie positively *begged* for mercy. It was *ghastly*, Lovejoy. They *snatched* that perfectly delicious painting.'

'Where were you?'

'In my car with . . . a friend.'

'What were they like?' I know it was night, but there

had been some light.

'Oh, quite *plain*, really, though one could have *really* improved himself with the right suit. Quite young, rather light hair for a foreigner . . . ghastly primrose leather jacket . . .'

'Foreigner? How do you know that?'

The bobby had decided to move into the Arcade. Sensing a bigger audience, Patrick immediately shrieked his way into frank hysteria.

I knew enough about lay-by scuffles to realize it was hopeless getting anything more definite. I kissed Margaret so-long and said I'd honestly see her soon. She told me to be careful and to come for supper one evening. I promised to and managed to say honestly twice more as I shot out.

I'm not much on the police force. Its useful bits are mostly hooked on its own problems, and the rest is a monstrous anachronism. Ledger'd tell me nothing, so they were best forgotten.

Instead I got hold of Tinker and told him to drum up news of any antiques genuine or fake, resembling the painting. He was narked at that because the boozer was still open but I gave him the bent eye and said get going. The lazy old devil went shuffling off, a couple of brown ales clinking in his shabby overcoat.

Then from the phone-box by the war memorial I rang Connie and asked her to lend me a few more quid and could she please fill her motor up with petrol and let me borrow it. I had a secret notion to impress the blonde bird instead of being embarrassed in my old Ruby. She hesitated. I said, 'If you don't I'll make you do all the sky bits in my next jigsaw puzzle.'

'Sadist.' Then she sweetly added she'd come along too, because we didn't want Lovejoy using borrowed wealth to pick up some bone-headed young tart, did we? Bitterly I

agreed that we didn't want that, and stood miserably by
the traffic lights near the Castle Park entrance thinking of
her bloody cheek. Women have no trust in their fellow
man, that's what it is.

CHAPTER 4

'Suss this out, love,' I asked Connie in the torrid heat of
her vast motor. We were parked among the trees by the
football ground for secrecy. One other good thing about
Connie is that she loves gossip. Attentively she sat in her
pale apple costume, with pearl necklace and earrings
revealing class. I gave her Patrick's account. As far as I
knew it added nothing, but Connie with her devious
woman's mind instantly saw a crack.

'Why didn't the police ask Patrick all this?'

'They did. He wouldn't tell them.'

'Why not, if he told you he'd actually seen those three
brutes?'

'Well, er, he was, er, with some bloke . . . You see,
love, erm, Patrick's, erm . . .'

'Another queer,' Connie said, nodding briskly. 'So now
we must find his lady friend.'

I had my doubts. 'Elsie? No use, Connie. I heard she
was in Ilford until late. And Patrick had some row with
Lily last night.'

She got excited. 'Don't you see? Lily must have learned
about Patrick going to meet his friend and followed.'

'So Lily maybe knows something extra?'

She gave me a sweet smile. 'You're learning, darling.
Close that car window. There's a draught.'

Lily was part way through a bottle of gin by the look of
things, and dark blue gondolas of sorrow hung fleshily

beneath her eyes. Worse, she instantly took against
Connie, even when I'd introduced them with my best
Edwardian gallantry. Plainly she would reveal nothing
while a strange woman was in the house so I had to ask
Connie to wait outside. She left Lily's hallway, managing
to slam three doors on her way to sulk in the car.

'Come through, Lovejoy. My husband's abroad again.'
I breathed a sigh of relief and followed her in. The telly
was on. Lily's living-room was a fug of fag smoke. 'Have
you seen Patrick?' she asked wistfully. 'How is he?'

'Upset,' I said lamely. I'm not much good at this sort of
thing.

'Is he?' she looked up hopefully. 'I suppose that crabby
geriatric rat-bag Elsie Hayward's smarming round him.'
When I said nothing she grew aggressive. 'Now you tell
me the truth, Lovejoy.'

'Yes. In the Arcade.'

'Bitch. She's had more false starts with men than all the
tarts in Soho. He'll come back to me, Lovejoy—won't he?'

'Erm, quite possibly.'

She subsided on to an armchair. 'Oh, Lovejoy. What a
mess. Why can't he *see* that it's *me* he needs?'

'Last night, Lily. You followed Patrick.'

'Mmmmh. He'd got some man in his car.' She looked
piteous. 'It's only a weakness, Lovejoy. This phase.'

'Sorry, love,' I said helplessly. 'But you saw?'

'Yes. It was that horrid sickly sailor man he usually—'

'I mean the goons, Lily. Patrick said one was foreign.
What accent?'

'I didn't pay much attention. I was frightened. The van
had been waiting for Mr Malleson and Crampie. They hit
them, really *hit* them, Lovejoy. Then the young man
shouted "Get the painting!" The men didn't care. They
jumped in the van.'

'And you rang the police, Lily?'

She shook her head. 'No. I just sat there and watched.

The lorry-drivers came running, but the van went.'

'No other facts, Lily?'

'He was continental, Lovejoy. Maybe Austrian, that sort of accent. And flashy.' She shivered and pulled her dressing-gown tighter round her. 'Lovejoy,' she said, heartbroken. 'He was laughing. The young one, in bright colours. Once they had the painting he ran back and hit Mr Malleson and Crampie. While they were on the ground. Oh, they lay so still.'

I consoled her as much as I could, saying thanks and Patrick was sure to come back soon. She asked tearfully did I really think so and I said sure, just you see. I felt I'd been through the mangle when I escaped.

Connie was freezing but excited to know what Lily had seen. I told her all of it, hoping she might do her helpful guessing trick again.

'Didn't she tell Ledger any of this?'

'And get Patrick in trouble? Ledger would ask what she was doing herself, parked in the night hours near the scene of an antiques robbery. After all, she's an antique dealer herself — on good days.'

'Darling. Who *would* want the fake so badly? It doesn't make sense.'

'That bird.'

'In the auction?' Connie's mental radar blipped hatred into her mind. 'That one trying to attract everybody's attention in the car park with the wrong hairstyle?'

'She bid a fortune for the fake even though she knew it was duff. Mr Malleson went bid-happy so she ducked out.' Maybe she had decided to acquire the painting by the most decisive of all methods — armed robbery. Thugs are easy enough to hire anywhere these days, God knows. 'Drive me to the High Street.'

'Only if you take your hands off, darling. Your fingers are freezing.'

'How else can I get them warm?'

We argued all the way back to the cottage. The rest of the day was full of pleasure, and therefore uneventful.

CHAPTER 5

It was coming dusk when Connie finally left. I was in good time and ready when the bird called. I cranked my zoomster's engine and lit its lamps while she went on at me.

'You're not coming in that thing?' The blonde leaned from her perfumed cocoon and gazed down at me. 'We'll take all night.'

'Race you,' I said with dignity.

Her car rolled, sneering, up the lane. My crate clattered reproachfully in its wake. It hates being out after dark. The bird was waiting by the chapel, deep engine thrumming and her fingers doubtless tapping irritably. Pricey motor-cars like her are all very well for a year or two. After that they go wrong and decay in forgotten yards. It's filthy little heaps like mine that keep going. Grandeur tends to rapid obsolescence. Unaware I'd reasoned my way to a conclusion which ought to have warned me of impending danger, I drove through the dark village. Wheezing, backfiring, creaking at every joint, Lovejoy Antiques, Inc. was on the move and full of confidence.

Sometimes I'm just pathetic.

Fingringhoe's one of these straggly villages a stone's throw from the sea. You can scent the sealands. Many of the inlets are reserved for birds and mice and whatnot to do their respective thing, making a crashing bore of the whole soggy area. I mean, not an antique shop for miles, a few scatterings of houses along lost lanes, a field or two with yawning cows, and that's it. Our diligent conservationists are busy keeping it that way. They've a lot to answer for.

Following the blonde bird's car in my horseless carriage was like rowing a coracle behind a liner. I kept coming upon it, lights at every orifice, revving impatiently at dark crossroads, but I kept cool. I've been humiliated by experts in my time so degradation at her hands meant little. We turned left at the pub. She tore into the black countryside behind her monstrous beams and I puttered after.

We were close to the sea when she hurtled into a gateway set back from the lane. Apart from a distant low gleam of the sea horizon and the bright windows of the Georgian house beyond the beeches there was nothing to guide you. The drive was paved, if you please, not merely gravelled or tarred, proving that pride had not yet vanished among the country set. Nor had scorn. She gave me some derision free, airily walking through the porch and leaving me to park my knackered heap and hurry after.

The house inside was beautiful. The inner chimes from the antiques all around reverberated in my chest so strongly I had to pause and clutch at the doorway for support.

'This way.' The bird was narked by the delay. Impatiently she waved away a motherly-looking serf who was coming forward to process this stray nocturnal visitor. There was a world's wealth of antiques everywhere on walls and floors and furniture. Mesmerized, I advanced reverently over the Isfahan carpet which partly veiled the mosaic hall floor. It was hard work. A Turner watercolour radiated its dazzling brilliance on the wall, and you can't say fairer than that.

In contrast, the study was not well lit. Panels of original

oak (none of your modern imported Japanese stuff), shelves of books with delectable white parchment covers, a Gainsborough nude drawing, furniture mainly by Ince and Mayhew and a real Canaletto I failed to recognize but which finally fetched out of my anguished throat that moan I'd been hoarding.

The old man in the chair was pleased.

'You are impressed by my possessions, Lovejoy,' he piped. His voice was a pre-Boehm glass flute, sonorous yet high-pitched and miles off. 'I cannot convey how gratifying your response is.'

'*Are* there people who puke at fortunes?'

He tried to roar with laughter, actually falling about and swaying in the great leather chair. His roar was practically inaudible. I've heard infants breathe louder. Politely I waited while he choked and the bird resuscitated him with well meaning pummels between his shoulders. She had to blot his eyes, blow his nose, find his specs and generally cobble the old geezer together. It took a hell of a time. I was drawn to a jewelled snuffbox set on an illuminated covered stand. It looked very like Frederick the Great's cartouche-shaped favourite which Christie's sold for nearly half a million quid. The Emperor was a great collector of them, but this thing was never one of his famous 300. It was a clear fake. Not a tremor of love in it.

Somebody gripped my arm, broke the spell.

'Sit down when you're told.' The bird, clearly an apprentice matriarch, shoved me at a chair. 'Grandfather shouldn't have to suffer your rudeness.'

'Caterina.' The gentle reproof was enough to shut her up and leave her seething with irritation. I sat and waited humbly.

Sometimes it's difficult not to grovel. If the old man's task for me was pricing the mixed antiques and fakes I'd seen so far, I was in for a windfall. Obviously this geriatric was the owner of a significant chunk of the antiques universe. The situation called for the classic whining Lovejoy fawn.

'I am astonished you are not older,' the old man said.

'I'm trying.'

'Mmmmh. Caterina recounted your behaviour at a village auction.' There was a pause. Good old Caterina had flopped across an armchair somewhere behind me. Her irritation beamed straight on to my nape. The pause lengthened.

I gave in. 'You want me to say anything in particular?'

'Mind your language,' Caterina snapped. 'Just remember the gentleman to whom you're speaking could buy you *and* your village.'

The old man winced at her bluntness and flagged her rage down with a tired gesture. Money was beneath mention, which meant the bird spoke the truth.

'Can you account for your perception, Lovejoy?'

'You mean about the painting?'

'Of course, dolt!' from the sweet maid behind.

'Is there,' the old man fluted, 'is there really such a person? A . . . a divvie? You can detect antiques unaided?'

Oho. Caterina had taken the trouble to suss me out pretty well.

'Yes. I'm one.'

He asked the girl to offer me sherry. She slammed about and glugged some. I was scared to touch it. Maybe it was polite to let it hang about an hour or so. Better wait till he'd slurped his, if he was strong enough to lift the bloody thing.

'How is it done?'

'I don't know.'

Caterina snorted more free scorn.

'Six out of six antique dealers with whom I have discussed the matter, Lovejoy, pronounce you to be an authentic . . . ah, divvie.'

'They're in league with him, Grandad!'

The old man smiled. 'Now, Caterina. Lovejoy hardly looks affluent. May I?' he added benignly to me.

'Yes,' I said, wondering what he was asking.

'Caterina. Lovejoy was given the freehold of his cottage by a lady now living abroad. Subsequently he has raised money on it by two mortgages, fraudulent. Both are now in default. The building society is suing for possession—'

'Here, dad,' I interrupted, annoyed. 'That's libel.'

'You mean slander,' he said absently. 'Furthermore, he has a police record. I was advised by all six dealers not to employ him. He owes money to nine dealers in Colchester, and approximately eleven others.'

I found my sherry had emptied itself into me of its own accord. This gentle old man was a deceptive old sod. Well, I had nothing to lose. I was unemployable after that heap of references.

'Which raises the question why you asked me here, dad.'

'Quite so, quite so.' Too much good literature makes these old characters talk Dickens, I suppose. He girded his loins for the plunge. 'I wish you to perform a task on my behalf, Lovejoy.'

A sweat of relief prickled me over. Maybe I was back in.

'A valuation? An auction deal?'

'Ah no.' The old man was suddenly apologetic, evading my eyes. And I remembered Caterina's determined bidding for a fake. And in a dealer's ring, that highly illegal enterprise. My throat went funny.

'Bent?' I asked. He gazed at me blankly, so I translated. 'Illegal?'

'Ah, well, you might say there *is* a rather, ah, clandestine aspect to the activities, ah, which . . .'

I stared. Dear God. Geriatrics were in on antiques scams these days. Still, a zillionaire with Turners and

Canalettos would not think in groats. Whatever it was, I'd soon be eating again. And the ill-tempered lass might revert in time . . .

'An antiques scam?' I struggled to suppress my exultation. Nicking antiques lifts the lowest spirits.

'No.' The old man's gnarled hand gestured to calm my alarm at his denial. 'Not *an*. The.' The scam of all time? I could only think of the British Museum and the National Gallery.

'How big?' I asked. Naturally I assumed the old geezer wouldn't want to reveal all, but I was wrong.

'It's Venice.'

'Venice, eh? Exactly what in Venice?'

'Venice itself. All. I am in process of, ah, borrowing everything Venetian.' His opaque eyes stared into me. God, he was wrinkled.

Well, lose some, win some, I thought bitterly. I managed to smile indulgently. You have to make allowances for idiocy. The daft old sod was rich, a possible future customer whom I couldn't afford to offend even if he was barmy. 'Look, Grandad,' I said kindly. 'You *can't* nick Venice. It's fastened to the floor in that lagoon. I've always wanted to nick the dome-dialled Castle Acre church clock, but I've more sense. The village bobby'd notice. Get the point? I'd give anything to possess its marvellous dead-beat escapement, but daren't risk trying it.'

'I'm serious, Lovejoy.'

I got up and said compassionately, heading for the door, 'Good luck getting Venice through the Customs, but don't say I didn't warn you.'

'Stop him, Caterina,' the old bloke quavered.

Some hopes, I thought. Short of undressing there wasn't a lot she could do, but women are wily. 'Money,' she said casually as I passed, not even bothering to look up.

'Eh?' My treacherous feet rooted.

She gazed calmly at me then, idly perched there on the chair arm, swinging her leg. 'How much will you earn in the next hour, Lovejoy?'

'Erm, well,' I lied bravely. 'I've a good deal on.'

'Unlikely. But we'll buy one hour.'

'To do what?'

'To sit and listen.'

I looked back at that walnut visage, then back to the bird. She too was serious. For a family of lunatics they seemed disturbingly sure of themselves. Well, money's nothing, not really. But without it the chance of acquiring any antiques at all very definitely recedes. I weakened.

'What's an hour between friends?'

The old man nodded approvingly at the luscious bird as I sat down.

'Lovejoy. You speak fluent Italian, I believe?'

How did he know that? 'Not really.'

'Oh, but you do. You learned the language to, er, rip the Vatican.' He leant forward earnestly, the elderly perfectionist. 'Rip. The word is correct?'

As a matter of fact he was right, but my past sins are personal property.

'You want to nick Rome as well?' I said cruelly.

'That'll do from you, Lovejoy?' Caterina spat.

'Shush, my dear. Lovejoy, you have never been to Venice.' The knowing old sod was reminding me, not asking. His gnat's-whine voice became flutier and dreamier. 'You poor man, never seen the Serenissima. It's the ultimate glory of Man.' His eyes were on me, but looking through to some distant image. 'I'll tell you a secret, Lovejoy.'

'Grandfather!' Caterina warned, but he shushed her.

'I've never experienced either contentment or ecstasy for thirty years.'

'Don't give me that crap,' I blurted, 'er, sir. With all these antiques?'

'True, Lovejoy.' He seemed near to tears. 'Thirty years ago I first saw the Serene Republic, a routine holiday. Within two days I'd bought the Palazzo and knew it was for life. Ah, the hours I have watched the *traghetto* men smoke and talk in the *campo* below my window on the Grand Canal!' He collected himself. 'I saw Venice, the greatest man-made structure the world has ever known. Paintings, architecture, sculpture, clothes, weapons, everything living and vital.'

'I know the feeling,' I said enviously.

'You do *not*, young man. You believe I am talking about greed. I am not.' Now he sipped his sherry, hardly wetting his lips. 'On that visit I learned of something so terrible, so near nightmare that I never recovered. I have never felt happiness since. Despair, too, is absolute.'

'You all right, mate?' His nightmare, whatever it was, had turned him grey.

'Yes. I thank you.' He replaced his glass and leant back, weary. 'To avert that nightmare I am prepared to give everything I own. You see, nightmares should vanish with the dawn, Lovejoy. Mine does not. It is descending upon that magical city with every minute that passes. In your lifetime you too will suffer it. And when you do, Lovejoy, you will never smile again.'

In spite of myself I had to clear my throat and look about to make sure we were all okay. 'My nightmares are pretty boring. What's yours?'

'Venice is sinking.'

That old thing. 'Aren't we all?'

'Silence!' cried the old bloke, enraged.

'That does it!' Caterina was rising, also enraged.

I'd had enough. Even hungry cowards get fed up. 'Shut your gums, you silly old sod. And as for you,' I said to the bird as I crossed and poured myself sherry entirely

without assistance, 'dial nine-nine-nine for the Old Bill if
you like. But just remember you invited me here to listen
to your lunatic crap. I don't have to agree that it's gospel.
Okay?'

After an ugly pause old Mr Pinder said unexpectedly,
'Okay, Lovejoy,' to Caterina's fury. I went and sat down.

The old bloke was simply watching. The bird was for
Armageddon.

'Right, then,' I said. 'Venice.'

He smiled with a gleam in his eye. 'Venice. If you saw a
lorry carrying a small parcel containing a Verzelini
drinking glass accidentally slewed over the wall of the
Chelmer canal, what would you do?'

I wanted to get the hypothesis absolutely clear. 'No
danger to me?'

The sly old devil shrugged. 'Well, Lovejoy. Broad
daylight. You can swim like a fish, I'm told. Canals are
only a couple of feet from the towpath. Surely . . . ?'

I thought, sensing a trick. Verzelini was a Murano
glassmaker from Venice who made it to Good Queen
Bess's London and turned out richly valuable Venetian-
style glass in his little City factory until late 1590s. A
single glass nowadays would give you enough to retire on.
Well, in for a penny . . . 'Okay, I'd try and save it.'

'Now. Supposing that Verzelini glass, in its precarious
parcel, was multiplied a million times.'

'Still no danger to me?'

His distant-reed voice cut in. 'Yes or no, Lovejoy?'

'Well, yes. But there's less than a dozen Verzelini
glasses knocking around. And Venice isn't a parcel on a
lorry.'

Grandad smiled then, his face like crumpled kitchen
foil. 'All Venice's art can be made into such parcels,
Lovejoy. And it is certainly about to fall into water,
Lovejoy.'

I thought about that. 'You mean . . . ?'

'Piecemeal.' There was a pause. He added, 'Bit by bit,' as if I didn't know what piecemeal meant. 'A UNESCO expert—'

'They're cretins.'

'—says that every year Venice loses six per cent of its marble treasures, a twentieth of its frescoes, three per cent of its paintings, and two per cent of its carvings.'

'That's not the sea, dad. It's collectors.'

'Which proves my scheme can be done.'

'This is insufferable!' Caterina said the words like aggressive teachers used to in school, only she didn't thump me on each syllable. She flung out, the door shaking my teeth.

In the newfound calm I gave the old fool a fresh appraisal. 'That's an awful lot of bits, dad. One parcel's fine. Two's not beyond belief. But three's just asking for trouble. And nobody on earth could nick four of Venice's precious antiques without all hell being let loose.'

'Ah,' he said, as if spotting some troublesome little flaw in my argument. 'You're apparently assuming, Lovejoy, that we don't replace each, ah, bit by the very best reproduction that money can buy. Paintings, stonework, carvings, statues. You'll no doubt remember your own escapade in the Vatican?'

I wished he would give over about that. I'd made my own repro to do the Vatican rip, so I'd known it was up to scratch. What this old duckegg was suggesting meant trusting a load of other forgers to be as perfectionist as me, and that was definitely not on. You can't trust just any faker.

'You'd need an army of superb forgers. I can only think of three.' What worried me was the Carpaccio fake that Crampie and Mr Malleson had been murdered for. As soon as I got a satisfactory explanation for that, I'd be off out of this looney-bin like a shot and he could do what the hell he liked with Venice or anywhere else.

'I see you're beginning to understand, Lovejoy,' Grandad said. 'There are many, many more than three. And I do assure you they are being produced at a Dunkirk rate, Lovejoy. Money no object.'

'But where and how?'

'Ah.' He pondered, grimaced, creakily raised a finger and said knowingly, 'Are you in or out?'

'In or out to do what?'

'You will check the authenticity of the items involved in our, ah, scam. We've lately had one or two unfortunate events.' A frown crinkled his face worse than ever. 'One point. I sought the derivation of that word *scam*: "scamble" is hardly convincing, yet it's modern currency . . .'

I waited for a bit. The old criminal had nodded off.

I cleared my throat. 'Dad?'

He partly roused, muttered, 'Ammiana . . . Ammiana . . .'

'Eh? You awake?'

No sound. The old man was snoring, a squeak of a distant bat. I poured another glass and had a think.

CHAPTER 6

Joyce the serf found me padding around the upstairs landing. The first I realized she'd caught me was her abrupt, 'Downstairs, Lovejoy!' Just shows how sly women are. She led me to the kitchen—takes a serf to spot a serf—and brewed up some repellent broth designed to 'warm a man's blood'. A learner grannie if ever I saw one. But her tea was good, and from the vestibule window I could see a gilt-framed George Webster seascape in oils hanging on the stairs so it wasn't all wasted time. The frame, a quite early plaster-gilt job, worried me. Maybe

I'd seen one rather like it recently, maybe in an auction . . . Joyce had an open kitchen fireplace and a lovely old cast-iron Mason's grate of about 1865.

'I was only looking,' I told the interfering old cow, in case she had the wrong idea.

'You put the map back?'

The question was off-hand, but I smarted inwardly. Women nark me, always suspecting the worst. The hand-coloured map, by the Dutchman Dirck Jansz van Santen, was dazzlingly illuminated in gold. The silver had oxidized a bit, but that's only to be expected for something done about 1690. (Tip: look for deep precise printing—showing the map was an early print from the engraved copper—and the more embellishment the better.) The thought of nicking it honestly never crossed my mind. No, I'm really being honest now.

'You're just like old Mr Pinder,' she told me. Praise indeed.

'Me? Like Grandad?'

'Mad about stupid old things.' She wet her wrists and started to attack the pastry. 'Of course, Mr Pinder's so taken with Venice these days he's useless for anything else. Him and Caterina's stepmother alike.' Her tone was disapproving. 'Things would have been different if her real mother were still here, God rest her. This house is like Piccadilly Circus some days. You wouldn't believe the sorts of folk get fetched here. Long-haired layabouts in fast cars, foreigners from boats, every language under the sun.'

'What does Caterina do?'

Joyce gave a sharp, inquisitive glance. 'Helps Mr Pinder to run the estate.'

'And Mrs Norman?'

'You'll need more tea, ducks.'

'Er, ta.' I knew a shut-out when I heard one. Caterina's stepmother was clearly not to be discussed. 'Does the old boy kip most of the time?'

She glanced at the hour, a highly-sought Lancashire Victorian wall-clock with the familiar keyhole stage and cased pendulum. Five years ago you couldn't give them away as ballast.

'He'll sleep till tea-time now. Are you going to help him with this foreign thing? Like Mr Malleson?'

Like Mr Malleson? Well, I thought. Let's see if her idea of 'this foreign thing' was the same as old Pinder's. 'Yes,' I lied.

'Then be careful. Mrs Norman has altogether too many hangers-on if you ask me. Though I must say Mr Pinder's pleased at how she copes with the big house there, Palazza whatsit.'

'How long do you think he'll want me to go for?'

'You'll have to ask him, dear.'

'Can't Caterina decide? She seems in charge.'

'Doubt it.' Joyce's lips thinned. 'That end's always left to Mrs Norman and her . . .' She petered out, maybe deliberately. The old shut-out again.

I said I'd better be off unless she had designs on my body, and got another smile. I like smiley women.

'Can I leave Mr Pinder a note?' Without letting Joyce see the words, I scribbled thanks, but the task wasn't quite up my street and some other time, and told Joyce it was private and she wasn't to look inside the minute I was gone, which made her cuff me amiably. 'My husband will run you down the road.'

She gave me an Eccles cake to be going on with, laughingly scorned my offer of thirty quid for her aspidistra—they're genuine antiques nowadays—and shouted her husband from the stables.

Mr Lusty drove me all the way into town, chatting laconically about the Pinders' benevolent support of poor artists. It seemed the old gentleman ran a sort of complicated trust, which was quite interesting, but not as interesting as the short cut we made as we left the Pinder estate. A cart-track ran down to the waters of the estuary. Mr Lusty was so proud of the new stone wharf that he stopped the car to show me. He explained that a sizeable ship could come up-river from the sea-reaches. I said I'd no idea it was such a responsible job, and was duly amazed at the size of the two boatsheds. There were two biggish yachts moored out in the tide-race, the bigger with two masts.

'Yes,' Mr Lusty said all modest. 'The *Eveline* came in two nights back. A young painter. Be gone tomorrow. Sometimes we're so busy we can't keep up with the routine estate work.'

'Is that so?' I walked on to the wharf.

'It's dredged,' he said, seeing me peer over into the river. 'The real thing, big dredgers up from the Blackwater.'

'It must cost a fortune.'

'All comes out of the trust, you see.'

'And these artists train here, I suppose, eh?' We walked back to the car. The wind was whipping at us from the sealands. Beyond the low banks and sedge lay the North Sea and the Low Countries.

'Heavens, no, Lovejoy. Most of them just pass through, except when Mrs Norman's home. Then maybe her, erm, erm . . .' He coughed, recommenced. 'A right motley mob they are, too. But Mr Pinder's a perfect gentleman. Always gets himself wheeled down to every boat that calls, even if he's not feeling so good.'

'Where do they come from?'

'Oh, all round the coast. You name it.'

He drove us beside a few acres of reforestation and we emerged on the Fingringhoe road, but as we'd pulled away I couldn't help looking downstream across the marshes. The Roman Empire had shipped its products up this very river. Somebody could ship things the other way, right?

I caught the bus after waiting with Mr Lusty in his car a few minutes. All the way back to town I kept wondering about Mrs Norman and her Erm-Erm who together seemed to be responsible for the Venice end of the whole scam—if it existed.

One thing was sure. Everybody trod very, very cautiously round Mrs Norman.

The next two days were hectic. I sent Connie to dig out the Pinder family gossip. She's a cracker at collecting gossip—God knows how, because she never stops talking long enough to listen to anything anyone else says. Tinker's job was to ferret out local antiques which were possible fakes of anything Venetian. My own contribution was to think, read, and find why my private antiques world was spinning off its wobbly little orbit.

The best way to think about crime is to work, preferably at something slightly less than legal.

Connie was only able to stay with me the first after-noon, so I had a lot of solitude. We got up about tea-time and put the divan away, with still a sizeable chunk of the day left. At the moment I was making an 'antique' papier-mâché chair. Don't laugh. In its time, papier-mâché's been used to make bedsteads, tables, practically any sort of chair you can imagine, picture frames, boxes, vases, clock cases, even parts of coaches. Elderly French women came into mid-Georgian London to chew (literally: *chew*) cut-offs from stationers into a gooey mash for pressing on to a metal framework. Varnished, pumice-stoned and decorated, it can be beautiful and anything.

In this cruel lying game of antiques, you take all stories with a pinch of salt. Respectable history's a pack of lies. I mean, an eighteenth-century bloke called Clay reckoned his papier-mâché hot-mould stoving process was new, but it's only the same old system speeded up. And that carver-gilder Duffour, who worked from a Berwick Street pub in Soho, even claimed he'd invented papier-mâché. That's rubbish, too; the Persians were making it donkeys' years before he got into bad company in The Golden Head pub in 1760. You can forge anything from papier-mâché.

There I was, in my workshop—actually a grotty shed deep in garden overgrowth—honing down the chair with pumice. It was to be a cane-seated drawing-room chair with a spoon-shaped back splat. Oh, I know quite well that this sort of chair's the favourite of the modern faker, but I have two secrets up my sleeve which can make a three-day old fake look an original 1762 piece from Peter Babel's place down Long Acre.

The robin had followed me in because it knows I like silent company. It stabbed its cheese on the workbench, cackling angrily to warn possible intruders off its patch. Very like women. I wear these leather gloves or your hands wear off. You need *many* varnishings and honings. I intended to japan the whole thing because black lacquer's easiest to make antique-looking. You do it with an electric sander, but for God's sake remember to replace the emery paper with a rectangle of buffing cloth. Buff the lacquer *anywhere on the chair a human would normally touch* until the lacquer's worn thin. Then take a 2-kilowatt hairdrier and from a distance of two feet blow hot air at every part of the chair a human *wouldn't* normally touch—underneath, the legs, the lot. My favourite bit is a touch of class: a spoonful of house dust at all the intersections before your hot-air bit gives an unnervingly authentic appearance under a hand-lens. Then buff (shoeshine action) the seat edges and the splat's top until the undervarnish begins to hint through. All that's my first secret. The second's the way a fake's pearl-shell inlays are dulled from their brilliant newness to a century-old opalescence—

'Sceeeeech!'

'Sorry, mate.' I'd reached out for the red tin in which I keep my McArthur microscope and inadvertently got the robin. 'Well, you're both red. Same size. No need to carry on like that.' I put the disgruntled robin back on the bench. It stood dusting itself down, glowering. The red tin was almost exactly the same colour as the robin. Not far from a Carpaccio red, actually.

I stood looking. Red?

The robin was the same size as the miniature microscope's tin can, which had luckily been just right to hold the instrument. But so what?

'So the same holds good for picture frames, right?' I said to the robin. 'Sizes count as well as colours.'

It cheeped in a rage and flicked on to my shoulder so I got the message. Time for the idle little sod's biscuit. I sighed and turned to go in for one.

'What does a robin know about picture frames, Lovejoy?'

The light was draining fast from the day. Odd, though, that Caterina should be framed the way she was in the sun's last glim. Some women are enough to stop a man's breath without even trying. Things conspire. 'Eh?' I said, cool.

'What picture frame? You just told the bird.'

'That conversation was private.'

She came in and walked round the chair. 'You're restoring it. Nice. Late Regency?'

'Early Lovejoy.' That shook her, made her think a minute. 'Your killer's got a posh car, Caterina. I'll bet he earned it by doing fakes nearly as good, eh?'

The robin cackled and flew off in a sulk. No biscuit. I shouted after it, 'Give you two tomorrow,' and explained to her, 'He'll be in a hell of a temper all week now. That's your fault. Trouble is, he suspects blackbirds. One knows how to undo the catch on my breadbin, and the robin's not tall enough. Gets him mad.'

'Did you say my killer?' She'd gone all still.

'You know, the murderer you go about with.' I was all affable. 'The de Lorean. Old lemon-shirt.' I spoke quite conversationally and started tidying up. 'He owns the *Eveline*, doesn't he?'

Still and pale all of a sudden, so I'd struck oil. 'I knew you'd be trouble, Lovejoy. How did you guess?'

'The frame on that Webster seascape in your grandad's hallway. You tried to lend that Carpaccio fake some authenticity by putting it in an old frame before sending it to the auction. Then you realized your mistake— Grandad missed it, so you had to try to buy it back. Something like that?'

'Nearly. But go on.'

'Feet.' I began to sweep round the chair. She moved her feet obediently, watching, listening. 'Mr Malleson went bid-happy and got the fake against your bids. So you had him and Crampie killed by your tame murderer, naughty girl. You told him to make it look like a routine motorway café rumble.' I emptied the workshop dust into the plastic bin and looked round for her verdict.

'Almost, Lovejoy.'

'Only almost?' I was so bloody sure.

There was a trace of bitterness when she spoke, but it was Crampie and Mr Malleson got done, not her. 'You obviously think the worst of me.'

'Almost, Caterina,' I said evenly, and went past her to switch the outside light on.

'You won't go to the police, Lovejoy.' No question there, only the assured flat statement of a bird in charge of everything which intruded into her world. 'They already suspect you of every local antiques crime. They wouldn't listen to your wild suppositions.'

So she had changed my accurate logic into wild

suppositions. I held the shed door for her to walk out, and locked up. We stood in the darkening garden, each waiting for the other to speak.

'Your mistrust means you won't work for my grandfather, I suppose?'

'Correct.'

Oddly, she drooped as if accepting a still heavier burden. 'Then that's the end of it,' she said resignedly. 'Can you be trusted to take no further action?'

'Where my skin's concerned, yes. But just remember, if my robin goes off his grub, it's your fault. And I can be very narked.'

'Are you never serious, Lovejoy?'

'Lady,' I said wearily, 'I'm serious all the bloody time. It's everybody else that's jokers.'

Nowhere. I'd got nowhere. I knew more or less how, why and who. And still I'd got nowhere, stymied in every direction. I was getting narked.

CHAPTER 7

Speaking of sex, so many things puzzle me. Like a woman's all chat immediately afterwards, then she zonks out an hour later. But the man's off into a melancholy twilight doom-riddled world, a comatose grief from which he only slowly returns to remember the ecstasy and delight. In particular, the last thing he wants is his bird prattling gossip into his ear, like Connie was doing to mine. The fact that she was only reporting the gossip I'd told her to collect was no excuse.

'Darling! It's so interesting! Mr Pinder's daughter, Caterina's mother, passed away. Her stepmother Lavinia—'

'Who?' I reared blearily out of coma.

'Lavinia married Geoffrey Norman. He's hopeless and she's a tramp.'

Rear and blear. 'Who? Caterina?'

'No, silly. Lavinia. I keep *telling* you, darling. Eventually she got so bad the village shunned her. Scandal, the lot. *Lovely*, darling! People are sorry for Caterina . . . Old Mr Pinder runs some sort of arts foundation . . .' Her voice faded. My mind went into neutral, and the world went away.

That old man had been on my mind half — if not all — the night. Clearly he was a nutter. Even if he and his syndicate were worth a king's ransom, a nutter's still off his rocker any way you look. What with Caterina's hatred and Grandad's whispery voice, his scam seemed more unreal.

'The steps leading down to Venice's lovely canals were for a lady's descent from the gondolas,' he'd said, eyes glistening. 'But the bottom steps never emerge from the water now. And the Piazza San Marco itself is underwater in the great yearly tides from the Adriatic Sea. The ground floors are thirty *inches* above sea level. Oh, the tourists pour in and see the Queen of the Inland Seas resplendent there in all her ancient glory. But they go, and the sea again takes over. Only each year Venice is lowered and the sea more rampant. Politicians promise. Engineers measure. But the duckboards, the *passerelle*, are left out now, to disfigure the loveliest of cities.

'And do you know what is the most shameful thing of all, Lovejoy?' he concluded, his cracked-flute voice embittered. 'Our belief in our own permanence. We little know that what passes for permanence —' he paused a second, wondering whether to be pleased at a possible pun, waved it away — 'is only the gift of constant endeavour. Man's priceless art treasures must be ceaselessly protected, or they vanish. Like Venice is emptying of treasures and people.'

'How can one man—?' I'd interjected, but he washed out my objection derisively.

'There are many of us in my syndicate, Lovejoy. Finance is no problem. Let me tell you a story. Vivaldi's church, the Pietà, stands on the Riva—the lagoon waterfront—and contains the most pathetic memento you could ever imagine. A marble rectangle set in the floor, inscribed that the church's Tiepolo painting was restored by American money.' He paused to allow the world time to prepare for his next utterance. 'Is that immortality? Lovejoy, the entire flooring, which records in immutable marble the generosity of the Samuel H. Kress Foundation of New York, USA, will soon have settled for ever beneath the waters of the Adriatic.'

'But it's a try,' I found myself protesting. 'Worthwhile.'

'Pointless patchwork, Lovejoy. Darning the cabin curtains on the *Lusitania*. Only success is worthwhile. Don't you see?'

Eventually I did see. The love, the old man's conviction had swept me along. I almost forgot he was bonkers.

Which was all very well. In the cold light of day.

That same noon, Connie, Tinker and me held a council in the White Hart.

'You first, Tinker.' I told him to be quick about it, because Connie was supposed to be on her way back from a shoe-buying trip to Northampton.

'Nowt, Lovejoy.' He took a note and got another pint for himself. Connie leaned away as he shuffled back. Some days he's worse than others.

'Eh? I told you anything Venetian, Tinker, you burke.'

'Don't blame me, Lovejoy. Worn my bleeding feet orf, I have.' He slurped his pint dry and spoke with feeling. 'There's not a single frigging Venetian antique, real, fake, nicked, bent or just passing through, in the whole frigging Eastern Hundreds.'

He rose to shamble off for another pint. 'Ted,' I called to the barman wearily, 'keep one coming or we'll be here all day.' I beamed a rather worried look at Connie, because she'd have to pay and I owed her a fortune already. By her reckoning I possibly owed very, very much more. Quickly sensing she was one up, she immediately asked Ted to stop the draughts which were positively *whistling* through the pub, and to please turn up the heating while he was at it and put more logs on the fire—

I concentrated. 'None? That's impossible, Tinker.'

'I know, Lovejoy. It's bleeding true. I went down Brad's, Ernie's, Jessica's, Mersea Island . . .'

With Ted rolling his eyes in exasperation and Connie enjoying herself giving him anti-chill orders all over the saloon bar, I closed my ears to Tinker's mumbled list of negatives, and thought: one or two negatives, fine; but a whole East Anglia of negatives is serious cause for concern.

There and then, my mind made itself up.

Until hearing Tinker, I'd assumed that sooner or later Ledger would find the three blokes who did Crampie and Mr Malleson. Now, it was all too clear that things were beyond reach. It was too big. Think of the resources to clear out every special item from East Anglia. It took expertise, men, time, knowledge and money, money, and more money. Old Pinder and his syndicate were not so daft after all, just wealthy and obsessed. I half-listened to Tinker's boozy drone. '. . . then Liz at Dragonsdale, who reckoned she'd seen an early Venetian black-letter book eight weeks back, but . . .'

Which left the question of what the hell *I* was worrying about. Caterina's warning was crystal clear: keep out of it, and Lovejoy will not be troubled in the slightest. Honestly, I wasn't feeling guilty. No, really honestly. It was nothing at all to do with me. Admitted, Mr Malleson wouldn't be dead if I'd dissuaded him enough. And Crampie wouldn't be dead if I'd maybe stopped, insisted on giving him a lift. Or maybe I shouldn't have shouted all over the pub car park that the Carpaccio was a fake. I can shed guilt like snow off a duck. Anyway, I always find it belongs to somebody else. No, I was absolved.

'Then I went to Jim Morris at frigging Goldhanger . . .'

'Ooooh, you poor thing! It must have been freezing!' from good old hot-blooded Connie. By now she'd got us all hunched over the pub fire. My mind was busily doling out absolution, mostly to myself. 'I was, too, in the library.'

That reminded me, and I opened the book she'd brought. It was the wrong one.

'But darling, the library was freezing—'

'I distinctly said the History of Venice, you stupid—!'

'It's a book on Venice, isn't it? It's not my fault.'

Of course it never is with women. I tried to sulk driving all the way to the Colne estuary but got interested in the book in spite of myself. The index listed Ammiana, the name old Pinder had mentioned. It was an island, one of the many which made up the Most Serene Republic of Venice. A thriving centre of culture, of religious activity, eight gracious antique-filled churches—until it had sunk beneath the waters, never to be seen again. There were others. Reading in a car makes me unwell, but it wasn't just that that made me feel prickly.

'It's perishing in here, love,' I said. 'Put the heater on.'

She did so with delight. First time we'd ever seen eye to eye.

CHAPTER 8

'I'm so frightened, Lovejoy.'

'Don't worry, love. Just do it.'

'When do I put the money in?'

Connie and I were crammed in the phone-box. One of
her stockings was tight over the mouthpiece. We'd had a
hell of a time getting it off her lovely leg in the confined
space pretending we were doing all sorts so people
wouldn't stare. She was shaking from fear.

'You don't need money for an emergency call.'

I dialled, pressing close. Connie whispered, 'Darling,
this is no time to—'

'I'm only trying to listen!' I whisper-yelled, thinking,
swelp me. I'd do a million times better without help.

'Police, please,' Connie intoned. I'd tried training her
to speak low and gruff for disguise but she was
hopeless—thought that pursing her mouth into a
succulent tube made her into a bass-baritone.

'Mr Ledger, please, Constable,' Connie boomed
falsetto into the mouthpiece.

'And don't keep saying please! You're supposed to be a
criminal!' I spread the crumpled paper for her to read
from.

'Hello?' She turned a pale face to me, eyes like saucers.
'He's answered, darling!'

'Read it! Read it!'

'Erm . . . get this, Ledger, mate,' Connie read in her
tubular voice. I closed my eyes. It was like a bad dream.
'I'll only say this once. Go down the estuary, please. Off
the old Roman fort there's moored the sea-going yacht
Eveline. She's full of fake antiques . . .' Her voice faded.

'What is it? Keep reading!'

She dropped the receiver in a panic. 'Darling. He said to put you on.'

'Eh?' We stared at each other.

'He said, Just put Lovejoy on the blower, lady.'

Slowly I unwound Connie's stocking and listened at the receiver.

'You there, Lovejoy?' Ledger asked wearily. 'Stop tarting about.'

'This is a recording,' I said, embarrassed.

'So's this. You seem to think we do bugger-all here. We've checked out everybody who was known to be at that auction, at the caff, on the trunk road—including your posh lady Caterina, especially as you've been seeing so much of her these days. You still there?'

'Aye.' I felt a right twerp.

'Then pay attention. I'll only say this once.' He sniggered at nicking one of our lines. 'You're meddling, lad. And I don't like it, because meddlers usually have a reason. And your reason is vengeance. Don't think I don't know. I can read you like a bloody book. Last warning. Understand?'

'You can't arrest me, Ledger,' I said weakly.

'There's such a thing as protective custody. Just remember that if you're on my patch I've signed for you. Oh, one more thing. The *Eveline* has sailed. She was clean as a whistle. We looked.'

My heart sank. What a flaming mess.

'I hear your lady is a cracker, Lovejoy,' Ledger said pleasantly. 'Funny voice, but I don't expect that worries you too much—as long as Ken Bridewell doesn't find out, eh? Cheers.'

Click. Burr.

We left the phone-box, me ashamed because the trick had failed and Connie still shaking. She looked worried sick. We were near the football ground in town.

'Darling,' she quavered. 'It's . . . it's become rather

serious, hasn't it? All this, I mean.'

She must have caught Ledger's final threat. I sensed an incipient farewell, the state she was in.

'No more serious than usual, love.'

She stood there drooping. 'The police, Crampie and the other man, the whole business. I'm frightened, darling.'

'Only temporary difficulties,' I said like a cheery weather-forecaster in an unexpected blizzard:

'You're going to Venice to find them, aren't you, darling.' Another lovely woman who could make a simple question into a flat accusation.

'Of *course* not,' I said, beaming. 'Honest.' And I looked into her eyes with all my innocence.

'Really honest, or Lovejoy honest?'

'Same thing, love.'

'Is it?' she shivered but only listlessly from habit and looked about. Her car was nearby. Women never trust a bloke when he's trying to be truthful.

I fumbled in my pocket to see what gelt I had left. Maybe enough.

'Come on, love,' I said, pulling her across the road to the shop. 'I'll buy you a replacement stocking. Can I put it on your lovely leg?'

'I've two legs, darling.' She managed a wan smile.

'A whole pair, then,' I said recklessly. 'Hang the cost.'

Any woman leaving is the end of an era. No two ways about it, Connie's absence was bad news. Lucky I was so busy, or I'd have suffered even more. The worst bit is realizing how sad she'd be too. I couldn't see the point of her going, but women are always boss in a relationship and, if that's what she felt was timely, I suppose it had to be. I mean, a man can't simply leave a woman, not off his own bat. Oh, of course birds complain about blokes 'leaving', but that's only punishment for failing to live up to her expectations. At least Connie had given me the sailor's elbow for a material—not emotional—reason, which is good going for Lovejoy Antiques, Inc.

I'd just put her stocking on her. It had taken three hours. She was overlying me the way she liked to afterwards.

'If I ask you not to go, Lovejoy . . . ?'

I gave her my million-watt stare of transparent honesty. 'Who said anything about going anywhere, love? Where's this daft idea come from?'

She sighed then, and dressed slowly because she knows I like to watch. I could tell she didn't believe a word, but women are notorious cynics. She came back to give me a kiss before she went, blotting her eyes. I waved her off from the bed. She was just in a funny mood.

A ten-point turn to negotiate the gateway, the engine sounding horribly final.

Gone.

I lay there thinking, money. I must get money. Venice is such a hell of a way. This called for one of my antiques orgasms.

By four o'clock I was going full steam. I'd sold my papier-mâché fake chair—as a genuine antique, of course—in a part-exchange high-mark deal to Elena on North Hill, coming away with a rough old oil panel of a long-haired bloke with lace cuffs and a cravat. Genuinely oldish—say late eighteenth century—but poor artistry. You can still get them for a song in any antique shop in East Anglia. I inscribed some famous-sounding name on the reverse, like 'Port^t. of Abraham Cowley' and an illegible signature, and decided to flog it for twice what Elena could, and before nightfall too. A high-mark deal is one where you part-exchange items and come away with money as well, because your item is worth more than the other bloke's. I did well out of Elena and my chair.

With the money I put a deposit down on a nineteenth-century wrought-iron church porch lantern, all bonny hexagonal panels intact, told Brad I'd pay him the balance by the weekend, and carted it to Patrick's (resplendent today in a vermilion poncho). There I sold it for a profit and used the gelt to buy a group of six French hand-shuttles, Georgian, from Margaret Dainty. These little things come in old engraved steel, ivory or wood, and are avidly sought by collectors nowadays. I borrowed John Cronan's phone in the Arcade to contact a Midland shuttle-collector from my book, priced them high and got him to promise to post off a money order within an hour. I told John I'd owe him for the phone call when the stingy swine moaned, and sent Tinker to the post office to wing the shuttles off northwards.

Ten minutes later I sold 'Abraham Cowley's' portrait for a good price to Markie and Beatrice in the Red Lion. I pretended to be broke — this comes easy — and desperate for money. 'I'd meant to restore it,' I said, hoping to God the marker-pen signature which I'd scribbled on the bottom corner wouldn't rub before they got it home. I'd thoughtfully pencilled a Christie's auction number on the frame angle beneath the canvas tacking, and pretended not to notice when Markie spotted it and nudged Beatrice surreptitiously. They claim to be Expert Antique Picture Restorers. They'd need to be, I thought fervently, pocketing the gelt.

Crossing the Arcade to Jessica's place, I took a deep breath and plunged into her incense-riddled alcove. Ten minutes later I staggered out stinking like a chemist's shop but happy with my loot (got on deposit, ten per cent) which consisted of a Waterford crystal comport dish, jug and decanter. I'd persuaded her they were 'new-factory' wares — post-1951 — instead of the 'old-factory' crystal which extends back from 1851 to the 1720s. Of course I'd lied in my teeth, and agreed to pop round her house tomorrow night and settle up what I owed.

Meanwhile, Tinker had a brass chandelier with a brass
'Bristol dove' finial at the top (no feathers, smooth wings
closed). It was mixed-period because some know-all has
always mucked about with them, but it looked fine. I
bought it there and then, added a thirty per cent mark-
up and told Tinker to phone Sandy and Mel (not got time
to tell you about them, thank heavens). They agreed to
buy it. Tinker would ferry the chandelier out, get the
money, zoom it to the Arcade and there buy Margaret's
small Japanese shouldered tea-jar outright. It had its
original tiny ivory lid (think of a decorated draughtsman
off a chequerboard). I told him to up the price by half,
phone a London dealer in Museum Street, say I had 'flu
but needed the cash by morning. It broke my heart. If I
clapped eyes on it again I'd never let its dazzling little
body out of my sight ever again. As it was, Tinker knew
enough to hand it to one of the long-haulage drivers who
run England's unofficial nocturnal antiques delivery
services nationwide faster and safer than ordinary post. It
would be in Museum Street by midnight. Then Big Frank
from Suffolk bought the Waterford crystal at a good
price . . .

I reeled on, hurtling Tinker about the town and
cadging lifts while I borrowed like mad, spending like a
civil servant. Oddly, sometimes when you go berserk
things go for you. We found antiques which were
unbelievably rare. Tinker even dug out a musical
book—Victorian 1880, little projecting tabs trigger a
cuckoo's call when you turn the cuckoo picture. I'd never
even seen one before. Naturally, you also pick up the
dross—two 1671 water clocks 'by Ed^{d} Larkins,
Winchester', for example. People get really narked when
you tell them that these are *all* repros by Pearson Page.

The day faded into dusk. In the Arcade, lights came
on. People scurried among the closing shops. Traffic

queued at intersections. Stores shuttered for the night. Night schools opened. Car parks filled for our one theatre.

I stormed on like a mad thing, dealing, buying, borrowing, selling—and above all promising, promising, promising. At the finish Tinker and I were knackered and swilling ale in the Three Cups. He's not daft, and got courage up to ask it after a couple.

'What do we do about all these frigging IOUs, Lovejoy? You wuz giving them out like autographs.'

'Do the best you can, Tinker.'

'Eh? Me?' He felt so faint he drank both our pints. 'Where'll you be?'

'Somewhere else for a few days.'

'Leaving me to cope with the whole mess . . . ? Jesus.' He stared at me, appalled. 'They'll have my balls, Lovejoy.' He slurped his new pint, and gave a sudden gummy chuckle. 'Hey, Lovejoy. I can't wait to see Jessica's face when she sees me turn up tomorrow night, instead of you. I knows you pays her in kind, randy sod.' He rolled in the aisles at the notion.

No real need to worry about Tinker. He's the sort who could scratch a living bottling fog. 'Hold them off payment till I come back.' I had the money to reach Venice. That was all that mattered.

'What about your woman Connie?'

I thought a minute. The beer seemed to have gone off. 'Forget her,' I said, and pushed him my glass.

Which only goes to show how useless I am at knowing women.

Early next morning, as I was putting together my spare clothes in my grotty battered suitcase, a special messenger arrived at the cottage with a big manilla envelope and an accountant's letter. It read,

I am informed by Mrs C. Bridewell, director, that you

have accepted responsibility for purchasing on commission ladies' Italian seasonal styles in pattern for the Bridewell shoe-shop chain. Please find accompanying this an open return air ticket to Venice, and funds calculated at average Continental daily rates, as permitted by HM Inland ˉRevenue. We estimate ten days.

They remained mine sincerely.

It was Connie's godspeed. My hand shook as I signed the receipt.

The lad proudly burned off on his motor-bike, with me standing there looking at the air ticket with vision suddenly gone blurred. She hadn't believed me one bit.

Bloody women, I thought, and locked up.

CHAPTER 9

Venice. If you've never seen it you can't believe it. And when you clap your eyes on it you still don't believe it.

I stood on the Riva waterfront utterly bemused. It really *is* waterborne, floating in the sunlit mist of the lagoon. I've never seen anything like it. Nor, incidentally, has anyone else.

Since meeting old Mr Pinder I'd read like a maniac. Even on the plane to the Marco Polo International airport—we'd left at an ungodly hour—I was scrabbling through a potted history without gaining much. Clearly, the little maritime republic founded on a mudbank on Friday, 25 March, in the Year of Our Lord 421, had done okay for itself. Venice had an eye for the old gelt. But when I got to the bit about the Venetian calendar starting on March 1 and Venetian days officially starting in the evening, I chucked it aside. I was confused enough. I even

started on my old Italian course notes, but what can you
do with a language where the words for 'need' and
'dream' are so disturbingly similar? I chucked those aside
too. My usual Lovejoy method would have to do—
osmosis, fingers crossed, and a penny map.

Like I said, pathetic.

The whole waterfront was on the go. Busy, busy. They
were all there, massive black and white tugs, barges, the
water-taxis, waterbuses, all nudging the Riva. I must say,
the poles to which they were moored looked decidely
wobbly to me, but there was a jaunty confidence to the
scene, as if Venice had had that sort of useless criticism
before and so what? Crowds ambled around the *vaporetto*
terminus. Early-season tourists drifted, gazed at the
souvenir stalls, peered into canals from bridges.

Across the lagoon the beautiful San Giorgio Maggiore
rose from the vague afternoon mist, and, away beyond, a
suggestion of the Lido's buildings showed where the
Adriatic Sea was kept at bay. To the left, the Arsenal
shipyard which had turned out a completed warship every
day when the Serene Republic was doing over the Turks.
To the right, across the water the gold gleams of the
Salute church, still celebrating the end of that bubonic
plague, 1681, and marking the start of the Grand Canal.

But where were the streets, the avenues, the cars? Odd,
that. I'd heard of Venice's canals, of course. I just wasn't
prepared for the fact that they were everywhere and
completely displaced roads. I stood to watch a big liner
shushing slowly past, turning in towards the long raised
spine of the Giudecca island. Another odd thing—despite
the bustle, no noise except for the occasional muffled roar
of a water-taxi. I finally got the point of Joker Benchley's
cable home: 'Streets full of water. Please advise.' You
walk in tiny alleys between the canals, on bridges over the
water, or in and out of tiny squares and that's about it.
The *fondamenti*, places where an actual pavement exists,

are practically major landmarks and rare enough to have special names. All right, I thought. Venice is simply one hell of a tangle, with hardly anywhere to put your feet.

But it was still the place where I would find that yacht-owning lemon-coloured smoothie and his two goons who did for Crampie and Mr Malleson. Ledger couldn't touch me here, and with luck some delectable antique might fall my way.

Right, now. Where to start? I looked about expectantly.

'You find a welcome, signore?'

The boatman was smoking nearby. I nodded, 'Yes, thank you.'

The water-taxi which had brought us from the mainland airport was idle at the wharf. From the way the driver was grinning he had spotted my deception. And I thought I'd been so slick, mingling discreetly with the Cosol tour mob who had flocked off our plane, getting a free sail into Venice. He offered me a fag. I declined with a head-shake.

'First time in Venice, signore?'

'Very first. It's beautiful.' No grass, no countryside, I suddenly realized with delight. Everything—*every single thing*—in sight was man-made. Boats, canals, houses, wharves, bridges, hotels, churches. Everything. It gave me a funny feeling, almost as if I'd come safe home.

'*Grazie.*' He read my glance with the keen skill of centuries. 'We have trees and fields, signore—out at Torcello island and places.'

'*Deo gratias,*' I said, thanking God with ambiguous politeness, which restored his approving grin. 'Your little signorina was uspet because I, ah, borrowed a ride?'

The Cosol courier was a pretty but distraught girl who had engaged in a ferocious whispered row with him at the airport. She was still inside the hotel seeing to complicated room allocations. He pulled a face.

'The other girl refused to come this week. Signorina Cosima will have to run all our tours.' He shrugged eloquently as if that was the ultimate calamity.

'Your boat wouldn't be free for a half-hour . . . ?' I said, a little too quickly. The penny had dropped at long last.

'Possibly,' he said in a way that left no doubt. 'Perhaps I show the signore the Grand Canal, the Rialto Bridge, the—'

'May I give directions?' I suggested politely.

He already had the painter in his hand. He nodded at my words, as if Venice constantly received complete strangers who knew their way about.

The weird familiarity of Venice is quite unnerving. Like coming across your own backyard in, say, darkest Abyssinia. Five minutes after leaving the hotel I was looking expectantly for landmarks which I *knew* would be there. 'Vivaldi's church of *la Pietà, non è vero?*' I said even before we cast off. It was only five or so buildings along the Riva wharf from the hotel. An instant later, the romantically misnamed Bridge of Sighs, the Doge's Palace, the great campanile and the Piazza of St Mark's. Every lovely thing exactly where you expected. We swept grandly past them, me rapturously thinking I was dreaming at the splendour of it all.

Thin crowds meandered between the long tethered line of nodding gondolas and the start of the slender Merceria shopping lane which runs off the Piazza. Harry's Bar was in action not far from the waterbus stop. We came abreast and ploughed into the Grand Canal. I asked if it was always this crowded.

'Worse, signore. *L'estate* . . . !' The boatman rolled his eyes at the problem of the summer. 'Even the Accademia Bridge groans then. The trouble is, everything in Venice is famous.'

'You must be glad—so many customers,' I said, 'though I suppose many bring their own boats?'

'Not many,' he replied, slowing to deflect his prow from a gondola crossing the canal up ahead. 'Visiting boats moor over the other side, facing the Giudecca.'

Important news, for when the *Eveline* arrived. 'I hadn't expected the Grand Canal to be so wide.'

All innocent, I asked him to let me watch the gondola. In it, four people stood solemnly upright while the gondola crossed the canal. Our boat idled by the little wooden jetties.

'Fixed fare from the *traghetto*, the gondola ferry.' He spoke with scorn. 'That's all they do—to and fro.'

My eyes were drawn to the adjacent buildings fronting the canal's splashy water.

'Do many foreigners have a palace here?'

'Palazzo,' he corrected politely. I'd used the English word by mistake. 'Merely means a grand house, in Venice. Yes, plenty come. Most stay in hotels such as that, in the campo there by the *traghetto* ferry.' His gaze idled across the campo to the tall pink-washed palazzo opposite. 'Others, the rich, buy their own palazzo.'

It was all I could do not to turn and stare at the building. What was it old Pinder had said so dreamily by his fireside when trying to persuade me to work for him? *The hours I have watched the traghetto men smoke and talk in the campo below my window in the Grand Canal . . .*

'No pavement,' I observed, my excitement barely under control. The houses just drop sheer into the water. Therefore no place to stroll casually past in the dark hours and test the strength of the palazzo's drainpipes, because there was simply nowhere to stroll.

'*Vero*,' the boatman said. 'Except one can walk in the campo, and even reach the Basilica on foot.'

The narrow space had once been a tiny field, hence its

name. One side, that hotel. The other side, the palazzo of
Mrs Lavinia Norman — if I'd guessed right. I needed my
map, where the palazzi were named.

'Are there many *traghetti* in Venice?'

'Very few.' He coughed to draw my attention. 'Signore.
The waterbus is approaching. And the *traghetto* has
crossed long since . . .'

'Ah. Sorry. Fine.' I nodded for him to go ahead,
irritated at being too obvious.

The waterbus was creaming towards its stop, a
wobbling T-shaped jetty with a cabin full of intending
passengers.

'To the Rialto Bridge, signore? Or the Fenice Theatre?
You'll know we Venetians invented opera.'

'You've a lot to answer for.' His face fell, but I honestly
can't understand why every little opera takes a fortnight.
I glanced forward. 'Show me the shape of Venice, please.'

'*Subito*,' he said, and we took off up the Grand Canal.

Everything is fantastic when you think about it long
enough. But some things are just simply mind-blowers by
nature. Venice is one of them.

It's a manmade universe of alleys, ancient houses, and
great — *great* — churches crammed on to a maze of canals.
And where? On 117 islets, in a lagoon of over 200 square
miles, that's where, with the Adriatic Sea muttering
sullenly just over a mile from the main island cluster of
Venice proper. Like the water-bloke said, everything in
Venice is famous. But to grow accustomed to Venice
you'd need a lifetime. I was amazed at everything.

Venice is singing cage-birds at canal-side windows.
Venice is exquisite shops and window-dressing. Venice is
inverted-funnel chimneys, leaning campaniles, wrought-
iron at doors and windows, grilles at every fenestration,
little flower-sellers, droves of children and noisy youths.
Venice is bridges every few yards, narrow alleys where you

have to duck to get under the houses which have crammed so close they've merged to make a flat tunnel. Venice is patchy areas of din — from speedboats racing to deposit their owners in cafés to do nothing hour upon hour—and silence. It's uncanny, really, how it can be broad day and all is silent. The canals glass. Nothing moves. The *calli* empty. Bridges hang in permanent solitude of space and time, as if the world was concentrating. Then, somnolently ambling round a confined corner, you're suddenly wedged in a dense people-jam pandemonium between glittering shops. It's the abruptness of the transition gets me every time: tranquillity into hubbub. Venice is a million separate sound barriers. Venice even has its methods—police boats, waterbuses, grocery boats, even funeral gondolas and barges conveniently moored facing the Madonna dell' Orto church on the side of Venice nearest the cemetery island. And the whole set of islands and lagoon on the go.

The boatman put me down exactly on the Riva. He had a high old time arguing the price for my two-hour jaunt, but deep down I was badly shaken. From every side I had been slammed by emanations from antiques—the buildings and the treasures they contained. I could hardly see, let alone breathe or argue sensibly. Even so, I had a shrewd suspicion the boatman surrendered too easily to a price which was almost fair. Something was wrong. I made great play of standing on his wood jetty watching the tourists stroll among the cafe tables set out along the waterfront.

'Apologies to Signorina Cosima if I made you late.'

'Cesare,' the boatman said. 'Like Borgia.'

'*Grazie*, Cesare. Lovejoy,' I said. He didn't even guffaw.

He tried the name experimentally while folding the money away. 'Should you need to travel to the palazzo of your friends, ask along the Riva anytime, *per piacere*.' He'd used the singular, palazzo. So he meant one in particular.

I said carefully, 'Friends? I know no one in Venice, Cesare.'

'Of course not,' he said with gravity. 'I meant should you wish to.'

'You know all about Venice.'

He smiled deprecatingly. 'We Venetians know some, though not all. Much is rumour—especially about newcomers in rich houses.'

There it was. He had detected my interest in the palazzo. I smiled and nodded. 'It's a deal. Give me a day to find my feet. Oh.' I stopped on the stone wharf. 'Give me a tip about Venice. Anything.' I explained away his puzzlement, 'I collect facts.' All too often they mean survival.

'Ah, *capisco*.' He thought a second. 'How long have you got?'

'Ten days.'

'Then it will be useful for you to know that we Venetians buy wine by taking an empty bottle for a refill. Make sure it's a one-litre bottle.'

Bigger bottle, same price. 'Very useful. Thanks, Cesare.'

'Wait, signore. In Venice we too collect useful facts.'

After a quick think I said, 'Santa Claus is also patron saint of prostitutes.'

He nodded seriously, coiling the painter. 'You are a careful man, Lovejoy. My tip will be most useful to you. Yours is without value.'

'Not everything is money.'

His audible gasp at this heresy gave me a grin. On my way past that daft plumed statue of Victor Emmanuel on the Riva, the Cosol courier Cosima hurried out, pretty with exasperation. Almost before she reached Cesare's water-taxi she was blasting him for being late.

Ten days, minus one.

CHAPTER 10

Food is definitely funny stuff. Miles from home, it takes on a weirdness that either turns you into a gourmet or repels you for life.

To me, a plate of spaghetti is a full meal. To Venetians it's no more than a windbreak. After noshing enough to sink a fleet they just soldier on through a jungle salad, then wade into half a fried calf followed by a *gelato* ice-cream all the colours of the rainbow. It's nourishing just to watch. Mind you, it takes nerve. Seeing a Venetian whittle a mound of whitebait is like watching a seal cull.

Go away from the Riva down one of those little alleys where your shoulders practically touch both walls, turn right, and you'll find one of the best nosh places in Venice. It's tucked under the shoulder of a bridge before the San Zaccaria. Venetian boatmen use it, so I felt it was as near to Woody's caff as I was likely to find, and in I went for a slammer of a meal. Some kinds of strange grub you can guess at, like how they'll do their veal. Others — fried rings of squid for example — you don't know until you take your courage in both hands. Then there's *polenta*, which I tried because I'd never heard the word before, and got this yellow woolly maize breadcake, toasted hot as hell. It's the local equivalent of our pasty — filling, cheap, eaten anywhere anytime. Made me feel quite at home, especially when I began to get slightly pickled on the wine.

Only a couple of rooms, and a counter by the door, everybody was in earshot of everybody else. That was half my reason for choosing it, but the talk turned out to be money, family, money, trade, money, and money. Not a whisper of antiques or fakes, and nobody mentioned the big house by the *traghetto* gondola ferry—the Palazzo Malcontento on my guide map. Of course, somebody within earshot mentioned the scandalous theft of St Luce's remains and the mysterious ransom demand of 1981, which focused brief attention on money. And no sight of Cesare. A longshot, really. After an hour—to me a good meal should last five minutes at the outside—I went out to explore Venice on foot.

It's easier said than done. During the meal I studied the map. Venice seems nothing but landmarks. In the end I'd picked out a few. St Mark's Square was a natural, and the Ponte di Rialto is the world's most famous bridge, sure to be well signposted. Two. And Mrs Norman's palazzo near that gondola ferry lay somewhere between. It looked easy. After all, the whole place was only about three miles by one. The canals were sure to be named, and Cesare's circular tour had shown me Venice's shape. The position of the other islands would show you which bit of Venice you'd reached. Simple, no? Answer: no. Unless you've a superb sense of direction, you're bewildered after a hundred yards and find yourself going anywhere but where you want.

A mist had descended. This seems to be the pattern in late March, foggy mist till mid-morning, then hazy sun till dusk when the mist comes back for the night. A bell was clonking monotonously out in the lagoon beyond the Riva wharfside. Tugs, ferryboats, water-taxis, and the rows of covered gondolas nodding between Harry's Bar and the Doge's Palace were inactive now. Few people, the tables and chairs stacked, the ornamental tubbed trees cleared away, a handful of young wanderers with haversacks waiting dozily for a night boat. It was all very evocative, listlessly beautiful. I'm not a sensitive bloke, but the melancholy quickly seeped into my bones. I wasn't cold, not like Connie gets. It must have been the unrelenting vibrations emanating from ancient Venice and sounding on my recognition bell. I shook myself, plodded over the Rio del Vin bridge, and was off, weaving slightly.

Lights guide you at all 449 bridges, and the *calle* alleyways are fairly well lit so long as you are near the main centres where elegant shops and posh restaurants abound. Yet it's an odd feeling being able to touch both sides of the high street as you walk. You soon get so used to it you're astonished when you come out unexpectedly into an open square.

Away from the main Merceria shopping thoroughfare, though, the tangle worsens. The canals develop an annoying habit of looking familiar when you know for a fact you are seeing them for the first time. The *calli* become narrower and more convoluted as you walk on. Bridges become more frequent and acutely-angled. I gave up trying to follow door numbers as a bad job. They are supposed to be supremely logical—start at nil and simply progress consecutively until the district runs out, but I couldn't quite get the hang of where Venice's six *Sestieri* or districts actually were, or which way the bloody numbers went at the trillion intersections.

In Cesare's water-taxi I'd worked out that the Palazzo Malcontento was less than 800 yards from the Riva as the crow flies. On foot it took me an hour, and I'm a quick walker. When finally I emerged into a narrow *campo* beside a church, and saw at the end the Grand Canal with the *traghetto* jetties, I knew it was luck more than judgement.

The place was ill-lit. The hotel one side was barely into its tourist season. A few tatty trellis-works marked off stacks of café tables, but the tub plants were dead and the ornamental electric bulbs trailed forlornly on frayed wires. The hotel seemed stuporose. The gondola ferry seemed to have jacked it in for the night. I strolled down the *campo* to the Grand Canal. Obliquely across and left was Santa Maria della Salute. Right, if I dangled out far enough, would be the Accademia bridge but beyond there the backward S of the Grand Canal concealed everything else. Well, well. Casual as any actor from amateur rep, I gaped left. Carrying a camera has always embarrassed me but I badly felt the need of one now. Nothing would be easier from here than to pretend to photograph the string of lagoon lights near the island of San Giorgio, and accidentally include the canalside aspect of the Palazzo Malcontento, but it was too late for good ideas like that. Typical. Several lights were on in the house, but mostly the windows were shuttered. No surrounding garden, of course, though there might well be a tiny courtyard hidden somewhere behind those house walls. I'd seen enough stray tendrils here and there to suggest that little manufactured gardens lurked out of sight. The two doors had that terrible implacable continental finality about them — doors are there to be closed, not necessarily opened. The lowest windows were firmly shuttered. No finger holds. It was all bad news.

The hotel reception clerk glanced up as I passed the door. He must have caught the altered shadows. The *campo* was better lit than I'd appreciated. An outside wall lantern on the big house and the hotel hallway shed more light than a thief would want.

Depressed, I found a dog-leg *calle* and came out on a little bridge at the back of the palazzo. The canal below ran at right angles into the Grand Canal. A small but elderly barge thing was moored in it. One of those water doorways, heavily barred, tunnelled its way into the side of the house, presumably where groceries and whatnot were delivered from supply boats. Great, I thought bitterly. The one nooky way in, and bars a mile thick.

By the time I'd found the wider *calle larga* which ran towards St Mark's Square I was miserably sober. The big house was virtually impregnable. I knew nobody in Venice, so no chance of wheedling my way in as a friend of a friend. That fashion-conscious killer who had smirked in his fancy yellow de Lorean would be on his guard as soon as he showed up in his posh yacht and spotted me. It was hopeless.

Even St Mark's Square looked hardly alive. A few strolling night owls crossed in front of the great basilica, peering up at the bronze horses which stand in front of the upper façade's central window. Venice acquired them in the Fourth Crusade, but they were made a thousand years before that shambles. Only one place was open, a crowded coffee bar where distracted young blokes slogged to serve late customers along the counter's entire length.

'Coffee, please.'

'Two, please,' a bird's voice corrected at my elbow.

'Two,' I agreed, wondering what the hell. The crush was too great for me to turn, but I glimpsed Cosima's drained face in the mirror.

No place to sit. I made it to the stairs where people were clustered. Cosima helped. We squatted on the fourth step.

'Upstairs is closed this late,' she said, huddling the cup to her and breathing in the steam. 'Nobody'll push past.'

'Lucky for us.'

'You look like I feel.' Her dark eyes held me briefly, let me go.

'Eh?'

'Exhausted. Fed up.'

She was right. I suddenly realized I was all in. Time to chuck in the sponge for today. I didn't quite cheer up, but it was close.

'I'm glad you happened along, Cosima.' I meant it.

'You stole Cesare,' she accused. 'Made me later than ever.'

'Sorry. Your partner didn't show, eh?'

'No. The bitch never does. One phone call from that lout in Mestre and she's flat on her back. Leaves me to do it all.'

'Extra money, though?'

'That's a laugh. I've phoned nine agencies for a substitute but it's too early in the season, you see.'

Honestly, for the first time I really looked at her. I mean, really looked, to see the person she was. Of course I knew she was a bit of all right from having seen her at the airport and on the Riva. Black hair straying and bouncy, with her distraught air lending her youth an added charm. She dressed in bird's clothes, too, which is something of a novelty in these days of scrapyard-lumberjack fashion. Travel couriers can go practically anywhere they like, right?

'Are you really desperate?' I asked, all offhand.

She looked at me, also probably for the first time. 'Yes. I've not stopped. Been doing tomorrow's reservations since your lot arrived, not counting the afternoon flight.'

We went quiet for a minute, watching the crowd.

I said, 'I'm a registered travel courier.'

'You are?' Her eyes widened so suddenly at me I nearly fell into their darkness.

'Except . . .' I hesitated for form's sake. 'I've only ever done the Portugal runs . . .'

'That would be all right,' she said eagerly. 'Do you have your cards?'

'Well, no. I'm on holiday leave. But I know my registered number. It's X-2911894, London.'

With some excitement we got it written down in her notebook. I invented a travel firm called Leveridge and Kingston in Bury Street, near St James's, because snobbery is a con's greatest ally. Anyway, it would take them at least four days to check. By then I hoped to have sussed the Palazzo's secret and be independent of Cosima. Optimism's always a laugh.

'This is very kind of you.' She was having doubts as we finished our coffee. 'Why would you do this? It's a waste of your own holiday. And the pay isn't . . .'

I looked away, working as much embarrassment into my face as fatigue would allow.

'Erm, look, Cosima.' I tried to go red, but you never can when you want to. 'I've never done this before . . . Follow a girl, I mean. I only hired Cesare to find out who you were,' I went on, inwardly a tortured soul. I turned on my most transparently sincerely honest gaze and looked at her. 'I don't know quite why, but when I saw you standing there at the airport . . .'

She flushed, glancing away and back. 'You mean . . . you mean you were . . . ?'

My shrug wasn't as Latin as I wanted, but I did my best. 'I suddenly had to . . . well, find out where you went . . . Are you angry?'

'No,' she said, still uncertain but trying for emotional distance. 'Not really.'

'I'm trying to be honest with you, Cosima,' I said hesitantly.

'Oh, that's very important,' she agreed.

We agreed for a minute or two that honesty was vital in relationships and finished our cappucini among the café's throng.

'Positively no obligation,' I said as a weak lightener. 'But I'll help. And I'll not bother you. Word of honour.'

'Only if you're sure . . .'

Worrying I'd acted too well, I assured her I wouldn't mention my catastrophic love-smitten condition ever again. Gravely she accepted the promise. We made pedantic arrangements for next day. I was to come with her to organize the morning arrivals, then do the afternoon airport run to collect tourists on my own. Cesare apparently knew the ropes well enough to help if I got in a mess. Self-consciously she wrote a telephone number and an address on a torn page.

'That's me, Lovejoy. For business purposes.'

'For business purposes, Cosima.'

'I'll arrange pay on a daily basis.'

We rose to go and I risked a joke. 'You mean I also get paid?' but I was so clearly trying hard to be brave she gave a relieved smile.

She needed the No. 1 waterbus so I walked her past the great campanile to the San Zaccaria stop on the lagoon waterfront. I couldn't help asking as we crossed into the Piazzetta.

'*Two* horses?' She squinted up into the gloom. 'You mean four. See?'

'Four, yes, but only two genuine. The two on the right are fakes.'

'Who told you? It's practically a state secret. They are being replaced by official authentic copies. The originals will go into the Marciano Museum.'

'In the interests of conservation?' I'd blurted out the bitter remark before I could stop myself.

She glanced at me. 'Why, of course.'

We made only stilted chat after that until the waterbus came and we shook hands like folk leaving a party gone suddenly sour. For all that, I stood on the undulating jetty and watched her go. I waved once. She didn't wave back. I suppose she needed to think, same as me.

CHAPTER 11

It being so early in the year, the hotel was only able to provide half-board. Breakfast was tea and a wad, unless you went mad and ordered English breakfast of eggs, bacon, toast and the rest, then extras were written on your bill. It looked like being a hard day, so I stuffed with everything I could lay hands on. Maybe the hotel management wouldn't care for the idea of a guest transmuting into a courier. So long as I didn't actually starve, I could always sleep dangling in some belfry.

Airports are all madhouses. God knows what they're like in high season, but on my first full day I learned the hard way that Cosima's exasperation was completely justified. Our own band of tourists were insane. Before we'd been in action ten minutes I could have cheerfully shot the bloody lot. Cosima had me stand in the thin crowd of couriers, depressives to a man, and hold up a placard labelled Cosol in red. I felt a conspicuous twerp, and Cosima said that's what it's all about. 'Believe me, Lovejoy,' she warned anxiously. 'If they can fall into the lagoon, they will. Last week I lost a whole Ami family—they turned up in Belgrade.' She stuck three badges on me.

Cesare had taxied us across the lagoon before nine. Cosima was lovely in the morning haze, her hair blowing as our boat creamed between the lagoon marker posts. She looked really stylish, almost too well turned out for a travel courier. We avoided each other's eyes and did a great deal of agreeing. I wondered vaguely if she was dolled up because of some bloke coming on one of the flights. None of my business. Still, my improvised confession of instantaneous love had worked a treat.

Before long I would be in charge of a tourist band and able to trail them anywhere. What more natural than select a 'typical' Venetian palazzo—the Malcontento, for instance—and call to ask if the lady of the house would permit visitors to inspect the elegant interior of so classical a dwelling?

That was the last coherent thought I had for a couple of hours. The tourists came through the Customs like a football crowd. We couriers held up our placards and bleated our firms' names, me carolling 'Cosol Tours, folks.' The whole row of us was overrun within seconds. I was engulfed by a motley mob, all ages, that plucked at my clothes, explaining mistakes, complaining, waving documents, showing me passports and tickets. One woman had lost a child and expected me to find it. One bloke had acquired two infants and wanted to hand them to me. One senile old crone had left her hand-luggage in Zürich. A tiny psychopath nicked my clipboard to play with. It was a nightmare. 'Cosol,' I kept calling, holding my stick aloft to attract more of these psychotics.

Cosima had to rescue me finally because I couldn't match up the sea of expectant faces with the names.

'They're all foreigners,' I whispered frantically. 'They aren't English or Italian.'

'German, American, Danes,' she whispered back. 'Talk English slow.'

She made me stand by the door and tick them off. Apparently the greatest mistake of all is to take away tourists from some other courier's group because you can never completely undo the documentation. Cesare loaded their cases—my God, did they bring frigging cases—until his boat was heaped high with the damned luggage. Cosima hung back to settle a Customs officer's apoplexy over something a young couple were bringing in, while I tried to put the flock into the boat in some sort of order. We had two hotels to call at, eighteen people all told. I almost lost an elderly bloke with a bad leg; another boat looked easier to board and he nearly escaped. It was only when Cesare noticed some old bird's anxiety that we recounted, and I went running hectically among the other water-taxis yelling the old bloke's name to get him back. Silly old sod. My head was splitting as we made space for Cosima and set off south towards Venice.

Trying to be a typical courier, I assumed a boisterous Italian accent and pointed out landmarks, mostly wrong, giving out exotic snippets I'd picked up about Byron, so much a part of Venice. That started them all asking breathless questions. Odd how people go for extravagant behaviour. We're all a bit like that, deep down, wanting to hear about Byron's Venetian roistering, scandals, his wild affairs. People are weird. Like, it's exciting to hear of the great poet-hero's splendid triumph in the swimming race from the Lido all the way up the Grand Canal. It's somehow less pleasant to hear that he loved to display his superb grace in the water because his ungainly club-footed lameness was so obvious on land. Hence his love of the night hours—the superstitious Venetians of those days would not stand within thirty paces of the deformed. I had the sense only to mention the posh bits.

We passed the cemetery island of San Michele that Napoleon got organized, and penetrated Venice proper. From then on it was bedlam. We separated our mob into two groups, luggage and all. Distributing them into separate hotels took us over an hour. Two people had not arrived on the plane and we had hell's own job persuading the second hotel we hadn't sold them into slavery, or—worse—to another hotel.

That gave us fifty minutes before I re-zoomed to the airport for the next horde. Cosima sat with me at one of the Riva caffs and went over the procedure. We were still very proper with each other, but I didn't mind. She would look after this morning's lot. The Ami tourists now due would be my sole responsibility.

'I like Yanks. I'll guide them round Byron's haunts.'

'You can't do the guide's job, Lovejoy. They're two different roles in Venice. I suppose they're combined in Portugal?'

'Mmmmh? Oh, mmh.'

More bad news. She saw me off in Cesare's water-taxi, calling worried last-minute guidance till we left earshot. I gave her my most confident grin and waved. She wore fawn and cream. All the way, till Cesare gave a bad-tempered swing of the bow taking us behind the Arsenale, I could see her slender loveliness showing against the pastel-coloured buildings. Well.

Cesare said very little on that trouble-free run back to the mainland. Almost as if he was furious at something. Still, the guidebook said Venetians were secretive, so I tactfully didn't ask him what was up. Deep down I'm a pretty sensitive sort of bloke.

That afternoon everything went right. Unbelievably, I found myself ahead of schedule. By two o'clock my tourists were ensconced in the hotels, signed for, the desk registries satisfied, Cesare's books made up, the Cosol dockets filled in on Cosima's clipboard, and not a single family in Belgrade. I kept my phoney Italian accent to lend authenticity and it worked quite well as long as Cesare wasn't too near and giving me the bent eye.

Even better, they were a talkative friendly bunch, as Yanks tend to be, and wanted me to be in the downstairs bar at three to advise on restaurants and other aspects. A pleasant, shapely bird called Nancy, mid-thirties, caught my eye, with Doris and Agnes, two attractive blue-rinsed middle-aged women, all towing a mild-mannered tubby bloke called David and forming a separate mini-group 'being from California, y'see'. Nancy explained she was David's secretary from Sherman Oaks, saying it as if the rest of California was a suburb and getting a laugh.

We reassembled downstairs in such high spirits I was more than a little narked that Cosima wasn't there to see how well I was doing. I dished out Cosima's little pamphlets full of shopping and dining hints, and gave them all a brief account of the tourist map in that dulled voice couriers use when they've said it a million times before. Though I say it myself, I was very convincing. The one hassle was something to do with a bathroom plug, easily passed on to the desk clerks.

David Vidal, the tubby Californian, suggested we take a quick stroll 'to catch the light', whatever that meant. Doris and Agnes eagerly agreed, and I was coopted to lead a small schismatic group out there and then, even though I explained their guide would be along to give them their private countdown at breakfast tomorrow. I must say, they're keen in California, and nearly as hot in Florida — two elderly Miami couples wanted to come along too. So it was that, under Cesare's sardonic eye, I emerged on to the Riva leading a party of eight towards St Mark's with David turning around judging the sky and holding up three little camera-like gadgets he had hanging on him. Still, it takes all sorts.

They wanted to dash into the Doge's Palace. Going all debonair, I paid the pittance entrance fee, pretending it was my pleasure to treat them. Actually it broke my heart but I was desperate to wheedle my way into favour. Maybe they'd insist to Cosima that I be promoted to a guide . . .

In the mad dash round the Palazzo Ducale before it closed, I was a real ball of fire. The faster we went, the more pleased my minimob became. We saw the Great Council Chamber, the Lion's Mouth letter-box where you slipped denunciations of treason — in the days of the Doges, Venetians got a hundred pieces of gold for each accusation, so a lot of it went on — and the exquisite ceilings. I was practically in tears as we zipped in and out of the chambers, corridors, prisons, galleries. To me speed is the modern disease. Dashing past Veronese's *Juno offering gifts to Venice* is a crime. It's the only genuine one of that set, as I pointed out to Nancy—the French kept the rest after 1797, though you're not supposed to notice. We were lucky and got into the Room of the Three Inquisitors, but Tintoretto's ceiling paintings have been replaced. David Vidal sympathized with my abject disappointment when I told him what was the matter.

'Look okay to me,' he said, quizzically peering upwards. He simply hadn't stopped judging the sky. Even surrounded by these massed treasures he was still glancing at windows, the bum.

'What *are* these things?'

'These? Light meters.'

'You a photographer?'

Agnes laughed. 'David's a movie-maker, here on assignment. We—'

A quick glance from David cut her prattle. I pretended not to notice and carried on my distilled guidebook patter. I had a few successes—the Bridge of Sighs, the prisons from which Casanova escaped in 1775—but mostly missed out. David was mad at Agnes. Agnes was pale. I was still trying gamely as we emerged on the quayside of St Mark's Basin, pointing out which of the 36 palace capitals were real mediæval stone carvings. Nancy was up in arms at the idea that half were modern replacements.

'That's cheating, if the guidebooks say only three are reproduction!'

I had to smile. Trust a woman. 'Mostly a harmless trick, love.'

'Well, so long as somebody keeps records.'

'I'm sure somebody probably does.'

'Don't you *know?*'

'Of course,' I said smoothly, thinking: Oh hell. I'd
forgotten for the minute I was a Venetian. 'Erm, in the,
erm, Venetian Antiquities Section of the, erm, Buildings
Ministry.'

'Well, *that's* a relief!"

David examined one of the phonies closely. 'How can
you tell the difference?'

'They feel, erm . . .' I recovered quickly, and gave a
convincing laugh. 'Well, actually we couriers are given
Ministry notices.'

He looked doubtful. 'If you say so, Lovejoy.'

The Floridans wanted to tip me as I got them back to
their hotel in the gathering mist. I refused, all noble,
saying it was my pleasure. Tom, an elderly Miami
boatbuilder, said how well I'd learned English for an
Italian. Nancy was the only one who'd cooled appreciably
during the brief walkabout.

'Almost too idiomatic,' she said sweetly. She was having
a good laugh inside, the way women do when they've
rumbled that you're up to something.

'I spenda two years inna London.' I did some hurried
bowing and scraping, but she gave me a sideways look.

They thronged the bar. I escaped by pious pleading
that it was too early for me to drink intoxicating fluids. I
was knackered and tottered into the lift amid a chorus of
bye-byes. My room was 214. It overlooked Ferrari's rotten
garish statue of Victor Emmanuel, but you can't have
everything.

I practically fell inside, looking forward to a hot soak, a
brief kip, then a long read about Venice and a quiet nosh
at the boatmen's caff near the San Zaccaria. The light in
my room was on.

Cosima was sitting on my bed, reading my Venice
book.

'Lovejoy. Where've you been?'

'Working,' I said. 'You?'

CHAPTER 12

The next two days I worked like a dog. We handled six planeloads of mixed tourists, two on charter flights, which necessitated taking on an extra two water-taxis for those. Cesare saw to them. He was great but ever more taciturn, not at all like the cheery bloke I'd met on my first day. The better our little trio functioned, the surlier he became. Odd. That earlier banter we had enjoyed was gone. Cosima on the other hand was blossoming, looking more radiant every day. Shrewd as always, I supposed her bloke had finally showed and that after working hours she was enjoying life to the full. Though I must say she wasn't getting much of his company the rate we were going. We hardly had time to snatch a bite in the waterfront caffs. We noshed like a Biggin Hill fighter squadron waiting for tannoys to shout the scramble.

For all that, I was oddly happy. It was as if I'd found a safe niche where the problem of Crampie and Mr Malleson, and the scam which old Pinder's grand-daughter and her killer boyfriend were supposedly helping the old fool to plan, could be comfortably forgotten. Maybe it was Cosima's accusation which had cleared the air, something like that.

That night I got back after showing Nancy and David and their pals the Ducal Palace, she had chucked the book aside but stayed on my bed, and demanded to know where I'd been. Women always have me stammering, as if I've really been up to no good. And honestly, hand on my heart, I honestly hadn't even thought of Nancy like that until Cosima said her name.

'I was only out walking,' I'd explained.

'With eight of the Americans,' she blazed. 'Including

that fat bespectacled Waterson woman who fancies herself—'

Nancy wasn't fat. 'They wanted to see San Marco. I thought I was helping you out.'

'Lovejoy.' She swung off the bed, furious but pretty as a picture. 'I've seen the way you look at these overdressed tourist bitches. Well, just let me tell you that if you step one single inch out of line I'll have your courier registration cancelled. On the spot! Do you hear?'

'But—'

'But nothing! Couriers and tourists are not allowed to . . . to . . .'

The trouble is, pretty women have the edge. They make you tongue-tied even when you're honest. It's bloody unfair.

'Look, Cosima, love,' I said brokenly, taking her arms. 'I didn't want to do this job. I was on holiday, remember? It's only that I, well, falling for you like I did makes me . . .'

'All *right*, Lovejoy!' She pushed away, not at all mollified. God, she was lovely. Her hair was sheer silk. I'd never seen any hair as lustrous as that. I bet it would be lovely spread out on a soft white pillow, just like Margaret's and Helen's and Liz's. 'All *right!* But you just remember.'

'I was only trying to do what you said, love.'

She spun round on her way to the door. 'What *I* said?'

'The tourist is always right.' Biting my lip, I subsided on the bed, clearly misunderstood and close to heartbreak.

She hesitated. 'Well, yes. I know I did say that . . .'

I shrugged, deeply hurt. 'You don't know how it feels . . .'

'Look,' Cosima said, but less firmly. 'I don't want you to take it too much to heart, Lovejoy. I just had to speak out before you got, well, *drawn in*. I've seen it happen.'

'I'll remember,' I said bravely, Gunga Din on the battlements.

'Very well. Then we need say no more about it.'

There was a brief pause. I didn't raise my eyes because we Gunga Dins are soulful creatures and don't particularly want our innermost feelings revealed.

She too was hesitant now. 'Lovejoy. Have you had time yet to find any more of those restaurants I listed for you?'

'No.' I heaved a sigh. 'I was going to have a bath, then go out with the map.'

She said seriously, 'As it happens, I was intending to, well, take a quick walk round the Cannareggio. Since neither of us has really eaten properly today, it might be convenient to take the opportunity . . .'

'So long as you're my guest,' I said. 'Please. It would give me such pleasure.'

'Very well. Eight o'clock at the Fondamenta di Santa Lucia? We needn't be too late.'

'Thank you, love.'

I waited until the lift doors clashed before recovering from my heartbreak. Already I knew enough to know that the Cannareggio Canal was not really a tourist area. If anything, it was somewhat out of the way. Still, another crisis was averted by the simple tactic of agreeing to spend the evening with such a beautiful bird as Cosima. Painless.

In the bath I bellowed some Gilbert and Sullivan, making myself laugh by trying to translate the words into Italian as I went.

What with the hectic state of our affairs I saw very little of my favourite group, that minimob of eight who had rushed and talked me off my feet in the Doge's Palace. Only after those two endless slogging days did I happen to bump into Nancy Waterson in the bar. Honestly, it really was accidental.

It was pretty late, going on midnight. As I entered the bar, worn out, a lovely but older woman beckoned me. Lovely perfume, bluish eyes, dressed to kill with that elegance middle-aged Italian women capture so perfectly. And tons and tons of make-up—always turns me on, that. She wore a seventeenth-century Florentine crucifix as a brooch pin, not quite her only mistake. A two-carat central stone of that rarest of gems Royal Lavulite, a translucent luscious purple, carried off its misplaced setting in the crucifix's centre with utter nonchalance.

She looked me over like they do horses. 'You the guide? Get me a Rusty Nail.'

'What for?'

She pulled me round. I'd been walking past. 'You're supposed to be a guide and you don't know the great Italian invention of the cocktail?'

The penny dropped. A rusty nail must be a drink. That wasn't quite as important as the fact that this high-class bird thought I was a serf. I shook her off. Venice was full of people she could order about without starting on me.

'French tradition, please. Amédée Peychaud was a Froggie pharmacist in New Orleans, love, and *he* invented the cocktail.' She still looked blank. ' 'Course, he did it mostly with absinthe and cognac in those natty little eggcups—*coquetiers*—now so highly prized as collectors' items—'

'Who are you?' she said, wondering.

'My grannie said not to talk to strange women in honky-tonks.'

I moved on, her chain-saw laughter following me as I pushed in. The barman tried. 'Lovejoy. A Rusty Nail's half-and-half Scotch—'

'Great news,' I said. 'Stick at it, Alessandro.'

The presence of Nancy in the far corner straightened my gaze. The older woman departing, that left nobody else about except the barman watching a telly screen, and Nancy. She flagged me over and gave me a glass of her wine. Her bar table was covered with notebooks. Too casually she shut them one by one. David, I learned happily, was out.

'Look,' I said. 'I didn't mean Agnes to get in trouble by asking—'

'Forget it. Movie people are like that. Touchy.'

'You too?'

She finally could not hold back and burst out laughing. And I do mean rolled in the aisles. She was helpless. The night barman smiled with the distant politeness of his kind but kept his eyes on the video-recorded football match.

'Your accent's slipping again, Lovejoy.'

Well, I was so tired I'd become confused. So many faces, nationalities, different hotels. I was bushed. And I'd told different stories to each lot. To the Danes in the Danieli—or was it the Londra?—I was a penniless music student working out my tuition fee. To the West Germans in the Firenze—or was it the Bisanzio?—I was an Australian spinning out the grand tour. To the Americans I was an Italian ex-waiter scratching a living . . .

Narked, I sat glowering while Nancy dried her eyes and made a gasping recovery, clutching her ribs. 'Oh, Lovejoy! That laugh did me good!' She touched my hand and refilled my glass. 'Don't be annoyed, honey. Only, it's so obvious. What exactly's going on, for heaven's sake?'

'Nothing.' Do Yanks really say 'honey', or was she mucking about?

'Come on. Don't sulk.' She was still laughing, silly bitch. 'We're all full of different theories about you. You know Tom and George are running a book? Dave Vidal's got six-to-four you're an antiquarian down on his luck.'

'Oh, he has, has he?' I said bitterly, thinking, I was

bloody well born that. 'What's favourite?'

'Agnes and Doris put ten dollars evens you're an actor practising different roles.'

'And you, Nancy?'

She quietened. Her smile vanished. 'Me, Lovejoy? I can't quite make up my mind between some sort of policeman—'

'They don't work this hard, love.'

'—or some sort of, well, criminal.'

'They don't work this hard, either.' I pinched the rest of her carafe and asked if her budget would run to a slab of nosh.

'Maybe,' she said, still grave. 'If you'll tell me what drives a man harder than hunters and hunted.'

It was bloody difficult, but I forced a buoyant smile. 'It's a deal.' I pulled her to her feet and helped her to sweep her books together. 'Come on. I'll introduce you to *polenta* in a boatman's nosh bar in a *calle* around the corner. Positively no obligation.'

She started smiling again and found her coat. 'Stop it, Lovejoy.'

I kept a weather eye out for Cosima all the way to the little bridge caff by the San Zaccaria. Not that I was worried. I just didn't want her getting ideas.

Then I nicked this gondola.

CHAPTER 13

Love's supposed to be the great pacifier. It is nothing of the sort. It's a torment, a stirrer, the ultimate hellraiser. Really great.

Oddly, Nancy and me were friendly, not at all like the usual carry-on with savage undertones, riotous misunderstandings, bitterness and suchlike. It only rarely happens. I found it very strange, almost weird, to be lying awake in Nancy's bed, hardly knowing who she was yet actually liking her. And not a scar on either of us. The mayhem was missing. A very disturbing sign, this. I was worried. It might be the way serfdom starts.

She was in the bathroom when I got dressed and slipped out. Luckily we were on different floors, so I was able to nip downstairs quite legitimately. Nobody was about. The phone in my room started ringing as I collected my map. That would be Nancy looking for me and ready to play hell. I didn't even pause. The reception-counter clock said three-thirty, almost too late to embark on a night prowl.

Turn right along the Riva degli Schiavoni in the mist under the line of waterfront lamps. Right at the Doge's Palace. Cross St Mark's Square obliquely left, avoiding the famous Clock Arch. Do a quick double dog-leg, and you are at a small canal basin between a hotel, a tiny pavement and a couple of side *calli*. A few bored gondoliers usually chat there in pre-season slackness, not really hoping for custom. Seven or eight gondolas are always aligned in the basin, the tarpaulin covers mostly left on.

Nobody on guard. No signs of life. No wonder, since there's nowhere you can go in a Venetian gondola except Venice. I took the end gondola with ease — no way of locking one, hence my brilliant choice of vehicle. Its cover was murder to shift and twice I nearly fell in. As a sign of good faith in case I got nabbed I took pains to fold the damned thing, and finally made a wobbly cast-off.

Living in the estuaries of East Anglia, I'm not too bad on a boat though they've minds of their own, but a gondola's the queerest craft I've ever tried to handle. For a start, it's deliberately built off balance. I mean it really is asymmetrical, with its bum leaning over more one side than the other. You propel it by this one stern oar. Easy enough, yet you have to keep guessing how much space you have over that toothy *ferro* thing at the front. Add to that the bridges which try to brain you every few yards, and you get the idea it's not plain sailing. It is so low down, especially in a night mist with the damp house walls rising into the night on either side.

There was only me afloat at this godforsaken hour. I poled out of the basin, turned a shaky left mostly by scrabbling along the canal's wet walls. Three bridges later, left again for two. Then three split fingernails, a few muttered oaths and two head thumps, and I doglegged out of the Rio di Fenice to see the Grand Canal in the gloom straight ahead.

So far nobody on the bridges on in the *calli* as far as I could tell. I pushed wearily into the thinner *rio* at the back of the great theatre, and a waterbus swished across about a hundred yards away, frightening me to death. From the vantage point of a gondola it looked like the *Queen Mary*, all lights and motion. The best about these little side canals is they get no tidal wave to speak of, so I was able to shove the gondola across the *rio* and ride out the minuscule disturbance. I'd no idea the wretched things ran at night.

Which meant that leaving the safety of the narrow *rio* was out of the question. That worried me even more.

I shoved the lopsided craft nervously forward beneath the bridge from which I'd examined the side of the Palazzo Malcontento. A few more strokes and I would be alongside that tunnel-like archway I'd seen, so thoughtfully barred against furtive intruders like me.

A silent Renaissance building, tiers of rectangular shuttered windows. Seen close to and from the water level, Venice is alarmingly tattered and patched. Even by the poor *rio* lights I could see that the palazzo was in the same state as the rest. I gave my gondola one more push and glided along the wall.

The barred archway allowed a head space of about four feet. I had no torch—me being stupid again—but beyond the bars, which seemed to be sort of padlocked double-hinged doors, there was a stretch of water about fifteen feet long running underneath the house. I had the idea I could make out a couple of wet steps and a kind of cellar space. Of course, there'd be no other way to move furniture in or out, there being simply no streets. This kind of entrance must be the Venetian equivalent of driving up to the front door.

Assuming I could somehow get past the barred entrance without springing some alarm, it was a way in. It was possibly wired top to bottom. But it only needed one—*one*—late-night bridge-stroller to happen by, and there'd be a hue and cry at a stray gondola poised outside a respectable palazzo in a distinguished part of the city. Too chancy.

Depressed, I handwalked the gondola back up the *rio* to the bridge. A small *fondamenta* pavement makes it easy to land there. I tethered the gondola, left a note under the tarpaulin and strolled nonchalantly off in the direction of St Mark's. I'd never felt so utterly down.

Lesson: Venetian cat-burglary using a gondola is simply not on. I'd have to think of another way, and fairly soon. I was running out of options.

I sat on my balcony overlooking the lagoon lights. I'd tried dialling Nancy's number but the phone maintained a sulky silence, so I gave that up. Some convenient lie would spring to my rescue when I saw her in the morning.

A big cargo ship was coming in, slowly threshing the night westwards between us and the San Giorgio. Soon she would turn leftish to avoid the Grand Canal by passing between the long shallow curve of the Giudecca island and the Zattere. Who would think that some of the most efficient docks in Europe lay beyond those beautiful churches and elegant rooftops?

By the time the ship's lights passed into the darkness I was pondering the curious spin-off problem of David's little group. Talking with Nancy while, erm, resting in her bed, I'd learned nothing. But what was wrong with being in Venice 'on assignment'? Their business, not mine. I should forget this side problem and concentrate on my main hassle of Mr Pinder and his lunatic scheme to nick Venice. I fell asleep trying to work out how you could fold up Venice and stuff it into a single palazzo.

When I woke from my doze, stiff as a plank and damp from the dawn mist on the balcony, I had at least one answer. If you can't gain entry into a lady's house by dishonest means like good old reliable burglary, you just have to resort to honesty. That's really underhand. Hard, but there it is. Nothing for it.

Plan X.

Incredibly, next day was free of incoming flights. All Cosima and I had to do was see off one taxi-load. After that, nothing. I tried being my usual pleasant unassuming self to Cesare but he was more sullen than ever and hardly responded. Maybe I'd absent-mindedly said a wrong declension or something.

Cosima was standing beside me on the Riva as our boat slewed into the Canale dell' Arsenale with the departing toursits. Cesare would be at least an hour away.

'What now, love?'

'You handle the first flight arriving tomorrow, Lovejoy. The rest of today is yours.'

Neither of us moved. It was blowing gently. Cosima had on one of those plain headscarves which even the tiniest Venetian girls wear to match their little sober brown boots in March. I could have eaten her.

'I, er, look, Cosima—'

'Yes?'

'I'll understand if you say no, but are you doing anything, well, particular today?'

'Well, no. Not really.'

That might have been untrue. Every day she was becoming more stylish. Today she would outshine the most elegant bunch of tourists. In fact I was a bit embarrassed just being with her because I look a scruff at the best of times. Vaguely I wondered who the bloke was, though it didn't matter. If she had a couple of hours to spare she could help Plan X along its thorny road.

'Would you show me the bits of Venice you like?'

She hesitated at that and I hurried to reassure her. 'I've a clean shirt I can put on. I've no other shoes but—'

'No,' she said quickly. 'Don't. It wouldn't be you, dressed up.'

I didn't know how to take that. It narked me, really. Everybody has their own twists. I admit I'm not exactly Savile Row, but I'm clean underneath. In fact my old Gran had this perennial nightmare I'd get knocked down and be carried into the doctor's surgery where All Would Be Revealed, and she laboured for years to pass on this paranoiac delusion to me, so it's second nature by now to de-filth daily. But some people can look stylish in anything, like Cosima, and others like me just can't so it's no use us bothering.

She was looking at her foot. 'I must call at the office first. Then I'll be free.'

'You mean you'll come? With me?'

She took my arm. It made me tingle. 'With pleasure, Lovejoy.'

Our office—I didn't know we had one—was near the San Giorgio dei Greci church, its tower inevitably leaning at an alarming angle over the canal. I only hope the people living nearby got danger money, at least a rent rebate.

You get used to Venice's leaning campaniles, but at first
you go about hoping you'll escape before they topple.
They all look scarily out of true, and I do mean a terrible
angle. Pisa's got one sloper. Venice has a forest of them.
You could plonk Pisa's leaning tower in Venice and
nobody would notice.

Cosima insisted I come in with her. Cosol Tours, Inc.,
seen close to, was less than munificent. One small office
heaped with forms, a small computer thing with its flex
unconnected, a couple of phones and Giuseppe Fusi. Our
big wheel. He was homely, portly, comfortable, and
proudly showed me photos of his numerous offspring
while Cosima delved irritably among the dust.

'Any tourist problem, Lovejoy,' Signor Fusi announced
grandly, 'I solve instantly!'

'Giuseppe, that charter special manifest,' Cosima said.

'Think of my office as the hub of the Cosol Tours
empire!'

'Great,' I said uneasily, thinking, God Almighty.

'Giuseppe,' Cosima said, endless patience in her voice.

Giuseppe's shoulders slumped. Work called. 'Yes,
Cosima?'

While Cosima gave him a drubbing over the tourist
manifests I had a quiet smile. Giuseppe was obviously one
of those blokes who love gossip and a glass. Everything
else was death. He must look forward to Cosima's visits
like the end of the tax year.

The canal below the window, wider than most, ran
straight to enter the lagoon where Vivaldi's La Pietà
church stands on the Riva. Lovely, strikingly unique
Venice. It really does warm you. I looked round to find
somewhere to perch and enjoy the view while I waited.
Smiling to keep out of her firing line, I gently moved a
pile of papers and sat on the desk edge to watch a small
motorized minibarge amble up the *rio*. These craft carry
everything from soft drinks to groceries, and are steered

with skilled recklessness by young blokes in overalls . . . *Norman? One of the papers I'd just moved had Signora Norman's name on it.*

'Ready, Lovejoy!'

I nodded, eagerly watching the barge go below the window. 'A minute, love, please. I want to see how he shoots the *ponte*. He might go left.'

'Ah, Lovejoy!' Giuseppe swiftly sensed a chat. 'No. He will go straight ahead, because the angle is too acute. Now, let me explain. If he wanted to make deliveries near the Palazzo Priuli, he would always come up the Rio del Vin, to meet this *rio* at a point below the Rio dei Greci. And why? Because—'

'Giuseppe,' Cosima said, too practised to waste a minute, bless her heart. 'This Geneva flight . . .'

Giuseppe's only satisfaction was that the barge went straight on. Mine was that, turning to tell Giuseppe that he had been proved right, I accidentally knocked over some of the desk papers. It took us a full minute to restore the heap to its original shambles. I of course was very apologetic, and took particular care the papers were all in order.

We left with Cosima happily calling exhortations up the stairs and Giuseppe shouting endless devotion-to-duty down. Cosima and I were laughing about Giuseppe as we crossed the bridge, but all the way along the narrow Fondamenta dell' Osmarin all I could see was Signora Norman's name. It had been on an invoice, address the Malcontento house. Mr D. Vidal and Miss N. Waterson had flown at her expense. I came to with Cosima shaking my arm.

'You've not been listening, Lovejoy. I said where to?'

'Sorry, love.' I went all misty. 'I was just thinking how happy I was, being with you like this.' Her arm seemed so natural linked with mine. 'You're showing me what Venice is up to, remember? Lead on.'

*

We combed Venice, exhilarated. Of course, I was constantly looking for something different from what Cosima was showing me. As the bridges came and went in a confusion of buildings, elegant façades, canals and alleys, Cosima blossomed. Her rather guarded anxiety vanished and we walked with what can only be called merriment. She astonished me with a zillion odd facts.

'Galileo's house,' she'd say. 'He showed our Doge his new invention at the top of the Campanile,' and you would know she meant *the* Galileo, his new invention being the telescope and his demonstration that business in 1609. No accident that the Flanders spectacle-makers zipped to Venice with their improved magnifying lenses, spying practically being a Venetian patent. Galileo just happened to hear of these lenses there. 'That place was Napoleon's,' she'd say, not even bothering to look. 'Your Lord Byron lived over there; a lady threw herself into *that* canal for love of him.' And occasionally her dear little face would frown with intensity as she asked a question to check that she was not leaving me behind. 'Casanova was born in that *calle*. You know Casanova?'

'Yes,' I'd say gravely, as if he was still around.

'Good,' she'd say, all serious, and her animated smile would return. 'That palazzo is Cristoforo Moro's. Your Shakespeare changed his name to Othello—you know Othello?—but Shylock lived across there—you know Shylock . . . ?'

Soon she was eagerly urging me along, anxious to show me her favourite spots and prattling all the time.

'Hitler toured Venice on his own at night—at a fast trot,' was one of her gems, supposed to be en-couragement. 'Didn't stay long, though.'

She had a collection of entertaining sights as well. One of her favourites was the rubbish collection. Household rubbish is collected at the lagoon-side entrance of each

canal about half-nine each morning. The brown
cardboard boxes and black plastic bags are lifted into a
long barge-like boat of military grey and black by the
steersman's two blue-overalled shore-based helpers. They
actually sweep up after themselves. Incredible. I couldn't
get over it.

As we walked, I realized there's this great trick
Venetians have, of pretending people from antiquity are
still knocking about. We have a similar knack in East
Anglia, but don't take things quite so personally. She
showed me Vivaldi's Pietà church, which old Mr Pinder
had practically wept over. I thought it beautiful, clean,
chill and excessively neat. 'So different from the Red
Priest himself,' I mused, as we gaped at Piazzetta's
Visitation painting. 'I wonder if that soprano Vivaldi
shacked up with was as attractive as her sister, and which
of them he really loved?' Cosima disapproved and quickly
pulled me out of the side entrance.

'Father Vivaldi's troubles were of his own making,' she
said sternly. 'If he'd paid more attention to his church
and less to . . . to his music, he wouldn't be defrocked.'

'Falling for the lady was perfectly natural, Cosima.'

She drew away, appalled. "You're not advocating free
love?'

'Is there any other kind?' I was a picture of innocence.

'It's Father Vivaldi's business, not ours.'

That's how I came to learn the Great Venetian Trick.
Antonio Vivaldi: 1678-1741; you must speak and think as
if he were still concert-master at the girls' school on the
Riva degli Schiavoni. You give the same courtesy to other
Venetians. You can mention Marco Polo, but not that he
came from China to knock on his own door and got
himself detained because nobody recognized him after a
score of years. You can praise Veronese's masterpieces to
the skies, but not his shameful trial before the Inquisition
about his *Feast in the House of Levi*. The Great Venetian

trick operates at all times: you can speak about Italians and all others any way you choose, but Venetians are respectable.

I wish now I'd thought about the implications, but it's no good crying over spilt milk. Especially when that spilled milk turned out to be Cosima.

The market near the Rialto Bridge was another of her favourites. ('Not the gaudy shops on the bridge itself, Lovejoy. They should never have been allowed there in the first place,' she said severely, criticizing the practice which began in 1592.) The Erberia vegetable market is everything women love to look at — raw grub in all its horrible pristine state of execution. Cosima dived in like a footballer, hauling me after her and yapping indignantly of the price of onions, greens, fruit, artichokes ('Look! A scandal! And Venice the fountain of all artichokes!') until she noticed I was pale about the gills and asked what was wrong.

'Those.' I indicated with a jerk of my head but didn't dare look. There was this stall selling dead seagulls and bald quail dangling on hooks.

'Poor dear! Is it the price? We might get one cheaper round the corner—'

'No, love. It's just . . .'

'Ah. *Simpatico!*' She hugged my arm as if enormously pleased, then remembered and dragged me among barrows to confront a granite statue, a little burdened bloke carrying steps which led up to the Egyptian granite rostrum.

'Our laws used to be proclaimed here. He's the Gobbo.'

The statue looked knackered, humping that enormous weight. She was smiling and reached out to pat him. We had to shove aside a heap of old vegetable boxes.

'When I was a little girl I felt so sorry for him.' She told me how in the old days wrong-doers had to run the gauntlet naked from St Mark's Basilica to touch the

Gobbo. 'He's a lovely old thing. If the bad men reached him all was forgotten. For a statue to do so much good!'

'And if they didn't?'

'Ah, well.' She was thinking of my faintness at the sight of the hanging seagulls and decided the fewer explanations the better. 'Now we go to our beautiful fish market!'

I didn't quite make that, and had to wait shakily at the San Giacomo for her after only a brief glance at the masses of stalls covered with eels, squids, every sort of glistening fish imaginable, crabs, shellfish. I know that grub turns a lot of people on. I mean, Cosima made a breathless return, hugely pleased with herself and carrying a parcel. 'What a pity you wouldn't come with me, Lovejoy! They're lovely fish today, but the *prices!* Scandalous!'

The single arch of the Ponte di Rialto has been severely criticized over the centuries, but as I paused to give it a last look I couldn't help thinking that Antonio da Ponte didn't do too bad a job. Cosima stood by me, looking.

'Is it true about Michaelangelo?' I asked her. I wasn't worried about her answer, but asking some daft question gave me time to glance casually at the motor-boat idling near the Riva del Ferro.

'Competing to design the *Ponte?* Yes. But he didn't get the contract.'

'Why not?'

She gave that lovely tilted Latin shrug I keep trying to imitate. 'He wasn't Venetian, of course.'

Of course. We had coffee in a *campo* near the Formosa church. Cosima told me how they used to have bullfights in the *campi* spaces between the canals. I don't know how much I took in of all she told me that day, but I wish now I'd burned every word into my brain. All I did was gaze at her lovely animated face, watch her delectable mouth move, and try to suppress the craving growing in me. The trouble is that hunger comes stealing into you when you least expect it. All I hoped was that her bloke wasn't an all-in wrestler, and that he wouldn't show.

She took us on a detour and paused at a *sottoportego*, a little alley going under a building. Politely she asked me to wait a moment please. I said of course, and watched her go through into a small courtyard beyond. She'd probably gone inside to make a discreet check that he hadn't arrived yet. Okay, so I was second fiddle. So what? Where was the harm? There was one of those disused well-heads in the *campo*'s centre so characteristic of Venice's tiny open spaces. While I waited I had a smile watching a pigeon bathe beneath a water tap. I wouldn't have smiled if I'd known what was coming.

The motor-boat idling up the Riva del Ferro was on my mind. It had been a weird pastel blue, with a thickset bloke at the wheel. And I was nearly certain that the affluent older woman seated in the centre was the rich cocktail bird who had argued with me in the hotel bar last night. The boat wasn't going anywhere, just idling. And again she had given me that incisive stare. Now, a bloke staring at a bird is merely being his usual magpie self. But a bird ogling a bloke is either on heat or the warpath. And us complete strangers.

Five minutes later Cosima appeared without her fish parcel. We solemnly linked arms and walked on like repleted lovers at peace with the world.

CHAPTER 14

At ten o'clock that night I ambled down the Riva degli Schiavoni, in absolute Paradise. It had been a magic day. Magic.

Cosima's bloke hadn't shown after all. Real luck, that.

A whole day going about with Cosima, and she had taken me back to her place—a cramped little third-floor flat, through the *sottoportego* as I'd guessed. I'd had her bloke's supper. Odd, but she'd enjoyed the whole bit, cooking shyly but with that determination women get. I didn't look, just read and watched her telly, occasionally calling out questions about things that caught my attention. She said the inky stuff she served the Seppie fish in was the right colour, and gave me polenta which she made herself. It was good stuff. I told her she was hired, and made her laugh. And she even promised to show me some of the lagoon's outer islands tomorrow. Magic.

Nothing happened much after that. No, honestly. I really didn't lay a finger on her, and she showed no sign of dragging me into the closed room beyond the tiny kitchen, stripping me naked and savagely wreaking her crazed lust on my poor defenceless unprotected body. And neither of us said it was a long walk back for me to the hotel. Or said how lonely beds are on your own. I have definitely nothing to report. Which is how I came to be ambling home along the Riva beneath its double rows of lamps in the night mist.

Two odd things, though. A boat started up suddenly as I neared the Victor Emmanuel statue. It sounded familiar, like Cesare's, but it tore off towards the Arsenale before I could see whose it was. That's the trouble with standing in a well-lit place, even if it is the mist-shrouded waterfront of the Venice lagoon: you can't see them, but they can see you. Daft as a brush, I thought nothing of it at the time. One boat in a nation of boats is nothing, right?

That night I fell asleep blissfully happy. Well, I would have done but for a silly game I used to play which sometimes comes back to me at the oddest times, like a daft jingle you can't get rid of. The game's called Edgar

Allan Poe. He once said the ingredients of a good con trick are minuteness, interest, perseverance, ingenuity, audacity, nonchalance, originality, impertinence—and grin! That's nine ingredients. In my game, you must assume that Poe was wrong. You are allowed only *three* of his nine, so which six ingredients do you chuck out? I always end up with minuteness, nonchalance, and the grin. Except I tossed and turned most of the night, ecstatically happy with memories of Cosima but playing my stupid game over and over in my head. It's usually a sign I'm worried, but what the hell could I possibly be worrying about? Cosima liked me. I was almost sure she did.

An hour before dawn it came to me: the worrying thing was that nobody was grinning at all, except me.

And when I woke and went down to breakfast at eight o'clock, Nancy, David, Agnes and Doris had booked out. Not a word. Sad, but no need to worry. It happens. And anyway nothing to do with my main problem. Right?

Cosima and I were down for the airport run for an incoming flight that day. There would be no afternoon arrival so I suggested she take the morning off but to my delight she said no, she'd come and we would do the run jointly with Cesare.

While I waited for her to arrive after breakfast I chatted with Cesare whose boat had been moored by then. Today he was at the Riva near where the big tugboats berth against those creaking, wobbling posts.

'Got a fact, Cesare?' I said to lessen his sourness.

'Yours are never worth any money, Lovejoy.'

That was a bit rough, but I trotted out a cracker. 'Turner the painter did a watercolour of the Rialto Bridge. It's lost.'

He nodded. 'Worth a fortune, eh?'

'Two fortunes. Your fact?'

He looked over the water. 'Every year, Lovejoy, people drown at night in the lagoon.'

I thought. 'That's not worth much.'

'It may be worth more than you know.'

Narked, I started to say something but chewed the sentence off. I shrugged and strolled over to watch the people embarking at the waterbus, nearly falling over that old geezer who sits there selling lottery tickets. White beard, tatty cap, his club foot thrust out to trip the unwary. I'd made him laugh the day before by nicknaming him Ivan the Terrible. He always looks asleep but he's not. Rustle a banknote within ten yards and his eyes are wide awake.

The Riva seemed to be filling early today. The San Zaccaria waterbus stop was thronged with people trying to get off. Cosima would arrive from the direction of St Mark's, so I walked past that daft statue as far as the bridge over the del Vin canal and stood watching.

My jubilation of the previous night had dissipated in the strange problem of Nancy. I had asked the reception clerk earlier if he had a message for me but no luck. That narked me. Nancy might at least have dropped me a line or two, even if it was only a 'See you again sometime.' I decided that was typical of women's callousness and leaned over the bridge parapet to see one of the pavement artists at work, a bearded lad with a small patient dog. Cosima couldn't miss me even in the crowd, stuck up here.

The bearded artist was really quite good and I became interested. He seemed to specialize in views of the Salute church and San Giorgio Maggiore, both easily visible from here—but he was not averse to dashing off the odd portrait masterpiece in charcoal. He was doing one now, of a coloured girl. She sat on the little camp-stool, aware of her attractiveness and the interest of the crowd.

Somebody made a remark, pointing at the sketch. The

artist was provoked by that. It's just the way artists are,
but this one was especially vehement and gave the critical
bystander a mouthful which made us all laugh. To prove
a point he pulled out an unfinished sketch and held it up,
gesticulating with his charcoal. There was a lot of good-
natured backchat, but I didn't care about joining in. All I
cared about was hurtling down the bridge steps, suddenly
and breathless, getting hold of that unfinished sketch.

'The sketch almost finished and she runs off,' the artist
was complaining. 'All my time and genius wasted!
Leaving me unpaid! Because of thoughtless comments
such as yours!'

'Finish it,' somebody suggested, amid chatter. 'Then
sell it.'

'Who to? Who would buy—?'

'Me, signore,' I interrupted, winded but struggling to
sound casual.

'Ah!' the crowd exclaimed, interest quickening. I
grinned amiably.

The artist was delighted. 'You know the sitter, signore?'

'Afraid not.' I made a comedy out of the denial and
people laughed because anybody could tell the sketch was
of a lovely bird. 'But you have caught a certain light . . .'

'I'll finish it for you—'

'No. That would be a mistake. I prefer it as it is.' I had
the sense to apologize to the coloured girl for
interrupting. Amid the babble of conversation I paid the
artist a full fee and went to sit on the bridge to examine
the unfinished sketch. Old Ivan the Terrible cackled a
laugh nearby. The old devil was watching.

'Such bad luck with the girls that you have to fall for a
picture?'

'Shut your gums, silly old sod.'

It was definitely Nancy. I didn't want to ask the
bearded artist when he sketched her because the presence
of the girl now posing for him made me somehow uneasy.

I was worrying sick about possibilities. Suppose Nancy had waited on the Riva to be collected. It might have occurred to her to have herself drawn . . . perhaps intending it as a souvenir? Or as a present she could leave me at the hotel? That was like Nancy. Which raised the interesting question of why she had done neither, and had left it in the hands of a complaining and unpaid artist. So she must have left in a rush, under sudden compulsion. David's special 'assignment'?

'*Buon giorno*, Lovejoy.'

'Eh? Oh.'

Cosima was standing there, smiling, absolutely dazzling. Hastily I scrambled to my feet, trying to roll the sketch up so she wouldn't see. I didn't want her, of all people, thinking I was loose or immoral or anything. We descended the bridge steps and moved along the Riva to where Cesare's boat was moored.

'Thank you for yesterday, love,' I said. 'Cesare's ready.'

'Not at all, Lovejoy.' She eyed the scroll I was clutching. 'Souvenir?'

'Only a little sketch of the airport.' My eyes were downcast and soulful. 'Where I first saw you.'

She paused. 'Oh, Lovejoy.' She said my name as if I was nothing but trouble. 'What sort of man are you?'

'Erm, only ordinary. What do you mean, love?'

Her enormous eyes made me dizzy. It was like looking down two deep wells. 'I feel so foolish. Sometimes you're just absurd.'

'Absurd?' I was just about to give her a mouthful when we heard Cesare yelling angrily and saw him at the jetty pointing at his watch. We walked along and boarded, a bit guiltily I thought, though God knows why either of us should feel guilty for nothing. Cesare's attitude hadn't improved. Cosima's brilliant mood had dulled somewhat. I sat there seething.

Absurd? Me?

Bloody cheek. That's the trouble with women. No judgement of character.

Somebody once said that death and Venice go together. Soon I would learn the hard way that they were right. If I'd had half the sense I was born with I'd have stopped daydreaming about sex and the precious ancient glass of the ancient glass factories, because all the clues were there for the asking. But, me being me and having only the brains of a rocking-horse, I ignored all the portents and simply sat in Cesare's boat and was wafted graciously to the Marco Polo.

At the airport Cosima bustled about with her clipboard in the arrivals hall. I stood like a suspect while she checked my three badges and my Cosol Tours placard.

I said lightly, 'Here, Cosima. What's happened to Agnes? You know, David thing's elderly bird. The hotel said she'd booked out.'

Cosima pursed her lips, pushing me into a more favourable position along the row of tour operators' reception stalls opposite the Customs exit. 'They were recalled.'

I tut-tutted. 'Holiday cut short, eh?'

Cosima said absently, frowning with concentration at the flight indicator, 'They flew out during the night.'

'Shame,' I said.

'Film people,' with a pretty tilted shrug. 'Sudden people, *non è vero?*'

'Lives not their own,' I agreed sympathetically as the concourse filled with our arriving passengers. 'Cosol Tours,' I started up. 'Cosol this way, please.'

CHAPTER 15

The trouble with some people is their heads never switch off. I'm the same. Even kipping's a busy time with me, all manner of guesses and frighteners swarming through a grey matter that's basically angry that the rest of the body's dozing just when it wants to play. What with all this free activity you'd think I'd be marvellous at planning ahead, a veritable Sherlock Holmes.

Wrong.

I'm a duckegg. Absolutely pathetic. There's proof: that bad day at Torcello.

It was all my idea. I admit that. But having an idea doesn't mean everything that happens is my fault.

Like I said, Venice is a mass of islands and Torcello was practically the first of the Venetian islands ever to be colonized by the people fleeing from troubles on the fifth-century mainland. In those early days it was even boss island, with tens of thousands all doing their thing in the new maritime nation. They say it's dying away, but aren't we all? It's the speed that matters.

Everybody's heard of Torcello and its famous detached campanile (again leaning at a perilous angle) and the lovely wood-domed Santa Fosca church, so I was all agog to catch the *vaporetto* out and see it for myself. Heart-rending to tear myself away from Venice proper, but we needn't be too long about it. In my mind I suppose was the notion of a last fling before I tackled the Palazzo Malcontento. Of course, I was here because I'm always genuinely concerned with justice and truth, with preventing that yellow-suited nerk from committing murder again.

But everybody deserves a rest now and then. So to think

up a day in luscious old Torcello with the delectable Cosima was perfectly reasonable. A well-deserved rest.

Among the mob I'd handled the previous day were two Australian blokes, doing Europe on a shilling with Venice their launch-pad. I'd shared a bottle of vino with them in the bar. One was a flaxen-haired drifter called Gerry, a real dreamer. Farthing-clever-penny-daft, my old Gran would have called him. He claimed to paint butterflies, and lived this great vision where suddenly the whole world rushed at him demanding canvases covered with acrylic butterflies. I asked him if he ever painted anything else and he looked at me as if I was off my nut. It takes all sorts. His mate Keith was lankier, cooler, more on the make and poisonously practical, daft on engines. Opposite poles attract and all that. Synergism implies difference. So clever old Lovejoy in a drunken stupor put the big dig when the fourth bottle was easier to lift than its predecessors, but they knew nothing about David and Nancy.

'Never met them, sport,' Keith said. That was as far as I got, because Gerry wanted to talk about painting butterflies and Keith about engines.

'Engines,' Keith insisted tipsily. 'They're the future. What's missing in Venice, Lovejoy? Answer: engines! What's missing in the air, in Europe, in outer space? Answer: *engines!* Same in Australia, Africa, India, everywhere!'

Nodding, I got blearily sloshed. Nancy had gone without trace. I felt so kindly towards this weird pair I got the next bottle, carefully charging it up to Cosol Tours to show off, and bragged to them about Torcello. In a drunken humour I told Gerry I'd heard it was riddled with butterflies and Keith it had lots of old engines.

I was still part-sloshed when for the umpteenth time I fell over Ivan the Terrible near the second bridge along the Riva, scattering his unsold lottery tickets. He was nearly as pickled as me and we exchanged a mouthful of friendly abuse while I helped him to find them in the lamplight.

'Drunk because you couldn't find your lovely American lady?' he demanded, to rile me. He made a crude gesture.

'Shut up, you old fool.' I paused. 'Here, Ivan. How d'you know she was a Yank?'

'She spoke like one. I'm not yet deaf.'

So he'd seen the whole scenario: Nancy being drawn by the artist, somebody coming urgently for her, the artist shouting rape because his fee went missing.

'Was he a Yank, too?'

'The one who took her? One was. But the other.' Ivan the Terrible spat into the canal and closed his tatty old case. 'One of them pretty-pretty boys from the Malcontento. Suit of many colours. They should all stay in Naples.'

In a fit of misguided generosity I gave him a note for another bottle and went to watch the reflected lights out on the lagoon. If I hadn't been stewed I'd have tried to think. As it was, I did nothing but watch the lights until I nodded off and woke shivering.

That next morning Cosima and I caught the boat from the Fondamenta Nuove. I was a bit embarrassed seeing Keith and Gerry already on the boat among the crowd in the bows, but was pleased they saw me with a beautiful bird. I was proud of her. Some things are so beautiful you have to look at them piecemeal or they blind you. Cosima was like that. They both waved back, Keith especially smiling wide. Cosima, I observed, pinked up and gave them only the briefest nod.

'Glad they came,' I said conversationally.

The boat goes to Murano and Burano before reaching Torcello. Naturally I'd forgotten my map so Cosima had to point out the places we passed. A true Venetian, to her Murano was a sort of industrial slum island and she barely glanced at it as the *vaporetto* chugged nearer, past the posh bright brickwork which rims San Michele cemetery island.

'We had to put all the glassmakers in one place safely away from the rest of us,' she explained casually. 'Their furnaces kept setting Venice afire.'

'Recently?' I was only joking, but her pretty-serious face showed concentration reflected in the boat windows.

'Thirteenth century. Of course, it was as well they were moved out to Murano, Lovejoy. It became a little . . . depraved.'

I'd heard that too, but never in such tones of reproof. Moral indignation from a Venetian is a scream, seeing they invented Carnival and the cicisbeo, that cissy upper-class version of the gigolo. Still, depravity makes you even more interested so I looked with fascination as we stopped to let droves of folk on and off, then puttered past the line of glassmakers' slipways and wharves. Lovely to see higgledy-piggledy industry flourishing exactly as it did six centuries gone. The pleasure-gardens are now all vanished beneath hundreds of tiny crammed glass factories but I thought it looked lovely. My sort of scene. Especially the idea of all those lovely special glasses made by those old-generation glassmakers on every mantel-piece. She'd made the glassmakers' banishment sound somewhere near Mongolia. It's hardly a mile.

'Pity Cesare couldn't come,' I said as our prow turned towards Burano. 'We could have gone to see the church of San Donato if we'd had his boat.'

She did glance at the gliding islands then. Her hair was moving in the wind that breezed down the length of the boat's interior, silkier than on any telly advert. 'I am content,' she said quietly.

'Yes, er, great. Me too.' For the first time I realized she

looked even more like a million quid than usual. Were
relatives lurking on Torcello? Were we going to drop in
on a mob of uncles and crones for *colazione?* An ordeal
loomed. God. I felt in a state, sloppy as always. 'San
Donato,' I said lamely. 'Not every day you see a saint
whose spit kills dragons. The Muranese say they've the
dragon's bones behind the high altar . . .'

She shrugged dismissively. 'The Muranese!'

The boat moved slowly into the northern waters of the
lagoon. Still a warming sun, still that lovely brittle
daylight. But as the occasional island stops came and
went and Venice's doomed city receded in the morning
mists the beat and rush of the boat seemed lonelier than it
had. The water seemed brackish, less blue. We could
hardly see the long lines of the islands and banks to
seaward, and the islands now seemed threadbare and
even desolate. Cosima touched my knee.

'Are you well, dear?'

I grinned with every erg, determined to show I was on
top of the world.

'The best day I ever had so far, love.'

She drew breath the way women do when checking they
won't be overheard. About us the passengers had
thinned, so out it came. 'Please do not jump to
conclusions, Lovejoy,' she said. 'I am merely anxious to
accompany you to Torcello, since you appear to have
read of the Teocota Madonna.'

I hastily agreed to whatever it was she was blathering
about, and dismissed her mood as one of these weirdities
they often have, because Burano was in sight, its splash of
blue, red, yellow houses a brilliant set of nursery bricks
crammed any old how among the drab lagoon marshes.
You can't help loving it. It is toytown. Its campanile leans
like a Saturday drunk. Everything, from canals to
doorways, is dinky. No wonder they're born lacemakers.
Delighted as I was, though, Cosima stayed aloof.

'They made a lace collar of blonde hair for Louis XIV,'
I babbled, delighted at the colourful island. 'They have a
museum for Venetian point lace—'

'Torcello soon, dear,' Cosima said, her face lighting
into a smile that dried me up.

'Er, good.'

Only love illuminates a woman's eyes with that kind of
radiance. Love and all its works. My instant conclusion:
lover-boy lives somewhere on Torcello, and we'd
presumably bump, accidentally of course, into this rustic
cretin which would give her the excuse to leave me
stranded. Don't get me wrong. I wasn't narked. I mean,
all's fair in love and all that. But even gigolos get paid. I'd
somehow got myself into the position of unpaid stooge.
For a few minutes, as the boat moved on serenely through
the bright delicate mists of the morning, I maintained a
pained silence so pointedly that Cosima shyly reached
across and took my hand, her eyes avoiding mine. My
frost didn't last long. It couldn't. Nobody's frost can last
long when that ancient warmth beats out of the waters
and the stones shriek at you of past human existence and
love preserved in the works of Man.

'Torcello, dear,' Cosima was saying. 'I hope you'll—'

But I was already eager to be on the landing-stage and
only later, when it was altogether too hopelessly late for
both of us, did I piece together the conversation on the
vaporetto with my lovely Cosima.

Like I said. Pathetic.

Torcello.

We'd gone a few hundred yards when I stopped.

'Where is it, love?'

She paused with me, holding my arm. 'This *is* Torcello,
dear.'

'But the city. The great palaces.'

Her eyes moistened, gazing at me. 'You didn't read

quite enough. Torcello is . . . ending.'

'There's twenty great churches,' I bleated, standing on
the overgrown path beside the canal.

'Two.'

'—and thirty thousand inhabitants.'

'Less than a hundred souls.' Her eyes were brimming
now, hers or mine. 'I'm so sorry, darling.'

The canal runs straight from the landing-stage into the
heart of what is left of Torcello's great square. Now it's
not even a village green. The great stone arches of the
fifteenth century bridges, the dazzling *fondamenta*, the
might of empire literally fallen and overgrown. A wooden
bridge crossed near a canal junction. A couple of
cottages, a scruffy field or two, a few lanes of artichokes
here and there in the dampish fields. A line of peach
trees. Weeds and reeds. A tiny file of ducks. I sat on the
canal edge.

'It . . . it sent a fleet of galleys to the Chioggia wars.' My
voice hardly reached a whisper. 'It was a whole empire.' It
had even sent two Torcello agents to steal St Mark's body
from mighty Egypt.

'Gone, dear.' She was hugging me, kneeling beside me
and rocking gently. 'Don't be sad. You live too much
inside your head. You must come out, darling.'

Lucky there was nobody else about. We were the only
ones to have disembarked at Torcello except for Keith
and Gerry who had set up Gerry's easel by the landing-
stage, so we were unseen. Cosima took my hand and led
me then into the orchard, me trailing like a heartbroken
schoolkid, and we lay beneath the spreading branches.

She hand-shushed me from calling out at the pinnacle,
then murmuring and rocking my head on her breast
while her fingers made sure we were decently clothed
again so as not to give offence to any ghosts which
happened by.

She talked to me, even though I was almost oblivious in

that small death which follows loving. We must have looked so incongruous, a delicious colourful bird with dazzling lustrous hair, sitting-kneeling in a lost orchard with her elegant new dress crumpled, nursing a slumbering dishevelled oaf who wasn't paying the slightest heed to a word she was saying. Odd, but women I actually love are the only ones who can switch off my nightmares. That hour in Torcello I dozed deeper and more restfully than I had for many a month. She did everything for me that magical time, with the reeds soughing and the stalks clashing softly all about the edges of the waterways. Once I half-woke to hear a couple of children shouting, but Cosima calmed me out of being startled. 'They're the little ones playing *al pangalo*, darling. Only a game of batting sticks. Shush.'

At the finish she had to wake me to get me moving. Our aim had always been to nosh at Cipriani's. Until Cosima explained how the famous restaurant had come to the rescue of poor old Torcello practically single-handed I hadn't realized that the famous *locanda* was the one remaining epicentre of life in Torcello. She had booked us in, and so we dined in sunshiny elegance looking out over the small vegetable gardens next the tiny central square of Torcello. Beneath us, around us, entirely covered and unseen, the ruins of one of the powerful mediæval empires of Europe. Around, an innocent spectacle of market gardening with a bloke hoeing vegetables, and a couple of buildings in view, with a farmhouse a little distance off.

I got up courage to ask her. 'What about your, erm, intended?'

'Intended?'

'Your bloke.'

'Cesare thinks too much of his own wishes.' Cosima reproved me at the impertinence by wagging her head so her hair swung.

'Cesare? The boatman?' I needed a minute to take that in. No big bruiser meeting us? No bloke back in Venice?

'Cesare. But only a little. Anyway, Lovejoy. He never has been so . . . close. Certainly not my intended.'

Hence the glowerings. Hence his growing surliness. Hence I'm as thick as usual, because Cesare saw me threatening his own ambitions for Cosima. That's what I needed all right, an enemy I'd picked unerringly to reveal my interest in the Palazzo Malcontento. He was also my one means of independent transport, apart from stolen gondolas. Which raised the question of what Cesare was doing back in Venice while Cosima and yours truly were whooping it up in Torcello.

'Listen, Cosima.' I'm always awkward saying thanks. 'Giving me, erm, love . . . My soul gets sort of damp when it feels antiques go wrong.'

'I know, darling. Learning about Torcello. I told you too suddenly.'

'My fault.' I got my money out to pay for our meal. 'But you have the right to know everything.' I meant almost everything. 'It's time for you to ask me about myself, love. I'll answer every question with complete honesty. Promise.' I meant almost complete.

'No.' Firmly she poured the last of the wine for us. 'It is time for *me* to tell *you* about myself. We shall exchange information while we examine the remaining pieces of Torcello. There are several hours of daylight left, darling.'

'It's a deal.'

'And I have arranged a surprise for you.'

I couldn't help wondering as we raised glasses. A deal of planning had gone into this day at Torcello. I only wished I'd been in on it, so I could work things out. I was beginning to think I'd been surprised enough.

The dusty little centre of Torcello pulled me up short.

The Piazza—its proper name—was once the great meeting-place for the all-powerful Tribune. I expected at least *some*thing, a sign, some spectacular ruins. Anything to ablate this terrible feeling of melancholy.

Instead, there's threadbare grass, dusty paths, and two or three little cottages. A building converted to a tiny museum. To one side is a low octagonal church, all fawns, and this taller cathedral with stone swing-shutters to protect its windows. A canal runs by. A lady in traditional dress had a stall selling unbelievably mediocre modern lace. A big stone chair stands improbably in the centre of the space, God knows why, just asking for a stray tourist to clown for a comical holiday snap.

And that's it. Get the point? That's it *all*. Exactly as if we'd gone to find a bustling Times Square or Piccadilly and found instead a derelict yard.

I felt ill.

'Come, darling.' Cosima hauled me to come into the cathedral. 'We'll sit for a while. I'm sorry about the tower, but lightning's taken its top off.' This temporary setback happened over three centuries gone. I watched her fold a headscarf to enter the cathedral. Most underrated of all woman's decorations, is the old headscarf. I touched her cool cheek to show I approved.

She said gravely, 'Dearest, I want to pray. Only to . . . explain. Not apologize. You can look at the Teocota while I do.'

I almost started a grin thinking, What is all this? But she wasn't joking, and moved towards a transept, her heels clicking echoes down the nave. Grumbling inwardly that there wasn't any need to put on airs or assume fetching little tableaux—she'd already hooked me in the most permanent way—I turned to move parallel, along the northern length of the nave, and saw it.

Maybe it was the sheer spectacle or its unusual form, though I'd been expecting something profound because everybody on earth's heard of the Teocota Madonna. Or maybe it was just having loved Cosima. Whatever the cause, I was blammed by it. The background's gold and faint, and the Madonna herself is somehow elongated like an El Greco, but those are just technical points. Ignore them. Technique is only the irreverent dogma of forgers and curators. Concentrate on technique too much and you miss love and feeling. The mosaic face weeps. The Madonna gazes above your head, not at you, but beyond as if at the things you've left undone and the cruelty you've enacted on the way to Torcello. Of course, I found myself reasoning, the Madonna didn't really mean me. She was reproaching the rest of the buggers, because I'm always reasonable and fair-minded and have a pretty good reputation for doing the right thing and never hurting people. Beautiful, stunning. I shivered, but only because it was colder in the cathedral than I thought.

Or it could be the lurking horror of realizing that the image of old Mr Pinder had suddenly shifted in my mind. He might not be a batty old lunatic. He could possibly be what he actually presented himself to be: an elderly man battling against neglect and ignorance with the only forces at his disposal to protect ancient brilliance like this Madonna.

Christ, I thought. The notion made me glance suspiciously at Cosima, but she was oblivious, contentedly crossing herself from having lit two candles. No artifice, no pretence, as she came across and whispered eagerly, 'Did you like the Madonna, Lovejoy?'

'Yes, thanks.'

'They say some Greeks made it.'

'They did a good job.'

'Darling! Your hand is freezing.'

'I'm cold.'

'Then it's time for sunshine, and my surprise. Come, darling.'

We left, the Madonna's tearful gaze burning down above the crown of my head.

CHAPTER 16

'We've come absolutely miles,' Cosima answered.

We lay on a reedy island no higher than a mud flat among a myriad small water channels. The day was still hot, but a steady breeze had sprung up causing the dense reeds to make a dry clattering sound. Here and there a duck splashed, businesslike, but that was it. Great for secret loving picnics, but nothing else.

'How far, love?' I hate countryside, and this remoteness was at least partly that.

She raised her head, finally kneeling up to see across the *palude* flats. We'd seen Torcello's campanile when putting the *sandolo* boat ashore. 'About two kilometres, I suppose. Almost.'

'Good idea, your lady's engine.'

Cosima laughed and fell sprawling, embracing me. 'Is the signore tired, then?' This witticism made her roll in the aisles when she came to the punch line. 'May one ask why?'

I had to laugh with her. The surprise had been a *sandolo,* a small curved-looking boat. You row it standing up like a gondolier does, but mostly with two oars. The oldish lady from whom Cosima had hired the *sandolo* had mischievously explained that the object humped in the stern beneath a black plastic dustbin bag was an outboard motor. 'Wise to take precautions against the lagoon,' she'd said. 'And for exhaustion, on your return.' Cosima had given her a mock scolding at such suggestiveness but the old Torcellana had cackled all the more and pushed us off. She'd used the ancient greeting

'*Salve*', showing she was local.

Cosima wanted to row but so did I. I felt I'd rowed a race but had a high old time losing my way before Cosima said we should stop. We had a picnic and love on the blanket she happened to have brought along. I called her a scheming hussy and she said she didn't care.

'What's that noise?' The dozy afternoon kept being punctured. 'It's nearer.'

'Shooting, beyond Santa Cristina. The Doge of Venice used to give five ducks to the noble families every Christmas. Folk still shoot.'

'I hope we scared some off to safety.'

We'd made rather a racket the second time around, which was okay because apart from the occasional shrill outboard and lazy squawkings from the dense reeds there was almost total silence. I reached for her again but she pushed my hand away.

'There's a boat coming. Listen.'

'Stopping.'

At the canal back in Torcello we'd glimpsed Gerry and Keith puttering past the *locanda* intersection in a motor dinghy. Keith had waved. Gerry was too preoccupied consulting a paper, apparently giving directions as they'd headed out into the lagoon. Hardly anything to paint around here, that was for sure. Except me and Cosima. And ducks, but they were being decimated.

Another shot sounded, not quite so distant. No echoes like the others. Cosima drooped over me, our faces inches apart in the hair-filtered sunlight.

'Maybe somebody looking for the San Lorenzo. It was a great church. Now it's just a mound in the water. People dig at low water for rubble.'

'Saint Francis loved the ducks when he came here,' I accused.

'Dear Lovejoy. Always looking for somebody else to blame.'

'Bloody cheek.'

'It's true. You should look at yourself, darling, instead of the rest.'

She was smiling and rubbing noses but it's the sort of chitchat that gets you narked, especially when you know for a start that you're twice as reasonable as everybody else.

'It's this place, love.'

'Vanished splendour?'

'Maybe.' I was beginning to feel lost, remote, altogether too far from civilization and safety. All this silence, these miles of empty shallows and tangled channels with only the occasional distant campanile slanting to catch the late afternoon sun.

'Want to get back? There's a *vaporetto* from Torcello and Mazzorbo in an hour. We've plenty of time.'

There it was again, the spooky reminder. Mazzorbo's name means 'great city', and I knew for a fact it was nothing more than a few villas, a boatyard, one cypress tree and an ivy-covered campanile. Perhaps I was letting myself become nervous. Silly, really, because there was nothing to be worried about. Especially not out here.

'Know why I came?'

'Ulterior motive.' She was smiling, kneeling up doing her hair, mouth full of hairclips, head to one side.

'Several.'

'How many are female, Lovejoy?'

'One. You.'

A warning shake of the comb at me before she resumed her hair. 'That's all right, then.'

'Then I wanted to find out why you've cornered the world market in television people.'

'That's easy, darling. They're a rich signora's playthings.'

I sat up. 'Eh?'

'We did a group charter — unfortunately through those

Milanese agents, absolute gangsters with their endless moans about commission.'

'Signora Norman,' I said, relief washing over me so I prickled with sweat.

'*Sì*. You'd think a rich woman wouldn't worry about a special price, wouldn't you, but she argued over every single lira . . .' She rapped me on my belly with the comb. It didn't half sting. '*Bruto!* You said *one* female, Lovejoy! How did you know her name?'

I reached, tried to pull her down while she elbowed me off, hands in her hair still. 'Never even seen the woman, love. I was only worried because it was you who approached me in the café that night.'

'Why are you so suspicious, Lovejoy? About what?' She nudged me with an elbow so I tumbled. There she was, kneeling up in the daylight above me, clipping her hair, head illuminated by the lowering sun, when they shot her and she fell with a cough on to me.

I was helpless laughing at her sudden slumping weight, not realizing. '*Now* you change your mind!' The hairpins rattled on her teeth. She was making a coughing noise, moving on me, pinning me down.

Another shot sounded. The dry reeds gave a concerted tap, loud.

'Cosima? Cut it out. Somebody's playing silly buggers.'

I'd stopped laughing. Her face was on my chest, eyes closed, and her breathing was a two-tone hiss between teeth where a hairpin clattered. There was a brown redness, wet and new, spoiling her white blouse above her right breast.

'Love?' I tried to get up under her weight. '*Love?*' Then I was scrambling, scrabbling erect and yelling for help and bawling abuse and fury at stupid careless pigs of duck-hunters who loosed off in any direction.

'Help, for Christ's sweet sake! Help!' Like a fool I stood up and waved both arms, any direction, anywhere over the endless expanses of reeds. 'Somebody's been hurt!' I even bawled for an ambulance. Hysterical, I turned because I couldn't see anybody, not a boat, between us and Torcello's distant campanile, and stood on Cosima's ankle and fell aside as the reeds did their concerted snap.

'What?' I remember bleating as if somebody had asked me a daft question. 'Eh?'

But I stayed down. Shooting. It was coming this way. At us. Then I grabbed for Cosima, careful and low and on my belly because she'd been shot and there was no chance of help, not from anyone except ourselves. And that meant me, because Cosima was lying in a strewn attitude, still breathing but no thanks to me who'd fetched her out here to get her beautiful lovely life shot to oblivion. I was blubbering all sorts, holding her and heartbroken because I hadn't realized and had been laughing my silly bloody head off when she was getting herself shot. She kept making that coughing noise, endless and soft.

I fumbled in her handbag. My own hankie's always months out of the wash, but hers was pristine. Gingerly I blotted the blood. There was a circular wound, a little swollen, no longer leaking blood. That was a good sign, wasn't it, on the pictures when the cowboy's shot in the shoulder and a single wadged bandage did miraculous things for recovery? I looked about helplessly, frantic. The reeds snapped again, once. Two shots. Two shots of that lighter, businesslike cracking sound of the rifle. No shotgun, that. If I'd not been so preoccupied with my own thoughts and my own selfish bastard schemes I'd have realized hours ago somebody out there had a rifle, not a shotgun. We'd have been safely back in Torcello, tea at the *locanda*, the crowded *vaporetto* on its tranquil way . . .

Cosima moaned faintly as I lay down and pulled myself and her along the ground through the reeds. It's damned hard, especially when you're still sobbing incoherent remorse and you don't know what the hell you're supposed to be doing. And you've no idea what to do next and . . . and that noise. Outboard motor, but which direction? There hadn't been any engine sound before. And definitely no boat in sight when I'd goonishly stood upright to wave to our murderers to show exactly where I was and how very sensibly I was responding to the whole frigging mess.

Think. I tried, but it's difficult when you're frightened to death. We were within a few feet of the *sandolo*. I'd wedged it among the reeds ashore as far as I could. God alone knows how big the flat island was, or how much of it got covered by tides. I tried thinking. The rifleman—two of them if they were Gerry and Keith—was being careful. No need to rush up through the reeds. After all, I might have a knife or even a gun and lie in the tall reeds in ambush. Wiser to wait until I made a move into the open water between the island and the mudflats.

Yet stay too long and we'd be awash. Anyway, Cosima couldn't wait. Move, and we'd reveal our track of escape by the movement of the dense reeds.

The engine sound was shifting. It sounded like a low-powered outboard motor on a *sandolo*, going once round the island. A patrol, just making sure. Clever sod. The rifleman was in the boat. I knew that for absolute certain because I'd raised such a hullabaloo in my first panic that any innocent fisherman or duck-shooter must have heard and would already be calling out asking directions as they came closer. It had to be him. Them.

Sprawling, I cradled Cosima. I was almost screaming with the fury of impotence, at my own stupidity and helplessness. We couldn't stay much longer. He'd come closer each circuit, more and more sure of himself. Swim for it? But how far could I get pulling Cosima through the water before he caught us up? He might simply see us and

shoot casually from where he was. Sitting ducks. No
wonder some maniacs go hunting. Bloody ducks can't
shoot back. No weapons. And Cosima's picnic was too
neat, too prepared. One plastic spatula between us.
Plates cardboard, little basket, nothing. Good for starting
a fire but not for making into weapons to . . . Fire.

'Wait, love. I'll be a sec.'

I laid her down and edged back to where we'd lain. Her
handbag was open where I'd fumbled for her hankie. No
matches, but a small lighter, heart-shaped, red enamel.
It could click, and fired a light damned near into my
eyes. Gas, flame height adjustable with one of those small
wheel things. I tried it on a blade of grass which flared, a
reed which shrivelled vertically almost in a flash, but
snuffed both immediately. Nothing must happen as long
as that outboard engine kept whining and the hunter kept
moving closer out there among the reeds.

Cosima was coughing less now, still comatose, still
breathing. I tried cupping my hands round my ears and
turning slowly to get some idea of where the bastard was,
but couldn't for the life of me fix the direction. I'd have to
stand up for that to work properly. Presumably he knew
more or less where our *sandolo* lay, but for an accurate
shot he'd actually need to see us clearly. He'd only hit
Cosima second or third go, so far as I could recollect from
thinking back on those noises the brackeny reeds had
made, and even then he'd been trying for me. If we'd not
been fooling about, up and down at the moment of
shooting, he'd have got me and then it would have been
anybody's guess what would have happened to Cosima.

It had to be done. 'I'm back, love,' I gasped, trying not
to quake, and reached up a hand to haul on the *sandolo*.
Obediently it moved down almost into the water, six
hauls. These boats are all curves, pointed up at the front
and having a funny wedge-shaped decking there. To get
Cosima in without being seen I'd have to pull the *sandolo*

somehow on its side. I got the boat round after shoving it out to the end of its rope, then pulling it hard round as I crawled. The stupid thing nearly rolled on to me, and I must have created quite a disturbance in the reeds, but at least I had it slewed on a thick clump so it showed its interior towards us.

That outboard was still whining away out there, and no more shots. Sooner or later the swine would have to land on one of the zillion creeks to loose off a reasonable shot. Teeth chattering in fright, I stripped and lobbed my clothes any old how near the front of the *sandolo*. I'd carefully put Cosima's little red lighter on a mass of dry sedge, some old nest built by exterminated ducks, I suppose. With gasped apologies and endearments to my lovely crumpled girl, I clasped her tight and shoved myself along through the reeds.

Easy to criticize, and I know everybody else could have done it better, but the only way I could think of getting her in was to lift her legs in, then shove her bum on the gunwale, then worm beneath her poor bloodstained trunk and rise up so she more or less rolled in. Hardly a fireman's lift, with me groaning in sympathy with every murmur of pain from her. The effort left me wheezing and in anguish at the needless hurt I'd caused her, but I kept going and slowly manœuvred the *sandolo* away from the ground until it floated.

Three or four minutes of waiting, with me whimpering at the slightest sound from the reeds and inwardly cursing hate upwards to where a jet trace indicated a planeload of selfish swine living it up while I was starkers down here getting frigging murdered in the mud. Then the hunter's boat cut its sound, then sounded louder and gave that diminishing whine. He was turning somewhere. Not closer, but definitely about to cut his engine and run ashore and . . . He'd glimpsed our *sandolo*, or seen my disturbance of the reeds. Even as I realized that this was it, that he'd pinpointed us accurately enough, his engine coughed into silence and I was scrabbling like a mad thing, ripping at the reeds and twisting them into vertical clusters.

Surprisingly they hurt like hell, maybe because they were so dense, but I clutched and twisted until I'd cleared about a square yard of reeds and got them all doubled over in coils. I'd seen the men do it often enough along the sea marshes at home, while idling down the estuaries. The watermen always clear a space as wide as the reeds are tall. He must have left his boat, and now be crawling among the sedge grass towards us. A click, a spurt of flame, and the looped reeds caught, the sedge grass caught. The nest caught. The funny low tangles of grass caught. Every bloody thing caught, swooshing up flame and sprinkling the air with sparks and black fluff. The reeds caught up the flame, passing it across the island, I ran at a crouch, scrambled at the *sandolo* and floundered the stupid slow thing out among the thinner reeds into the channel, swimming like the clappers at the stern. Smoke spread everywhere, lying over the water.

None of these channels is very wide, and they're all completely irregular. That whole area of the lagoon is a jigsaw of islands, *barene* flats covered at high tide, with shallows and treacherous mudbanks everywhere. You can hide, but always only temporarily, because if you can take a boat anywhere down these labyrinthine little channels, so can the hunter. A shot sounded, clearly angry guesswork on his part. No buzzing and reeds cracking about us. The fire was spreading fast. I was going too slowly. Smoke billowed over us as I swam on, praying for a hidden creek where I could lay up a few minutes unseen and fix our outboard engine. With that thing mounted—if it went—I could make a run for it. And I'd not stop till I reached the Fondamenta Nuove in Venice where the hospital was.

Opposite where we'd beached the *sandolo* there was an inlet about twenty or thirty feet off, but it was too obvious. Instead, retching and spluttering, I kept to the smoke and shoved to the right following the channel, the silly boat's curved stern bumping on my head as I swam and pushed. It was then I made the most miraculous and ecstatic discovery. My knees—not my feet, even—touched something down in the water. I'd squealed and let go of the boat before I realized it wasn't a shark jawing my poor defenceless flailing limbs. It was mud, glorious mud. The lagoon here was shallow enough to stand up in.

It takes some doing if you're as terrified as me. But honestly I actually did drop my feet and start shoving, still hunched from cowardice yet thrusting that *sandolo* now at a hell of a lick. The hunter's engine still hadn't started up to show he was coming after us when I swung the *sandolo* to penetrate the thick reed-beds. We hadn't come this way, and heaven knows where we were heading, but I shoved on and on, moving always where the reeds were thinner but now never breaking out into any of the tempting open channels which sometimes showed to either side. Definitely I avoided the thick patches of reeds. Already my fire was proving as much a risk to us as to him. Sparks were carrying the fire across the reeds in jumps rather than a slow spread, and somewhere to the left a new fire had begun. Worse, the wind seemed erratic and once I practically choked in the smoke which seemed to stick to the water. Cosima was coughing again at the bastard smoke. I'd lost all direction, staggering on practically on my knees, shoving as hard as I could go and trying to guess which way to take by peering along the side of the *sandolo*.

How long it was before the sound of the outboard motor penetrated my consciousness I'll never know. By then I'd adopted this method of gaining momentum by using my weight. Head tucked down, left shoulder rammed hard against the stern and my hands raised to clutch the gunwale and take my weight partly on my arms, I could then kick my legs down into the muddy lagoon bed and keep the boat moving at a fair speed. Now, though, I let my legs trail me to a gurgling stop. No use giving our position away by unnecessary motion. I relinquished my hold and slumped my head against the curved wood, gasping and retching water. Smoke covered us once or twice, thinned, thickened again, thinned. Cosima coughed gently, moaned occasionally. I blurted out a whispered assurance, thinking, What a bloody mess.

The hunter's boat sounded no nearer. A few yards off, the reeds caught a floating spark and flared vertical fire and soot for a moment. Away in the distance I actually heard a man's voice call in one prolonged hail over the sound of his engine, but it was never repeated and there was no way of telling from which direction. Or whether he was a friend or foe, for that matter.

The engine sound was dwindling. Varying a bit, as he swung in and out of the inlets, but very definitely receding. Odd, that. No sense in rising to risk a look. One glimpse of us, and he'd come at us. We'd be lost. I let it go on for another minute, put my skinned shoulder at the stern again, took hold and got my aching legs going. Nine or ten shoves and we emerged into an open channel. I almost infarcted doing a frantic back-pedal but should have realized the only straight waterways in the Venetian lagoon are the manmade canals. All the rest are snaky shaggy thoroughfares, no two alike, and bending any way they want every few yards.

My brain managed to insert a reasoned logical thought among its waves of terror: So long as that droning engine didn't sound nearer, and so long as the channels didn't straighten out to give a clear long-distance view, it was better for us to move along the open water. That way, no reeds would waggle to reveal where Lovejoy was panicking his untidy shambolic passage through the water foliage, and no traces would be left of his movement.

Mentally I measured the intensity of the swine's outboard, then edged cautiously into the channel and rotated to move off along it. As I resumed my shoving, unbelievably I glimpsed a campanile in the distance. Only a glimpse, snatched between two coincident channels between slightly raised *barene*, but it was real and definite. I'd recognize those great stone shutters anywhere. Torcello. It was to the rear, back over my poor old knackered shoulder, now scraped raw and bloodied. We were moving away from it.

Still smoke everywhere. As I floundered on along the narrow channel, I was becoming certain the bastard was between us and where I'd glimpsed the great campanile. Difficult to judge, but the sound was constant. Maybe he thought we would head for Torcello and was patrolling between the burning area of the lagoon and the tall cathedral tower.

Sickened at the implication I kept on, ploughing my legs down into the soft mud, thrusting, dragging my weight on one hand or the other to keep to the channel. I wanted to avoid the wretched boat running aground and jarring Cosima, but was terrified of creating any more reed-shaking.

When you work at a particular horrid thing—like blindly sploshing a tiny boat through a muddy lagoon—your mind detaches and floats off somewhere, leaving your poor old hulk timelessly slogging away down there in the clag.

Eventually, though, two events filtered through to my basking brain. The first was gradual awareness of that engine sound. It had all but dwindled away. Whether we'd simply moved apart, or whether he'd stayed put as

I'd blundered further and further away, was impossible to say.

The second thing was this long white wall.

CHAPTER 17

The smoke had diminished by distance and eventually, I suppose, lack of reed fuel by the time the long white wall really made its mark. Of course I'd been dimly aware for aeons of a vague blur up there, but what's one blur a million miles away when you're being drowned, burned, smothered and shot, hour after bloody hour?

When I finally halted and groaned a few sloshed hunchback paces into the reeds the wall was there, across a wider spread of water than the narrow channels through which I'd slaved. I couldn't straighten up and stayed mud covered and gasping, hands on my knees and waist-deep in lagoon water. Blearily I noticed with astonishment that, the further I looked away from the white wall which rimmed the island, the darker the world seemed. It took several re-thinks before the penny dropped. Daylight was leaving the lagoon. No bright sun, no brilliant blue. That ochre sediment was washing upwards making a dusted haze out of an azure sky. It was approaching dusk. All I'd done was knacker myself, and get Cosima no nearer to a hospital. What I needed was a stray *vaporetto* or a holiday cruiser to happen by. Instead, I thought bitterly, I find a long white wall sticking upright out of the frigging lagoon.

No engine sounds now. Nothing. Not even a duck's quack. The island seemed fairly tallish for this part of the lagoon, raised vegetation showing over the wall. It didn't look inhabited. Except for some low water-steps over to the right, where a solid gate interrupted the line of the wall, there was no indication that anybody had ever even lived there.

I had to chance it. A bit of solitude, with Cosima carefully concealed out of sight beyond the wall, and I might even get the chance of mounting the outboard motor and possibly making a run for it in the manner to which I was accustomed—namely, with a hell of a lot more speed than trogging across this reedy expanse like a stranded cod.

Weeping at the bloody futility of everything, I bent to the stern and strove my slow course out into the open water separating the reed channels from the island, making for the steps. To my alarm the mud vanished underneath my flailing feet and I was back to swimming, pushing the boat with my head or hands or wherever my dwindling strength made me meet the useless frigging *sandolo*.

The sudden stop had slammed the stern's long curved rib into my shoulder. I blubbered and wailed in agony. I was sorry for myself, quite justifiably, but Cosima moaned, thank Christ, and I looked to see what had stopped us. It was the water-steps of the white-walled island, hit straight in the middle.

Above me was a tall barred gate, padlocked, chained. The wall was continuous and quite tall, but over to one side was a bit dishevelled and lower where scrubby wild bushes and undergrowth showed. Admittedly a low-lying sort of place, but still high enough to be a better vantage-point than anything else in the lagoon except the campaniles.

By now I was utterly flaked. How I got Cosima out and over the wall I'll never know—that's untrue: I know only too well the way I handled her, finally just straddling the wall in the lessening light and letting her slide in an untidy heap on to the surprisingly white ground below. I hate to think of the pain she must have been in because I was too scared and shagged out to lower her properly.

From the foot of the wall the island sloped almost immediately into the water, only a few feet of rim at most. Even that was whitish stonework. Funny bloody place, I remember thinking, hauling myself along the pale slope back towards the steps. Why, even the ground inside the perimeter was whitish. Clever old trees to stay green in all this ghostly pallor. No signs of a house, though, from the one quick dazed glance I'd had.

An engine. An outboard engine. The sun was gone, and the sound was distant, but there hadn't been one a minute ago. Same sound. Presumably our same old faithful hunter.

'Oooooh.' That was me, scrabbling down to the *sandolo* and all but rupturing myself lifting the outboard in its plastic bag. The only place was over the wall, so clunk it went among the bushes any old how. Fine thing if I'd ruined it. My clothes too and the oars went over. Which left our swine of a boat.

The stones were loose, possibly dropped there by one of those dredgers to reinforce the base of the wall. I got a monster one, put it into the *sandolo* and tilted the boat by sitting astride the gunwale. She filled with maddening slowness, and even then hung about below the surface with her prow and stern tips showing. No good if she bobbed up just as our hunter came cruising past. I kicked her to one side of the water-steps, in case the bastard landed and saw it. Even in my state that *sandolo* astonished me. I'd thought that one puncture finished the average boat, but this wretched thing kept cheerfully floating up even when I'd actually sunk it. I hauled more dredged stones from the artificial shore. It took eight of the damned monsters to keep the *sandolo* convincingly down and I could scramble over the wall into the scruffy brush.

No signs of life here among all this perennial whiteness.

Not even a dilapidated palazzo or other building. Stiffened into a hunchback, I found it murderously hard getting to where I'd dropped Cosima. The white ground seemed to be made up entirely of these irregular pale stones. They gave a hollowish clatter as I stumbled along so I had to steady myself with a hand on the wall. A rum place, with its patchy mini-jungles of undergrowth. Odd that the Venetian authorities had taken so much trouble—dredging, the wall, the gate, that expensive littoral shoring with valuable masonry—especially since nobody lived here.

My teeth were chattering when I found Cosima and straightened her. It had become quite cold . . . but of course I was in my nip so I went and collected my clothes and tried arranging them round her. No good me hugging her till I dried because I was perished and I'd only wet her through. That horrible whining noise of the boat on the lagoon was coming closer. Queer how menacing a slow approaching threat can be.

Any movement on these white-mound stones might create a clatter I couldn't quieten so I froze. He was here. The engine droned, dropped a tone. Closer. To look at the gateway? Me and Cosima were about twenty yards from the gate, very close to the wall. I couldn't take the risk of looking because I suddenly might have had to duck back into cover, and set these hollow stones rattling.

He didn't stay, just cruised slowly past between the island and the reed channels from which we'd blundered. Once, he returned with his outboard deeper and slower. Not too close, I prayed, or you'll run into my sunken *sandolo* and get yourself sunk. Then he might climb out of the water and I'd have a scrap on my hands. I was in no shape to start hide-and-seek in this loony place.

The engine snapped into higher pitch. He was off. I listened as the note gradually dopplered off into the gathering dusk. Of course, he could be encircling the

white island to come at us from the other side, but I was
beyond working it all out any more. For the minute I was
safe with Cosima, which was more than we'd been ever
since we left Torcello.

Light was now surprisingly poor. I clambered to my
feet and did some exercises. Once I got myself unperished
and that outboard had dwindled to zero I'd chance a look
out over the wall. Maybe then I could think about getting
away.

Twenty minutes later I'd realized two things. One was
that I was a million miles from Torcello. Vaguely, the
slender line of Torcello's campanile showed against the
sky glow which must be Venice itself. So that was south. I
must have struggled northward all afternoon long. Not by
reason of skilled knowledge of the lagoon, but only
because the reed-beds and the channels and the smoke
had given most chance of concealment. Well, the lagoon
had to end somewhere even in that direction, but it might
prove all too easy to waste away the night frantically
careering among the marsh channels. And an outboard
motor makes a telltale sound. No, getting the boat up
and Cosima to a doctor was our priority. Since the killer
had only to sit in Torcello and wait for us, which was
presumably where the bastard had gone now, we had to
go travel in the opposite direction.

The second thing I realized was what all these mounds
of white stones were.

I was sitting mournfully by my lovely wounded Cosima
when it dawned on me that I could maybe arrange some
of these hollowish white stones into a pillow and make her
breathing a bit easier. My trousers could be wadged on
top for softness, and the movement would keep me from
freezing to death because it was now becoming bitter.
You can die from cold. Every muscle screeching, I
listlessly fumbled for a rounded stone, got one, and felt it

to see which of its aspects was most regular. My finger waggled. I felt some more. My thumb was on teeth. My index finger was in an eye-socket. It was a skull. I screamed and leapt, flinging the bloody skull away so it clacked and clattered among the foliage.

And I felt the ground. No soil. Only long bones, thin bones, round skull bones, spine bones, shoulder bones and hip bones and skull, skull, skull bones. The whole frigging island was one great charnel house. We were on Santa Ariana, the *osseria*. The bone island. A world of bones. Gibbering, I danced clumsily, trying to keep my feet off the bloody things before I found myself over the wall and dementedly floundering down into the water where I'd sunk the *sandolo* and lobbing those great stones out of her as though they weighed nothing.

It seemed years of shuddering feverish activity hauling the *sandolo* on its side up the sloping margin to get it empty, then screwing the outboard in place, all by feel and murky peering. Probably it was no more than half an hour or even less before I got the damp *sandolo* floating in soggy obedience. Going back for Cosima, my clothes and the oars was the hardest thing I've ever done. I didn't even wait to dress. The old woman's engine started first yank of its string, and I was off into the gloom any old where. My own noise, my own engine, choice surging back into me with all the power it brings.

CHAPTER 18

Choice is power. Some poor bloke enjoying a well-earned nosh in that roadside *trattoria* west of the village church of Altino found that out when I nicked his car in the time-honoured way (comb through the window rubber, join the starter wires under the dashboard) and recklessly

drove it down the path as near to the water as I dared. It
was quite fair, really. If the people of Altinum hadn't
migrated into the lagoon fifteen centuries back to found
Torcello and Venice, Cosima and me wouldn't have been
in all this frigging mess. If anybody owed us, it was
Altinum.

I'd chosen — well, guessed — landfall where shore lights
showed and where the black-pointed hulk of a boathouse
promised there was access for a car. Cosima hadn't
coughed now for some time, maybe hours. Speed. I
wanted — *had* to have — speed, but making a safe landfall
wasn't easy. Once I almost ran full tilt into a marker post,
and twice I tangled with those projecting tops which
crisscross patches of the lagoon and mark the limits of the
valli fish farms, and had double nightmares ripping
myself free. Somehow in my mad scramble away from
Santa Ariana I'd lost Cosima's lighter, my only source of
light. I had to go by what glimpses of road lights showed
to the north and west, and even then had to cut speed to a
slow crawl in case I ran aground or entangled again. In
the conditions I was lucky to reach the lagoon shore as I
did, only having to shove the bows off a dozen or so times
when clumping into the *barene*.

There was a clear reach of water and a channel
running to the north-west from the boathouse. That
structure was pretty derelict, maybe even unused. All the
better, because I didn't want telltale clues like *sandoli*
showing we'd got away.

'Come on, darlin',' I said to Cosima as I lifted her from
the boat. 'We're nearly there.'

I swear she almost muttered something but there wasn't
time to chat. I staggered up the truckle landing-stage and
with only two rests made it to the car. No lights. She had
to go in the passenger seat upright, head back, because
like a nerk I'd stolen one of those small two-door things
without a lift-up rear door. I'm pathetic when it comes to

planning. The position she was in made her breathe funny and hissing. I rushed down to the *sandolo* and untied it. It was only a couple of hundred yards down-channel to open water.

That engine was great. I used the stern rope to fix the outboard handle to dead ahead and opened the throttle to half speed. Then I pointed the *sandolo* out into the mid-channel heading into the lagoon and let go.

Away she went, straight as an arrow. I found myself shouting, 'Thanks, mate,' as the little boat trundled off on its own into the darkness. For a few seconds she showed blackly against the pallor of the waterway, then only the faint scut of white water gave her position. Then that too was gone and only the engine sound remained, receding as she ran the channel. With luck she might even get an uncontrolled mile, or even further, before she struck and exhausted her fuel aground on one of the *barene*.

Utterly knackered now, I lurched up to the car. As the channel ran inland, it widened to include a couple of small reedy mid-river islands. A road crossed above there, showing bits of the terrain when motor headlights swept over. Probably the road from Altino village. Follow that coastwise, and you'd reach Mestre, Venice's oily landbased neighbour. It had to be that way.

No signs of agitation as we drove grandly past the *trattoria*. Altino is now no more than a village, maybe only a hamlet. Signposts told me it was a few miles to Mestre, to Treviso, to Padua.

'Hold on, love,' I told Cosima. 'We've a little way still to go.'

A little way meant twenty-five kilometres. I decided to aim for the hospital in Padua. The motor clock placidly showed it was ten past ten. Astonishingly, the Marco Polo airport lights showed to our left after we'd gone barely a couple of miles, and we were in Ca'Noghera. Unbelievable. The whole swinish world had been living normally while my poor Cosima got shot and I'd been terrified out of my skin. I swallowed my hate and concentrated.

We drove serenely towards Mestre as if we'd been out for a quiet supper. There was an overcoat in the car. Useful, for a born planner.

'Johanne Eich,' I explained, beaming, to the admission nurse. Going the whole hog, I gave that brilliant Regency gunsmith's Swiss home address as well. 'Though,' I added with a flourish of invention, 'I work in Geneva.'

'And you found the lady . . . ?'

'A short distance from Vicenza. There she was,' I said, graphic and eager, 'staggering along the road. She actually fell! I actually saw her! Naturally I thought she was drunk, until the headlights revealed her condition.'

'The doctor says she appears to have been shot.'

'Shot?' I was a picture of the flabbergasted Swiss businessman. 'Then how fortunate I urged you to contact the police! Who knows,' I speculated grandly, getting carried away with jubilation now Cosima was safe in hospital, 'what disorders have been perpetrated? You must order the police to investigate instantly!'

'Do you know her?'

'Certainly not,' I lied. 'Incidentally, shouldn't you ask for my car licence number? Identification. You must also ask for my detailed account of—'

'Of course.'

The lass was plump and fetching, and swiftly becoming irritable. I was sorry to rile her, but I had to portray the classical image of solidity or I'd never get away before the police came pouring in.

Heel of my left hand to steady the admission form, because fingerprints and characteristic skin impressions end at the wristline. Meticulously I recorded the number from the Swiss-registration saloon I'd memorized from among the cars in the street near Padua's railway station.

'It's a company car,' I solemnly informed her. 'Now, signorina, you must record that the injured young lady gave me her name. Maria Guardi, she said. Please write it down.'

'I am, signore.'

'But you must not simply take my word 'for it,' I preached maddeningly. 'You must demand to see the documents. They are in a special double-lock compartment in my auto-mobile,' I announced affably, twinkling what I thought might look like a Swiss businessman's affable twinkle. 'I'll get them. The signorina will not mind if I leave one or two of my company's business cards . . . ?'

'There's no need for all that,' the poor nurse said wearily.

'No trouble, no trouble. All records must be *complete* at all times. It's practically my company motto. An incomplete record is no record at all. You agree, I'm sure . . . ?'

I strolled out, then ran to the car. I was on the main road as the police car zoomed in the hospital entrance.

Half a tank of petrol. Quite enough for what I wanted. Well, not *wanted* exactly. Had to do, more like. Compelled. Everything was out of my hands now. The others, whoever they were, had forced the issue. They'd tried to kill me and Cosima. After my trick with the *sandolo*, perhaps they even thought they'd succeeded.

The geography of Italy's a mystery to me, and the car's owner proved to have been an uncooperative blighter. Not a single roadmap. Sometimes you can't depend on anybody. Vaguely I had a notion that Padua lay between Verona and Venice, but exactly where was anybody's guess. I'd told the nurse Vicenza because I'd seen it on a sign pointing in the opposite direction to that indicating Mestre.

Trains would run from Verona towards Switzerland. If the police found this car and news got about, the hunter might assume I'd lit out for Geneva and safety—as long as it was found nearer the Swiss border than Padua, since he might learn of Cosima's presence in hospital sooner or later.

Before carrying Cosima so dramatically into the hospital's casualty area bawling for assistance with the exaggeratedly odd accent, I'd used a ballpoint to write in her palm *One. You.* That way she'd realize I was in the land of the living and probably still somewhere around.

The other bastards were going to discover that fact the hard way. I'd make sure of that.

For a steady thirty-six hours after I dumped the stolen car by the railway, I slept in the station at Verona, ate, rested in the museum, noshed, went to the pictures for another kip, noshed. And phoned the Padua hospital asking how Maria Guardi was coming along, please, and giving the name of the Verona newspaper when asked for my name by the diligent ward sister. I was a wreck, but with a vested interest in recovery of all kinds.

The day after the day after, I felt at last I'd returned from outer space, and caught the train to Mestre.

CHAPTER 19

A heartfelt love message before this next bit: Dear ugly town of Mestre, Lovejoy adores you.

Now, nobody likes Mestre. Worse, nobody even *pretends* to like it. Everybody who works there wants to work somewhere else. People who live there loathe it because it isn't beautiful. Tourists zoom on into Padua or Venice. Nobody likes it.

Except me. I thought, do think and will forever think that good old Mestre is great. Ten out of ten on the Lovejoy scale. One corrosive breath of its poisonous smog, and my heart warmed with love.

For a start, it's horribly industrial. Its traffic is a shambles, its buildings ridiculous. It is definitely shop-soiled. Its docks are full of oil and all the greasy activity which that undesirable substance brings. Love on sight.

Soon after arrival I stood watching traffic along the Ponte della Libertà, comparing. At one end of the long causeway sits sluttish old smog-riddled Mestre. At the other lies queenly Venice, glittering, spectacular. And make no mistake. Venice is a luscious sight, pulling and compelling.

The sky was a balmy blue. The lagoon shone the azure back into the air about the Serene Republic, imparting a fluorescence so bright it almost hurt your eyes to look.

It was over to the left, out there in the lagoon from where I was standing, that my little Cosima had nearly died. The hospital said she was now over the worst and was expected to make a steady return to health and who was speaking because the police . . . ? Don't get me wrong. I wasn't actually planning revenge. I'm not that sort of bloke. No, honestly. Ask anybody. All right, I admit that revenge is a pretty good way of getting even, but it's hardly my style to hold a grudge. Reasonable old me, always trying to be fair. The bad temper I'd felt, the hatred, the panic and sick fear were all gone now. I was my usual smiley self.

Standing there near the causeway in the sunshine, I thought of Venice.

These days we can't even begin to perceive what 'Venetian' meant to the ancients. Oh, the factual bit is clear: Venice was viewed as a strong maritime power simply because she was. And okay, Venice meant self-interest. Like when the thousands of knights and soldiers of the Fourth Crusade arrived at the Venetian Lido asking for help in the name of God, charity and compassion, the Doge of Venice actually demanded what was in it for him.

But beyond Venice's blunt greed there was something deeper and especially horrid. To the ancient people of the past centuries Venice simply meant fright, evil, everything sinister. Venice meant perverse secrecy of the most surreptitious and malevolent kind. Venice meant secret trials, silent stabbings, spies, clandestine murder and sudden vanishing without trace. Venice meant a slit throat while sleeping, and violent unfathomable assassination. Venice meant poison — it took a Venetian priest to murder a communicant by slipping poison into the very Host. Venice meant sly crime and refined treachery and skulduggery. Venice meant a reign of hidden terror, brutal but stealthily quiet imprisonments. Venice meant stark cold cruelty.

Throughout the long centuries of her prime, Venice was a permeating fear, a cloud of terror over Europe, a world of malevolent horror. Strong men quaked before her. Wise men shunned her. Rich men durstn't trust her. Poor men were simply out of Venice's reckoning, and thankfully praised God for being so. Even her glass industry was partly tainted by this weird fame: Venetian glass was reputed so delicate that it would shatter if poison touched it.

Her reputation was not undeserved. Venice's secret councils saw to that. Venetians learned to go about their business with a cool disregard for the abrupt absence of friends. One morning, the feet of three miscreants were observed sticking up out of the paving in St Mark's Square where they'd been buried alive — and all Venice passed by this fearsome execution blandly regardless: God was obviously in His heaven, and the dreaded Council of Ten was simply doing its usual Venetian stuff in the dark hours. Naturally, other nations were at it too. Like the time the Venetian ambassador was shocked to find his current secret correspondence, neatly labelled and bound into volumes, pointedly displayed on the shelves of a London library—possibly the all-time put-down for a spy. Despite these occasional setbacks, though, it was generally conceded that for dank dark deeds Venice took the biscuit. Nobody argued.

Well, with a reputation that formidable against me, I'd have to fight fire with fire. And forgery is the only skulduggery I know. Somebody had to knock on the door of the Palazzo Malcontento. Old Ivan the Terrible had given me a good enough clue: the fancy bloke from there had whisked Nancy away.

I thought, Right, you bastards. Here I come.

The money I had left wasn't a fortune. It'd have to do, though, because there wasn't all that much time. A sense of urgency was coming on me.

By evening, I'd got a part-time job as a kitchen help washing up afternoons and evenings in a biggish nosh bar near the docks, not far from a toolmaker's workshop I had my eye on. Day pay.

About a mile from the nosh bar I found Signora Lamberti. She was one of those massive affable ladies who understands every customer's need. To her, speech was a necessity, but only for purposes of agreement.

'Is it quiet here?' I asked, meaning were people of the district inclined to be nosey.

'*Certo*,' she bawled over the whistle of a passing train. 'You cannot even *hear* the station!'

'*Molto tranquillo*,' I yelled in agreement, paying her a day's advance for a tiny but clean room. She took down her 'Vacancy' sign as I howled promises to fetch my non-existent but voluminous luggage.

'At the signore's convenience!' she shouted understandingly as a goods train rattled by. We smiled at the fiction. Words are fine up to a point, her bustly attitude said, but don't let them get in the way of money.

That was the easy bit. It took me two whole days more to find the little piece of wood I needed. It was in a small lumber-yard, nothing more than a squat piece of sycamore with closer grain even than usual, taken from some nineteenth-century furniture. None of those distinct rays you sometimes see in sycamore wood, so I was happy. The driver in the yard said I could have it for nothing. I told him ta, my warmth showing him he'd done somebody a really good turn.

In case you don't know, sycamore's one of the Acer genus. Like Mestre, it's a real pal. For a start it is a strong, hard, pretty heavy wood. It can be artificially weathered by rotten crooks like antique dealers to look much older than it actually is, if you know how (tell you in a minute) and it stains up and polishes like an angel. The point of all this is you can work it quickly and accurately and expect very little trouble even if you're not expert. Its 'comparative workability' is 3.0 (white pine, that corny old stuff you can carve practically with a bent pin, is the basic 1.0).

You get the idea. Sycamore is faker's wood. The wood of the forger.

The bloke slogging away in the toolmaker's workshop looked up and saw me grinning at him on my fourth morning in gorgeous old Mestre, and he said good-morning. I'd passed by there and paused on the third day, but he'd tolerated my presence in his doorway without a word. He'd not once nodded or let his work be interrupted. Evidently he had no helpers. His wife, a hurrying tub of breathlessness, came out and gave him a coffee, glanced across at me with curiosity but said nothing.

I'd already decided this was my scene: a man

scratching a living, working a one-man show with no time to rest, crucial orders due for delivery and all that. Politely, that fourth morning I replied good-morning, still watching.

'Nice to have no work, eh?' he said. I liked the look of him, a short and beefy baldish bloke who worked without fuss and whose eyes were steady as his hands.

'I'm a hard worker, Signor Gambello.' The faded name was flaking off a plank nailed over the yard door.

'But not this morning, eh?' He had a ready if wry grin.

'My job is kitchen help. Over at the *trattoria*.'

'You, is it? I'd heard they got a stranger as kitchen skivvy.'

'But the mornings bore me.'

'Looking for another hour, eh?' He shook his head. He was lathe-turning short pieces of metal rod about eighteen thou. 'Not here, I'm afraid.'

'Tomorrow morning,' I suggested. 'Free work.'

'No pay?' That interrupted his work all right. He leant away, cut the machine. 'Why would anyone do that?'

'For an hour's use of your lathe. Private job.'

He wiped his hands on a cloth, gauging me. 'What's the catch? Key for your employer's safe? An illegal gun barrel?'

'Wood, signore. I want to make a present for my auntie's birthday. A surprise.'

'That's original.' The bloke was cynical too.

'You can watch me if you like. To check.'

He still eyed me. 'Maybe I will. What's the present?'

'Eh? Oh, only table mats.'

'Very well. Tomorrow, right?'

He watched me go, disbelieving. I left, smiling again. I'd turn up if I had to crawl.

Our agreement was that I'd slog in Gambello's yard from nine till eleven each morning. From then until noon I'd have free use of those tools not in use.

His actual job was lathing cylindrical metal rod into spindle-ended mini-shanks, and putting a screw-thread part way along it. God knows why. Something to do with engines. Signor Gambello had to make six thousand before the end of the week. I tried explaining how much more interesting the job would be if we rigged up a sapling gear like the Benedictines used for furniture, but he only stared, mystified. So we did it his way, on this shrill electric Woods lathe that turned his little metal sticks out like shelling peas. Great, but bloody boring.

The first morning I just helped and saved my own hour. Second morning I lathed for him while he did his books, and then got out my sycamore dead on eleven. It took me forty minutes to turn my piece to a perfect cylinder. First I needed a thin slice four inches across and three-eighths thick. Ten minutes flat. Then a flat cylindrical box, perfectly round, made to stand squat. That meant machining it in two bits so its lid settled easily inside—never an external-sliding lid for Elizabethan table-mat holders, remember.

There was an old tin in the yard. I half-filled it with pieces of bark I'd flaked off the elderly Quercus tree standing near the eastern crossroad traffic lights, on my way in. An old brown leather shoe I'd got from a dustbin, cut in slices, filled the tin; top up with water, and set it boiling in a corner of the yard. Signora Gambello touchingly brought me out a coffee and some *panini* breads and cheese. I explained I was only doing my own thing, that I'd really finished the proper yard work at eleven, but she said to have it all the same. I thought that was really kind.

Waiting for my stew to darken, I had the nosh and then fetched out my pound of black grapes. I only wanted the seeds and skins. It nearly killed me eating the pulp and sucking the skins clean, but I did it after an hour. Added to the stewing mess with as much Chinese green tea as it would take, and my tin ponged to high heaven. Twice I crossed the yard to apologize to Signora Gambello. Before going to work at the nosh bar I put the horrible mess to cool in the corner by the gate.

Next day my flat circular box and the thin disc went in and out of the dark mess about ten times while I worked the lathe between times. Gambello had a coke furnace for annealing wrought-iron, and he said it was all right if I dried my wood pieces on the flue between each soaking. Neither of the Gambellos asked anything, but their curiosity was more and more apparent as the phoney Elizabethan place-mat and its container became increasingly warped and stained. A split developed in the thin disc about noon — I worked on at the lathe unasked — and Signor Gambello was itching to point this out, but still I pressed on. He'd want to weld it. Every few minutes both pieces went into the tin of stain for a soak, then were warmed to dryness on the furnace flue.

That noon I postponed my nosh to impose coarser turning-marks on the surfaces, using a coarse bastard file and setting the Woods lathe to a laborious two hundred revs, then had my *colazione* while Gambello resumed the metal work in my place.

Next day at ten-thirty we knocked off the last of his mini-shanks and got them boxed and loaded on his truck. That gave me nearly three hours before I'd have to leave for my washing-up job.

The inscription I'd chosen was something vaguely remembered from school. Old Benkie, our literature teacher, once clipped my ear in a temper over forgetting a Chaucer quotation: *The answer to this lete I to divines*. Which divines, and answer to what, was anybody's guess, but the quotation was enough to fill the centre of the disc if I arranged a dot-and-vine-leaf pattern round the edge. At least it was the right period. Ordinary red ink, diluted, for the inscription, and a tube of artist's black acrylic paint for the pattern. The quill and steel with which the Elizabethans wrote was a difficulty. The way out is to take the cap of a ballpoint pen — use a Bic top for forging everything except parchment or paper manuscripts — and file the projecting bit down to a sixteenth of an inch tip. Cut a part-thickness groove all the way along, and perforate the top to hold a bit of dowelling rod. Epoxy resin to fasten, and there's your Elizabethan pen. I nearly spelled the inscription wrong like a fool, but at the finish held it up proudly. One more fast dry to fade the ink (remember phoney reds fade faster than phoney blacks) and . . . and . . .

Signor Gambello was watching me. Oho.

'Nice job,' he said, coming close to look. 'You know,' he went on, examining my piece, 'if I hadn't seen you make it, I'd swear it was really . . . old.'

'Good heavens,' I said evenly.

'*Certo*. It has that look.' There was a pause. 'I'm sure your auntie will be very pleased.'

'Eh?'

'Your auntie. It's her surprise present, *non è vero?*'

I remembered. 'Ah yes. Let's hope so, signore.'

There was a pause while we looked around the workshop and out into the yard. Signora Gambello was listening, arms folded, by the door.

'You will not work more, eh?'

'Just the *trattoria*. One more day.'

'Then, thank you.'

'Thank you, signore,' I said fervently. 'The debt is mine.'

Next morning I left Signora Lamberti's establishment — a bawled farewell over the racket from the shunting engines — and made my special purchase. With the money I'd saved from washing-up I had enough.

Mestre isn't exactly bulging with antiques. It had taken me a lot of searching to find something Venetian and genuinely antique. The book itself was ordinary, a third-edition Venetian dialect dictionary, falling to bits. It contained a few scraps of paper, though, on which people had doodled and drawn occasional shapes. This only goes to show how you can pick up a fortune. I bought the book, went around the corner and chucked it away. One doodled-on paper I cherished: only a figure study, pen with brown ink on a greyblue wash. Even with four elementary figures there was a lot of vigorous activity going on in swirly-clothed classical tableau round a sprawling babe.

Art has a million mysteries. Many of them occur in Venetian art, which was pre-eminent by a mile in the eighteenth century. To me, one of the most fascinating of all art mysteries is the great R.V.H. Mystery — R.V.H. for 'Reliable Venetian Hand'.

It must have been really miraculous in those days. Walk around the corner in Venice and you met artists like Canaletto, Tiepolo, Piazzetta, or Ricci, or bumped into musicians like the Red Priest, Antonio Vivaldi already on his way to getting himself defrocked. It was all happening in Venice then.

The tragedy is that artists die unrecognized, obscurely, in poverty. I mean, we don't know enough about Mozart or Constable, while the discovery that Shakespeare's dad sold a few condoms, 'Venus gloves', on the side — quite customary for all glove-makers those days — is treated as a major revelation. Not even collectors take enough notice of artists, until the artists pass on and it's all too late.

But once upon a time one collector *did*. Back there in that miraculous eighteenth century in Venice one collector bought the doodles, sketches, plans, any little drawing he could afford, from the original artists themselves. And he saved them, tidily, in complete safety until the day he died. By then he—she?—had scores of them, and of course they were dispersed to the four winds after that. But this collector did one last inestimable service for Art. In lovely copperplate handwriting, he labelled each tiny scrap with the name of the original artist. And he's always—*always!*—absolutely correct in his attributions. Museums the world over reflexly search every old stray paper for the names of Venetian artists in that precise elegant give-away handwriting. We don't know who that collector was, so we call him the Reliable Venetian Hand. Now, promise you'll never go browsing in old junk shops again without a fervent vow to remember old R.V.H. of blessed memory. And just occasionally light a candle for him/her. He did a greater job for civilization and art than the lot of us will probably ever do.

The dashed-off drawing I'd picked up had the name 'Sebastiano Ricci' evenly subscribed in that immortal copperplate. In my whole life I've seen three of R.V.H.'s items found, and the great museums of Europe abound with them, so you've no excuse for ignorance. Sebastiano Ricci, as far as I remembered on the spot, painted a chapel apse in Chelsea Hospital, but most of his stuff is in Windsor Castle or at Venice's Accademia.

Fully armed for battle, I got the train across the causeway. By eleven I was disembarking from the No. 2 waterbus at the Rialto on the Grand Canal, and cutting through the narrow *calle* that brings you out by the Goldoni Theatre. Ten minutes later I was ringing the brass push-bell of the Palazzo Malcontento, and smiling with fright, but in sure anticipation.

Looking back on it now, I think how reasonable I was to go berserk.

CHAPTER 20

The bloke who eventually opened the door was twice my
size. All curly black hair and droopy moustache. Nothing
to match Ivan the Terrible's description this time. He
might actually be the man in the waiting motor-boat who
watched me the day Cosima showed me round the
Gobbo's market. We greeted each other politely, friendly
politicians.

'Name of Lovejoy.' I offered the information into his
longish silence. A waterbus rushed past. The *traghetto*
man cursed in his rocking gondola.

'The *locande* are—'

Cheeky swine. I didn't want a place to doss down. 'I
want to see the lady of the house, please. Signora
Norman.'

'Not in.' Slam.

Ah well. I idled over to watch the *traghetto* come and
go across the Grand Canal, keeping an eye on the Palazzo
Malcontento. I'd never seen so much wrought-iron. Even
the balconies of the great tall rectangular windows were
covered with the damned stuff. Lovely and antique, but
you'd need oxyacetylene and a Sheffield gang just to let in
some fresh air. Clever Mrs Norman.

No sign of any motor-boat moored alongside the house,
but then there might be all kinds of sneaky little private
canals which we tourists never even see. No action by the
time the *traghetto* gondola bumped into its pier on its
eighth rocky trip, so I went and pressed the bell again.

He came out ready for a dust-up, moving with
aggression written all over him. I begged with the speed
only cowards achieve for him to accept a gift for the
signora. He halted at that.

'A gift. Personal.'

'Where is it?' He stood vigilant and still while I drew out the flat cylindrical box. I rattled the sycamore disc inside, tempting.

'It's a genuine Elizabethan coaster, signore.' I opened it and showed him, passing the box but keeping the inscribed coaster. 'Hang on, though.'

Signor Gambello had let me have—well, I'd nicked it, actually—a ten-inch piece of his metal rod to sharpen on the lathe. While this goon looked on in amazement I put the coaster flat on the palazzo wall and slammed the pointed metal through the wood. Quick as that, I chucked it to him to keep both his hands occupied.

'What—?'

'*Grazie.*' I smiled, swiftly backing off to where the two *traghetto* men were now still, looking at our little scene. No arguments, not even with aggressive goons, until I knew whose side I was on. Or better, who was on mine. The nerk went in slowly, staring at me with malevolence. He'd remember my face now, but then I'd remember his.

Ten minutes later he came for me. I was sitting perched on the *traghetto* pier railing reading notices about long-gone gondola regattas, and let myself be invited in.

'The Signora's assistant will see you now,' he announced at the air over my head.

'Ta,' I said, slipping round him and into the palazzo's doorway at a rapid trot, slamming the door behind me so he was left outside. Assistant, indeed.

These Venetian palazzi have an aroma all their own. Some find it claustrophobic, even musty. To me it's beautiful. It's antiques, antiquity projecting from the lovely ancient past into this crappy modern world, and still going strong. Still lived with, despite the folly and stupidity of our modern-day daftness. It's love, hallowed and enshrined—

'I don't *believe* it!' A staccato laugh ripped down the stairs at me. Ugly, shrill. 'It really is the tramp with that ridiculous car!'

A young bloke wearing a pink cotton suit and a cravat was staring down into the hall over a luscious oak balcony. The wall lights were subdued greens, yellows, rose colours in ghastly Murano glass, but I recognized the laugh from the day Mr Malleson had outbid the ring dealers and Connie and me were in the Ruby at the pub. I'd found the Norman family's hatchet man. The one who'd done in Crampie and Mr Malleson.

'Good day, signore.' I spoke up the staircase, swallowing my hatred and smiling. 'Lovejoy.'

'What have you done with dear Placido?'

'Locked him out, I'm afraid. Sorry.' Placido was a laughable name for a ten-ton mauler.

'You have?' the pink apparition said with awe. 'He'll be in such a temper!'

'What *is* it, Tonio?' a woman's voice called.

'Some scruff, dear. No need to come. I'm getting rid of him.'

The door was being pounded. Excited people outside were asking what was going on. It was all getting rather out of hand.

I yelled, 'Signora? Don't come out if you're ugly.'

'*What?*' the voice demanded.

'You heard.'

The enemy was coming down the stairs, practically quivering with anticipation at the excitement of taking me apart, when she appeared on the landing above us.

'*Wait.*'

Tonio halted his pigeon-toed descent. 'Don't spoil it now, dear.'

'You're the cocktail man,' she observed to me.

'Eh? Oh.' That middle-aged aggro over the cocktail in the hotel bar the night me and Nancy made smiles. I went

up, ignoring the burning hatred in Tonio as I passed.
'You're the lady with more money than sense. I
remember. I'm Lovejoy.'

She was being amused at it all when I finally stood
beside her. She was holding my skewered coaster.
'Explain your insults.'

'You've got to be rich to buy a two-carat Royal Lavulite
stone. You've got to be senseless to plonk it in the middle
of a Florentine-set gold crucifix like you did.'

We processed, me first, into a grand chandeliered
room of rectangular windows, darkened paintings and
heavy furniture. A telly was showing muddy red lines
across peoples' faces. The clue to her amusement was in
her screaming boredom. Well, if the script called for me
to be a diversion, I'd divert all right.

'It was done by a great craftsman, Lovejoy. Are you a
jeweller?'

'I'm an expert forger, love. That's a million things a
jeweller isn't.'

In the room's light she was lovely. No, gorgeous,
rather. Her hair could only be called rich, obviously
shaped daily by dedicated salon slaves. Her clothes had
that casual fawn style only wealth brings. She'd not been
expecting visitors but her make-up didn't war with her
earrings and her opal nail-varnish didn't drain the colours
reflected from a single one of her three rings.

'Or an expert lunatic who impales a genuine
Elizabethan posset coaster?'

Her eyes never left me — God, her black eyelashes were
a mile long — as she failed to take a cigarette from a
carved box of Bengal ivory. Failed because my fingers
were there first, crushing the cigarettes into an
unsmokable mess. She recoiled slightly.

'You're insane.'

'No smoking where there's these lovely oil paintings,
missus. Even the rich shouldn't be that dim. *Especially*

them.' I looked sadly at my ruined handiwork. 'And *I* made the coaster. Finished yesterday.'

'You?' Tonio came sulking beside her as she spoke. 'I suppose you've witnesses?'

'Two in Mestre. One here—me. I'd never do that to a genuine antique.'

'You're always stopping me, *cara*,' Tonio grumbled. I was beginning to hate the way he kept his opaque stare fixed on me. It's the way folk look at the salad in a restaurant—dull stuff, eating a chore, something to be got on with, then forgotten.

She sat to show how beautiful her shape was. 'Hush, Tonio. Bring us a drink. What else can you make, Lovejoy?'

'Not for me, thanks,' I said quickly. The sudden pallor round Tonio's mouth meant he was determined to keep Venice's mediæval reputation alive even if it meant poisoning my sherry. 'What else? I can fake anything.'

Tonio pigeon-toed out of the room, a lot of paces before he looked away to see which way he was going. I'd made a real friend there. Shallow eyes unnerve me. I get to imagining there's nobody behind the corneas.

'Prove it.'

I fetched out my little Ricci sketch for her.

'*You* did this?'

'*Certo*, signora.'

'How?'

'Mind your own business.'

Tonio returned, with Placido carrying a salver. She reached unlooking for her glass. The nerks guided it into her hand. I'd found the boss all right. I presume the brownish fluid was her famous Rusty Nail cocktail, but the glass was a perfect glowing example of Venetian eighteenth-century ware. I almost wept with longing. The two goons stood about in hope of an order to exterminate.

'*Cara*,' Tonio said as she placed her lips loosely about

the rim. 'This man's a dealer. I saw him with your daughter.'

His putting the relationship so spitefully into words shocked me, but I did my innocence bit, glancing about with quizzing curiosity before letting my brow clear and recognition show. '*You're* Mrs Norman?'

'Yes.'

I sat, unasked, nodding slowly as if realizing. 'I see.'

'You see what exactly?' She hated me for knowing Caterina. Notions of aging thickened the atmosphere. We all ignored them, but I wouldn't like to be in Tonio's lemon-leather shoes when she got him alone. Odd how older women don't realize they're twenty times better than young popsies.

'If I'd known you were the lady in charge here, it would have been a lot easier for me, signora.'

'You have one minute,' she said. 'Time him, Tonio.'

I spoke from a dry throat. 'I'm a dealer, true. And I've forged a few antiques in my time. The woman in the dealer's ring took me to see old Mr Pinder. He told me about some scam in Venice, a lot of forgeries and fakes. Wanted me to work for him.'

'Why didn't you agree?'

'I'm no glue-and-saw hack, love. I'm superb.' Tonio snickered and nudged Placido but I kept on. 'The old man seemed nice enough, and the girl said the wages would be high. But that's not enough. I've given you proof I'm a great forger. So I want a percentage. No flat rates for me, love, if it's a really big scam.'

'To which Mr Pinder replied . . . ?'

I shrugged. 'No offence, but it was obvious that the boss was here in Venice, not him.'

'The address!' Tonio spat, putting a hand on her shoulder. There was a lot of possessiveness in the air, and none of it anything to do with me, worse luck.

'Daddy and Caterina would never tell you, Lovejoy.'

'Mr Pinder got reminiscing. I pieced it together.'

'He's lying, *cara!* He's some sort of agent—'

'No. Babbo does, all the time.' She held out her glass as if in disdain. They leapt to collect it. 'I want this sketch examined. Bring Luciano.'

'He's on the island.'

Tonio bent and whispered into her ear. She smiled, gleeful, like a little girl given a pleasant surprise.

'Yes. Give Lovejoy the cigarette lighter.'

Placido passed me a gold cube. 'Ta. But I don't smoke, missus.'

'And pass him the sketch, Tonio.'

Lighter. Ricci's sketch. I held them both. There was no danger to anyone, but I felt my chest chill with that awful cold which true terror brings.

'Let me look!' She came across, knelt in front of me. 'Now burn it, Lovejoy.'

'Eh?'

'You heard the lady, tramp.' Tonio toesied over to enjoy the fun. 'Light the lighter. Burn the—your— sketch.'

He clicked the thing in my hand. The flame was blood red, some fancy gimmick. She had her forearms on my knees. Her eyes were enormous, dark, made into deep tunnels by the reflected fire. Excitement was making her breathe quicker. Our faces were inches apart, her lovely arms on my knees.

'Well?'

Neat. A true forger would burn it uncaring. He could dash off another fake in a trice on the back of an envelope. A phoney—especially one with some vested interest—couldn't or wouldn't, or would risk his neck with some hesitation . . .

The sketch hurt my fingers. It was already charred, fell on to her carpet. I'd lit it practically without thinking. I watched the flame move casually along to the corner, eating away Ricci's name in that painfully meticulous copperplate. Gone.

Her hand lifted my chin, exposing my mind to those luscious, fevered eyes. I gave her a delighted grin which felt from the very depths of my soul. I knew I'd kill her now. It was out of my hands. Tonio and this lady had not only done for Malleson and Crampie. They'd just foully murdered a precious antique from the hand of Ricci himself. My own laborious crap could be crisped or slung out, for all I cared. But people who murder antiques shouldn't be allowed. Everybody knows that.

I pulled a face, almost laughing now the responsibility had passed from me.

'Sorry about your carpet, missus, but you told me.'

For one instant she seemed a little puzzled. Then she shrugged and rose.

'What's your preference, Lovejoy?'

'Faking? Oh, furniture, jewellery, sculpture, if I'm on my own. Tapestries and oil painting, with the right help.'

'Stone work?'

My grin was wider and more heartfelt than ever. I even felt happy. '*Anybody* can fake stonework.'

'Take him on, Tonio.'

'Don't, *cara*. There's something wrong.'

'Nothing that a new suit wouldn't cure, Tonio.'

She snapped her fingers and they fetched her another cigarette box. I drew breath, glanced at her oil paintings. Her eyebrows rose inquiringly. I answered with an apologetic shrug. 'Light, Lovejoy.'

The same red fire, miles inside her exquisite pupils. She blew the smoke into the air with an upward jerk of her chin, and gave me an amused glance of understanding. I was one of her serfs now. I cleared my throat.

'Any time you want your oil paintings cleaned, lady.'

'Clean yourself up first, tramp,' from Tonio.

'Do you always dress like that?' Her interest stung me.

'Geniuses are allowed. And if I'm to work anyway.'

'Working clothes are different, tramp.'

I looked Tonio up and down. 'Apparently. Mrs Norman, that percentage.'

'Two things, Lovejoy. First: the money from our scheme is so vast that your pathetic little requirements are insignificant. You'll see in good time. Take him out there in a few days, Tonio.'

'Better be tonight *cara*. There's an *acqua alta* due soon.'

'Tiresome. Tonight then.'

'Out where?' I asked.

Nobody spoke until she said coldly, 'And the second is speak when you're spoken to. Understand?'

Everybody paused while I assimilated her last instruction. 'You mean like them?'

'Well.' She flicked ash on the carpet just too quickly for them to streak for ashtrays. They'd both twitched. I hadn't moved. 'Well, almost.'

Placido gave me a handful of money at the door. Tonio told me to make myself presentable, bloody cheek, by fitting myself out at a tailor's near the Calle delle Bande, to be on the Zattere, tramp, by eight tonight. He shut the door without waiting for my reply.

The San Moisè's hardly the prettiest church in Venice, but even ugly churches do for lighting candles. As I lit the four — Mr Malleson, Crampie, Cosima and a just-in-case for Nancy — I saw again those huge wells of eyes with their distant reflected scarlet flames. A second later, thinking, I put more money in the slot and lit a fifth candle for her.

On the way out I thought, Oh what the hell, returned and did a sixth though Tonio didn't deserve it. He was just lucky that generosity is my strong suit.

Pleased, I went shopping among the crowds, looking for Goldoni's shop where they sell the big navigation maps of the lagoon.

CHAPTER 21

Resplendent in a new off-the-peg, I tasted the coffee and sank a couple of giant *margherita* pizzas in the corner nosh bar on the delle Bande. Not that I was pleased about being well-dressed. As my usual grubby self I could fade among the mob. Immaculate as any wedding guest, I'd stand out like a daffodil in a goalmouth. The lady brought over my omelette and some of those thick *torta* slices that make Italy a green and pleasant land, so I was in good nick to wrestle the problem of the vast nautical chart I'd tried to spread on the world's narrowest counter while perched on the world's most pointed stool. One thing's sure, I thought fervently, in the nosh bar din, it's a hell of a lagoon. When I saw where I'd been, pushing Cosima to safety, I had to order some more cakes to stop myself throwing up from sheer fright. It's those deep blue channels and pale green sedgy *barene* that scare me.

The big problem was how an ultra-nervy supercoward weakling like me could make headway in this game. It had all escalated in a way I couldn't understand. Easy, though, to see why old man Pinder was eager to employ a divvie—best to be careful even if a bird as aggressive as the luscious Signora Norman was here at the business end of so much syndicated money. Clearly Caterina didn't trust dearest Mama. Her mistrust had reached Grandad Pinder—perhaps the penny only dropped when he realized that his lovely quiet scam was going awry after the savage assault of Mr Malleson and Crampie. Hence he suddenly needed a divvie that bad, to seek exactly which fakes had gone where.

Another big curved-horn *dolce* with cream, and I could look my own enormous ineptitude in the face.

What the hell did I do now? Not just the ultimate in cowardice, but an incompetent one at that.

My one bonus was that Cosima was fine, so they told me on the blower. From their guarded inquiries they taped incoming calls but I was past caring. Anyway, I changed my voice each time, talking through combs, tissue paper, doing it in funny accents and being different relatives and whatnot. No worry there.

Ranged against me was my monumental ignorance, my thoroughly chicken-hearted nature and innate incompetence. I didn't know practically everything. For example, what Mrs. Norman was up to. Tonio's role anybody could guess but was he Mrs Norman's bloke or Caterina's? Both? Playing one against the other, with Mama's money as encouragement?

There were some meagre bits of knowledge. The scam was painfully real. Cosima had nearly died, and gunshots were proof of the most absolute kind. And now I knew some of the participants. Mrs Norman was boss, with gelt *and* power. They'd mentioned Luciano, presumably an expert faker. And an island. And if Luciano the faker was there, with Lovejoy the newly-recruited forger being taken there, the island was the centre of the scam, right?

'Another two of those cakes, signora, please,' I asked, to keep out the cold, and settled down to memorize the islands of the lagoon from my chart.

As long as I got the direction and distance of tonight's boat journey, I'd be able to identify the island, then find my own way there whenever I wanted, right?

Answer: no. Because there's such a thing as a blindfold, and such a thing as suspicion. They turned out to possess both.

Curiosity made me peer from the St Theodore's column in the direction of the Riva. Curiosity drove me among the crowds past the dozing Ivan the Terrible, past my

artist — still grumbling to all spectators about money — to
the second bridge where I sat to watch for Cesare.

His boat was there. He was there, too, with a harassed
new girl courier I'd never seen before, clipboard and all.
Maybe Cosima's ex-partner, now relieved of her
boyfriend, and holding the fort?

Cesare's boat left with a load of tourists about five,
probably to the Marco Polo for the departing Alitalia
294, which meant a good hour even if little boats like his
don't have to go all the way round through Murano like
the big ones do. Reluctant to risk being accidentally
spotted from the hotel or by the boatmen, I ducked down
past the San Zaccaria, long way round, and popped into
Vivaldi's Pietà church, the one which old Pinder got so
burned up about.

I should have gone round to the Cosol office and
steamed Giuseppe's garrulous mouth open, demanding
all he had on Mrs Norman's private planeloads of
moviemakers, but I was tired and dozed off in one of the
pews. Dozing is a mistake in Venice. The vibes of ancient
life come out of the walls at you. Bound to, in a place like
that. I dreamt of wading and drowning, woke in a cold
sweat when a drove of chattering children came pouring
in to draw the orange, white and black mosaics in their
school exercise books. Then I realized my dream was true,
except it wasn't me drowning. It was children. The lovely
church which harvested Vivaldi's music and Tiepolo's
magnificent artistry belonged to the foundation which
reputedly harvested the newborn illegitimate babes
thrown alive into the canals, to drown in the filth and
darkness. What with the men of Venice away on the war-
galleys for so long, the Pietà did a roaring rescue service.

The little bar on the Garibaldi was open. It's the only
one in Venice without a big glass of coloured water for
you to drop tips in. Six o'clock and dark when finally I
left. Seven-thirty I was outside of another three pizzas and

waiting for action at a table on the Zattere waterfront,
watching the big ships thrash by. Never know why, but a
ship entering harbour always looks reluctant, and one
setting out looks eager. With me it's the other way about.

This boat taxi picked me up exactly at eight.

The water-taxi man didn't have to ask my name. He
simply walked up among the tables, tapped my shoulder
and led me to his boat. Shoddier than Cesare's, the
boatman wore the air of a part-timer, not an authentic
Venetian taxi.

'Where are we going?' I asked chattily.

'Talking not allowed.' No information, but no secrecy
either. I sat inside the cabin, able to see us head noisily
away from the Zattere waterfront cafés.

His crummy boat just about made it to the Giudecca, a
long thin island which curves round Venice's bottom
forming a wide natural harbour. He dumped me quite
illegally on an *Azienda* waterbus jetty where the No. 8
stops near the Santa Eufemia church and chugged off
without waiting to be paid. An all-time Venetian first. It
unnerved me more than any rip-off.

Ten minutes later, wandering and wondering if Tonio
and Placido had forgotten, I was collected by an equally
decrepit but open boat steered by the hairiest boatman on
earth, a real Cromagnon. He transferred me in the
darkness to a more respectable cabin craft, an unnerving
experience which left me shaking. They could have
drowned me. A cheerful geezer hooded me with a bag
thing. There were no lights. He tied my hands and sat me
on a bunk in the cabin.

'Look,' I said in an appalled muffled falsetto. 'What if
we sink?'

'We drown, signore,' he said pleasantly. 'I can't swim
either. We Venetians have this superstition: learn to swim
and the lagoon thinks you distrust her.'

'She does?' I bleated, scared out of my wits.

'And takes revenge. Especially at the time of the *acqua alta*.'

'High water?' That's what Tonio had warned Signora Norman about.

'Signore, *acqua alta* is one hundred and ten centimetres above sea level. When the sirocco meets the north bora winds, it will rise twice that.

'But Venice is only thirty inches above sea level as it is. You mean she could go *four feet under?*'

I gave a bleat. He fell about at that, so much that the boat swung and I lost my sense of direction. I'd never met such poisonous hilarity before. Before that, I'd been sure we were heading in towards the Fusina channel. Portia had set out from there to defend her lover's friend from the wrath of Shylock.

I listened. For anything. That clonking lagoon bell. The long cacophony of bells San Giorgio Maggiore sometimes stuns you with, warning women to keep away. Well, hormones and monasteries don't mix.

'What's up?' I croaked inside my hood. The engine had cut. 'Are we okay?'

'*I* am.' A guffaw, the sadistic pig.

Then it dawned on me. You can detect the way a small boat is turning sometimes by its engine sound, depending where you are. The swimmer's trick in the water. Cut power, and a boat can bob in any direction. Bitterly I sat cursing the time I'd wasted memorizing that bloody massive map. We did the engine-cutting trick four times in the next hour. At the finish I didn't even care where we were, much less know, and nodded off in my hood.

And screamed. The boat had touched something solid, immovable. Feet clumped, hands pulled me and blokes talked quite casually. I tried kicking and holding on to the cabin door but was prised loose by a simple nudge. They shoved me, wailing inside my hood, on to the gunwale step and over the boat's side. Legs together in a panicky attempt to hit the water feet first, the jarring concrete nearly popped my head off. Land. I was on land. I'd nearly peed myself from fright, tumbling over and lying shivering while everybody had a good laugh and a boat bumped small vibrations into the stone. Then I was tugged to my feet and hustled up some steps, me holding back and trying to foot-feel my way while they hauled me along, telling me, 'You're all right,' as I stumbled behind my captors. My elbows kept being brushed, first this side, then that, and now and again my hood was scratched.

'Duck,' my merry boatman advised every few yards. I did, slow to realize it was another joke to make my blind antics all the more comical. I blundered on, pushed and pulled by anybody that felt like an ego trip. A born duckegg, I decided the joke had gone too far and kept going without crouching—and brained myself on some low arch. You can imagine the jollity and all-round merriment as I was lifted and elbow-walked down two flights, eighteen steps each. Twenty-seven paces one direction, a right turn. Thirty paces, a door. Twenty more paces, another door.

Hood off, and somebody untying my hands. Light so blinding my head felt lasered. Vision returned with some pain. The first person I saw was Tonio. The second was my boatman, still making everybody laugh but this time acting out for Tonio's benefit my blind falls on the way from the boat.

It was a massively wide bricklined room, strip-lit. Huge. A ventilator hummed but the place's scent was dankish, cool. A score or so men worked silently at easels, on wall-benches, at desks. One chipped at a piece of masonry in a screened corner. Hardly a glance from the lot of them. Clearly a dedicated bunch. From a tall monastic-looking lecterned desk at the far end an old grey-haired bloke peered down at us. It was a factory.

'Another scratcher, Luciano.' Tonio gave me a bored jerk of his head to report. Luciano the expert, presumably foreman of all this faking industry. 'And you can go, Carlo.'

My friendly boatman and his two goons were actually at the door when I said casually, 'Oh, Carlo. Sorry about your chart,' and I headed for Luciano's desk.

'*Wait!*' I paused agreeably at Tonio's command. 'Chart? What chart!'

'Eh? Oh, Carlo's.' Tonio's pale stare worried Carlo. You could tell that from the way his smile had frozen.

'I keep no chart, signore,' Carlo said, his voice an echo of my own terror-stricken croaking.

'It was an accient,' I explained, ever so anxious to avoid misunderstanding. 'I nudged him. Carlo said I'd spoil this chart he was keeping, if I wasn't careful.' The two goons took a quiet step away from Carlo. Nobody was laughing now. I was really pleased at that. 'But it wasn't my fault, you see. I couldn't see a damned thing, for that hood.'

'Shut it, Lovejoy. You keep interesting secret charts, Carlo?'

Carlo went grey. 'He's lying. There are no charts . . .'

'I never actually saw it,' I put in, so anxious. 'Does it matter?'

'Carlo.' Tonio's reproachful voice was a sickly purr. I went cold. Carlo began to sweat.

'Signore. I swear before God . . .'

'Find it, you two.'

The goons whisked him out of the door before I could grin and tell Carlo to mind his head. It would have been my little quip, but my throat had clogged. I still feel rotten about Carlo, God rest his soul. Not wanting to face Tonio's gaze, I ambled down the factory towards Luciano, who had my skewered Elizabethan coaster on his high desk. He looked straight out of Dickens: tidy dark suit, if you please, neat dark tie and white cuffs showing, even pebble specs. His voice was the quavering of a lamb in the next county.

'What was all that about?'

'Dunno. Some chart or other.'

'Crummy piece of work, this, Lovejoy.' His eyes bubbled at me through the thick lenses.

'Never said it wasn't.'

That tickled him into twinkly humour. 'Not had time to put the word round to see if you're any good as a faker, Lovejoy.' The unyielding complaint of the disciplined serf.

'Faker? Me? I'm an authetic antique dealer.'

An artist painting nearby overheard and snickered, a sound I heard with a glow of pleasure. So long as we were all being sensible.

'You did a perfect sketch, I'm told,' old Luciano said. 'And burnt it.'

'Hardly perfect.' I cleared my throat. 'Yes. The signora was playing games.'

He harumphed, nodding, indicated the nearby artist. 'Take a look. Tell me what you think.'

I went over, asking, 'Where'd you get the photo?' The artist, a skeletal bearded geezer shoddied in smeared denim, took no notice, working steadily on at his canvas. It was laid horizontal on a trestle, first time I'd actually seen that trick used. As long as your paint's consistency is exactly right, once the canvas is dry enough you can lift it erect and judge the craquelure as it actually develops. This is great for artificial aging. I'd have to try that when I got a minute. A huge photograph was mounted on the wall, skilfully lit. 'I thought cameras aren't allowed in the Correr.'

'They're not,' Luciano said.

'Well done.' The Correr museum forbids cameras and handbags. It makes you deposit them in the ticket office anteroom at the head of the stairs, and that's the only permitted entrance. So a marvellous colour print of Carpaccio's *La Visitatione* spoke volumes about Tonio's powers of organization. 'Isn't your photo a bit small, though?' The canvas looked about right, four feet by four ten or so.

'It's the way I work,' the artist said.

'Mmmmh.' Fakers sometimes do this, copy from smaller photographs because it prevents that telltale woodenness from creeping into the fake, the bane of all art forgers since the beginning of time. Don't try it when forging watercolours, incidentally. Doesn't work.

He was 'squaring'. This means dividing the photo of the original into squares, and painting his repro square by square. Makes faking easier, but is a dead give-away to seasoned connoisseurs — especially if they have an X-ray machine handy. Almost anybody can create a fake which will pass for original at a quick glance. It takes somebody like Keating or On to do class jobs. Or me, on a good day. This bloke was using a *camera lucida* to cast reflected lines on to his canvas. It saves drawing them and leaving telltale marks, and seems like a good idea. I raised my eyebrows. Luciano gave me a rueful shrug as I strolled back.

'Is he careful enough, Luciano?'

'He's not bad.'

'I can't see his reference lines.' Forgers using squares from a *camera lucida* must have a standard measured square, because you have to adjust the damned thing when you switch it on at the start of every session. Most of us — er, I meant those nasty illegal fakers — nail a piece of card to the top rear of the canvas frame and focus in on it for accuracy.

'Domenico does it by eye.'

'Two cheers for Domenico.' A steady but faint thump-thump-thump came from behind the brick wall.

Somebody must be forging the Great Pyramid with a steam-hammer. As I listened it faded into silence.

'Decided, Luciano?' Tonio called.

The old man quavered instantly, '*Si* Tonio. Lovejoy can start helping Giovanni on the Doge's Palace stonework. We're behind with those.'

'Eh?'

'Over there.' Luciano pointed to the far corner with his quill, a real quill.

'Me?' I said indignantly. 'I'm only here to advise, you ignorant old sod.'

He shook with inaudible laughter. 'I work too, Lovejoy. Look.' He showed me what he was doing, a large Missa Solemnis on his high bench, faking away at a hell of a lick. He had black and red inks. It's a saying among forgers that a fake must be even better than the original. Well, grudgingly I had to admit his massive pages looked superb. The cunning old devil was even annotating the margins in a diluted ochreous brown as he went. Lovely work. 'Get to it, Lovejoy,' he scolded amiably. 'Remember. Idleness was a capital offence among the Incas.'

'They're extinct, right?' I groused back, and ambled over towards the screen in the corner.

Tonio saw and nodded. 'You do exactly as Giovanni says, Lovejoy,' he ordered. 'We want our money's worth.'

'Cheek. What money?' I peered behind the screen. The corner space was rigged out exactly like a mediaeval stonemason's workshop. This thinnish bald bloke, presumably Giovanni, was chipping away at a supported capital.

'The signore will explain.' Tonio wasn't smiling so presumably he meant it. 'Get to work.'

'I already told him that,' Luciano piped querulously.

'Yes. Get to work,' the stonemason said, not even bothering to look.

'Coming, bazz,' I greeted Giovanni cheerfully. 'Call that carving? Shift over and give me a go.' I'd made it. A worker in old Pinder's factory of forgers and fakers.

CHAPTER 22

'Cocky bastard.'

That was Giovanni's greeting, almost all he said during that long working night.

'Ducal Palace, eh?' I said chirpily, coming in and shedding my jacket while I gave his stone carving the once-over. 'Name's Lovejoy. Why'd you choose the Judgement of Solomon, Giovanni? You should have started with that lovely stuff by Bon.'

'Get to work.'

'It's from the capital next to the Basilica, isn't it?' I fondled the stone, checking its progress against the plaster-cast mould he had ledged on a chair. 'Look, Giovanni, old pal. D'you really believe it's old Jacopo della Quercia's work? I mean to say, 1410 AD's a hell of a—'

'Get to work.'

'Your Archangel Gabriel's head's too protruberant.'

I reached for the sander. Giovanni moved aside and called, 'Ventilator's on, lads.' I looked about inquiringly. The others all down the factory called fine, okay. Giovanni nodded, pushed down a boxed switch, and a hood above us hummed into action. The lazy blighter sat while I smoothed part of the angel's form. He also had his lunch from his sandwich box, offering me none. Lucky I'd stocked up with that bellyful of pizzas. He didn't offer to lend me his goggles, either.

I slammed into the task of copying the plaster cast. Go to the corner of the Doge's Palace and look at the capital

nearest the actual Basilica. These capitals are grand stuff
as sculpture, but they're too grim for my liking. All with
the same despondent message of mortality, and what a
horrendous business life is. Not a smile anywhere.

Still, I was happy, doing what comes naturally. Don't
misunderstand. Forgery's not as bad as it's painted. Not
even factory-sized.

I mean, generations of collectors have enjoyed their
'Canaletto' paintings sublimely unaware that the young
William Henry Hunt actually painted many of them as
copies in Doctor Monro's so-called academy, (for 'one
shilling and six pence the hour,' Hunt's little fellow-
slogger John Linnell said bitterly). Some were sold as
originals, as Linnell knew, but that doesn't really worry
me. Why should it? The 'Canaletto Secret' was to paint a
series of colour glazes over a monochrome painting. That
extraordinary light effect he achieved in his natural-
history pictures has given a zillion people pleasure. So if
little William and John painted just as brilliantly, what
the hell. And I don't mind that El Greco by 1585 had a
cellarful of minions turning out titchy copies of his own
efforts while he dined grandly upstairs — to the scrapings
of a private orchestra in the 24-roomed pad he'd hired
from the Marqués de Villena. The morals of fakery are
the same by the ounce as by the ton. Make a note of that.

As I worked I tried merry chat as a way of collecting
some news. Giovanni was impervious. He chomped,
swilled his vino. Then he sat, dozily coming to every few
minutes to see how I was getting on.

'How many of us are there, pal?' I tried, and, 'How
long you been at this game, eh?' And, 'What's the going
rate, Giani? Paid piece by piece, from the way you stick
at it, I'll bet!'

Not a word. A Venetian's silence when the subject's
money spoke volumes. Gossip was therefore forbidden,
the penalties very, very heavy. I began to worry about

that ashen look on Carlo's face. Worried sick about being worried—now about the flaming enemy, I ask you—I gave the somnolent Giovanni a friendly kick and told him to start roughing out the next stone capital.

Luciano put his head through the screens at this point, smiled and nodded and moved on. Doing his rounds of the forgery factory to see we were all doing our stuff, I supposed. Whatever the rest were like, I was determined Lovejoy would be exemplary. I'd see I would do twice as well as these fakers. If they worked fast, I'd work faster. And I'd make their natural forgers' versatility look like the ploddings of pedestrian hacks. I told Luciano not to interrupt the workers.

All that long night we worked, and I learned nothing useful. A couple of odd details, though. One was that thump-thump-thump, which recurred occasionally. Another was that Tonio disappeared once I'd got settled in and working. He was replaced by the two goons.

And there were other oddities. For instance, I'd never seen a forger worth his salt simply stand aside and let another bloke take over his handiwork, because forgers consider themselves artists of a high order. Yet Giovanni, the slob, had let me take charge of his sculpture. And, at least as strange, nobody talked. Three times I went past the other busy forgers on my way to the loo, and paused to make a friendly comment. No avail. Even Domenico gave me the bent eye.

The loo was a chemical can. No chance of flushing into the lagoon a message in a bottle, or a marker dye to trace. And no watches. No clocks. No radios. No apparent ventilation except the hood which hung suspended over Giovanni's masonry corner.

The goons knocked off after about four hours, and were replaced by a bloke who whistled through his teeth and read a kid's colour comic. Occasionally he chuckled, and sometimes read a difficult passage, moving his lips, with his forehead frowning in concentration.

They took us away one by one about an hour after this Neanderthal was replaced by our two originals. Home time. I was last to go apart from Luciano.

'Why the ten-minute intervals, Luciano?'

'It's the arrangement here.'

'Who makes the arrangements?'

Silence. Luciano polished his specs and had a good look at my carving. 'Not bad. Good and fast.'

'Better than your crummy plaster cast of the original. Careless.'

He murmured apologies. 'Done officially while they restored it a couple of years ago. We weren't really organized and used all sorts of rubbishy labour.'

'At least tell me about my pay, Luciano.'

'They'll tell you.'

I gave up and wandered about looking at the others' progress. For all my criticism of Domenico, he'd fairly shifted. A youngish bloke across the other side was faking one of the monumental arched Tiepolo paintings from the Madonna dell' Orto apse, but I noticed he'd had the sense not to use the *camera lucida* trick for that majestic piece. As the goons called me I felt a gentle bong of recognition in my chest and went past Luciano's high desk. An illuminated page lay fully exposed on it among his forged pages. The forgetful old lunatic had carelessly left a priceless original, beautiful and redolent with age, glowing in all its serene tempera brilliance for any careless nerk to scrape its wonderful surface with a ruinous elbow. Luciano must be past it. I tutted and manoeuvered it gently under the protection of a new sheet of parchment. Then I cursed myself. Luciano was regarding me quizzically. The sly old sod had done it deliberately, been watching all the time.

I said pleasantly, 'You're not a bad advert for senility, Luciano. Keep it up.'

'Don't talk so much, son,' he said. Not a smile. 'Go home and rest.'

I went up to the goons and obediently bent my head to be hooded.

'Be at the same place, same time, tonight,' the nerks said. 'Understood?'

'Carlo's day off, eh?' I asked jokingly into my hood, but nobody answered.

A stranger in a stranger's boat dropped me off at the Zattere waterfront after four blundering and scarey switches of craft out in the darkness of the lagoon. It was getting on for five-thirty.

When you think of it, having no place to sleep's no hardship for an hour or two. Or three. Or five. After that it gets to you. Gradually as the hours pass a kind of restlessness seeps into your soul. You don't *need* a place to rest, but the idea that you haven't got one to go to eventually becomes pretty horrible. You become desperate.

Maybe that's what made me burgle Giuseppe's Cosol office.

It's less than a twenty-minute walk from the Zattere across the Accademia Bridge, even going a long way round to avoid my old pals of the Riva wharf. True to the style of the Venetian early worker, I whistled, kicked the occasional carton and generally made myself part of the local scene.

Giuseppe's precautions consisted of a chain with a padlock, and the old double-lock. Two keys are supposed to make it difficult. As if two hands and two bits of bent wire were rarities.

Half past six o'clock in the morning when I found the lists. The garrulous chatterbox hadn't even filed the damned things. Cosima would go berserk at all this untidiness. I risked the light after shutting the door to the staircase. The lists were almost complete. Giuseppe was hardly in for Venice's Dedicated Worker award, so he'd probably bowl up no earlier than nine a.m. Plenty of time. I made myself some instant coffee on his office's mini-boiler, and settled down comfortably to read.

Signora Norman had truly forked out. First class for David, Nancy and the older pair. Which raised a lorry-load of new questions. Why exactly did a lady pulling an antique scam so huge that it needed a whole factory full of forgers need a movie mogul? And why had he vanished so suddenly that his secretary Nancy wasn't even allowed time for the entirely harmless purpose of leaving her erstwhile lover a thoughtful little souvenir?

Nearly seven o'clock when I'd finished searching, and the dawn showing and the mists clearing. Nothing, except more suspicions. Grumbling, I nicked the paltry sum of ready cash scattered around in the drawers, and left.

I didn't shut the door. Let somebody else worry for a change. Even if it was only Guiseppe.

My first two goes on the phone were hopeless. Something to do with time zones. Third go I got a secretary after spending a fortune in these *gettoni* you have to buy in order to use the Venetian blowers. My accent was phoney as anything.

'Iz zatt joo, David?'

'Mr Vidal's at a signing conference today, sir.'

'I particularly want speaking wiz eem. Eez ee reeturned from Venice, ja? Ee said me ring most urgent. Zee financial contract—'

Uncertainty crept in, thank God. 'Hold, please.' I was down to my last three tokens when the girl said breathlessly, 'You're through, sir.'

And David's voice said, 'Hello. Vidal here.'

Lips pursed, I gave a crackly electronic splutter and

downed the receiver gently.

Message: David vanished fast, but made it home. And it probably was the same for the other three. I'd have to think some more when I wasn't so knackered.

Happier now the possibilities were narrowing, I went down the Lista di Spagna looking for lodgings.

Not far from Harry's Bar is the Giardinetti near where poor distended tourists queue for a million years to go for a pee. Always there are the relieved halves of couples hanging about while the other half, still bulbous with agony, wait in agonized lines clutching their 200-lire tickets, praying for an empty loo. Sitting by the trees, I decided it might be my last chance to see Cosima so, knackered as I was, I'd have to take it. I went among the mobs to the boat terminus at the San Marco.

Maybe it was because I was so exhausted that I accidentally made an astounding discovery. A Lido steamer was pulling out as I plodded towards my waterbus stop. What with the droves of children and the engines I put my fingers in my ears. There was an odd beating sensation. I stopped, removed my fingers. Stuck them in again.

Block your ears, and the big boat's engines went thump-thump-thump. Remove them and the engines whine and growl amid the pandemonium of the crowd, the rush of water. I did it so often, just to check, that two little children on the concourse started laughing and imitating. With a sheepish grin I moved away, then went into a café for some wine and a quick change of mind.

The walk to the railway station took me thirty minutes and half a litre of bianco. The train journey to Padua was about the same.

CHAPTER 23

For the purposes of visiting Cosima I became the excitable relative of a patient in the women's surgical ward. My mythical sister was suffering from some unspeakable — not to say unpronounceable — malady, and my anxieties knew no bounds. I explained this to everyone I met in the hospital corridor. The most baffled country cousin in Padua that day, I managed to blunder into the outpatients' entrance and got myself redirected. God, but they're patient in Padua. If I'd been that nurse in Outpatients I'd have flung me out.

Cosima was up! I mean it. Really sitting up and having a drink. No tubes, no drips. And bonny as a bird, in a new nightie with her hair done and her face shining. Her face lit to see me. And I too was all of a do, until she asked me where Cesare was today.

'Cesare?' I hadn't mentally cleared him of shooting Cosima, so her mentioning his name with such expectation pulled me up short.

She searched my eyes. 'Didn't he find you? I've had him searching all Venice for you.'

'Lazy old Cesare.' When I'd glimpsed Cesare he hadn't looked at all like a boatman doing a desperate private eye. And there are ways of putting the word out which only boatmen know. Cesare hadn't searched very hard.

'Then how did you know to come today? I go to convalescence in an hour.'

We talked of our day out on the lagoon. The police had maintained a bedside vigil until she'd given her story. Mercifully, she'd told them I was just a casual acquaintance, that we'd met somewhere at a party . . . She actually remembered very little of our escape, except being lifted ashore and the *sandolo* rocking, and having this dreadful cough which pained.

'And hearing you blaspheme, Lovejoy.'

'Me?'

'In a car. Everything was dark. Your face was lit by the dashboard's glow. You were threatening fire and slaughter against everybody on earth. Even Cesare.'

'*Me?*' I was appropriately amazed. 'I'm not like that. Delusions, love. Common in gunshot wounds.'

She shook her lovely hair. 'I tried to ask you to stop shouting, Lovejoy. But you looked . . . possessed. A fiend.'

'When did Cesare show?'

'Giuseppe and Cesare come almost every day. And the two Australians. They've all been so marvellous.'

I was so busy crossing suspects off my mental list that I had no response. My silence was her big moment.

'Where did *you* go, Lovejoy?'

'Go? Me? Well, I was so exhausted—'

'You vanished.' She looked aside along the ward, colouring slightly. 'I read your message on my hand. The police said a Swiss businessman found me and fetched me in. They thought you'd drowned.'

'They're always red-hot.' I'd made the bitter crack before I could prevent myself. The comprehension in her gaze was unnerving.

'So you were simply keeping on running. I knew it. Why?'

'I had to, love. What did the police tell you?'

'Nothing. They thought some madman had shot me, or a stray bullet from an illicit marsh hunter.'

'Accidental, eh?' Good old police. Same everywhere, desperate not to get too involved in troublesome mischief.

'Lovejoy. If Cesare didn't find you to bring you here today, why did you not keep on running?'

Honestly. Women are always after motives.

'That was me phoning,' I said indignantly. 'Didn't you get messages?'

She smiled, my downfall. 'Practically every two hours. However did you manage to dash around to all those different places so fast?'

'I was in Mestre all the . . .' Caught.

'All the time?' she completed for me. 'So you only pretended to run.' No smile now. Just a terrible sadness and eyes slowly filling. 'Darling. What is it that you're doing? Even before this . . . accident, I wondered about you. So many things unexplained. And your mind's always miles away.'

See what I mean? Women are really sly. Even when there's nothing wrong their busy little minds are working out different angles. It's no wonder most of the world's bent with all this suspicion going on.

After that it wasn't a lot of use. I tried hard being happy and friendly and she tried hard to match my poisonous chirpiness, but we parted a few minutes later, me with the address of her convalescent home written out and her with my bunch of chrysanthemums. She'd be gone a few days.

'I'll phone, love,' I promised.

'Where will you be, Lovejoy? In Venice?'

'Certainly,' I said heartily. 'Where else?'

'At the same hotel? Honestly, now.'

'Of course! I'll keep in touch, through Cesare.'

'And you'll look after yourself? Promise?'

'Hand on my heart,' I said fervently. That was how we parted, truth and lies approximately half and half. I was heartbroken, because I sincerely really honestly loved Cosima, and now she'd as good as told me it was goodbye. That's always heartbreaking. But at least things were a lot clearer.

From Padua railway station I phoned my lodgings along the Lista di Spagna in Venice and explained that

Lovejoy, who'd taken a room there today, had just died in a plane crash over the Aegean and wouldn't be needing it any more, thank you.

Another two half-litres later I broke into Cosima's little apartment, locked the door after me and went fast asleep.

Watching Cesare and that thin lass going over their clipboards in the dying sunshine made me quite envious. It's the humdrum blokes of this world that get on. The meek really do inherit — if not the earth, at least the leavings. Cesare'd kept a low profile. Then, when the Lovejoys and other scatterbrains have blundered on their lunatic way, idle sods like Cesare inherit the birds.

When he was on my list of suspects it was simple to hate him. Now he was proving a real stalwart trusty loyal pal for Cosima in her adversity I hated him even more. The smarmy creep.

Because of the coming night's labour I'd had a couple of tons of pizza along the Garibaldi. As I walked towards Cesare's boat a bottle of wine clinked in my pocket and I carried three spare pizzas for the late hours working on Giovanni's stone capitals.

'Wotcher Cesare. Got me a tip?'

He jumped at that, recovered enough to keep calm and finish his list. The thin girl eyed me speculatively, tit for tat, and asked what time Cesare should report tomorrow. He simply said, 'Later,' so it was him and me in the late afternoon on the Riva jetties with crowds all about having a last *capuccino* before getting sloshed for the night.

'Lovejoy. You're back, then.'

'Never left, did I,' I said, quite pleasant. 'As you well know. I went to see her today.'

He shrugged, unworried. In a scrap with him I'd last half a minute. 'You're no good for her, Lovejoy. You know it. Now Cosima does, also. You went through four of those tourists in as many days. Randy sod. Leave Cosima alone.'

'Three,' I said indignantly.

'Three plus Nancy. Four.'

'Tell me who shot Cosima, mate.' I leaned crossed forearms on the wobbling handrail to show my pacific intentions.

'She was shot,' he said thoughtfully, gauging my motives. 'The police said so. And somebody took her to safety. I've that to thank you for, Lovejoy—'

Bloody cheek. *Him* thank *me* for Cosima? 'Get on with it.'

'—But without you, she'd not have been shot in the first place.'

'Does all this paranoia mean you don't know?'

'If I did . . .' He let me guess what the silence meant.

I wondered for a second how useful another falsehood might be. Could do no harm, so I said, 'She sent you a message, Cesare. Before she left.'

'She has gone?' The alarm of a thwarted lover leapt to his eyes.

'Yes. Sorry about it. She's going to convalescence and she wanted me to see you got the address.' I scribbled a fictitious name of any old mythical sanatorium.

'In Palermo?' he said, suspicious sod. 'Sicily?'

I nodded. 'There's a special team of doctors there, for the, erm, thoracic oesophagus. Wise to go far afield. That shooting was an attempt on her life, no?'

'Very wise.' He folded the paper and put it away carefully. 'Thank you.'

I didn't altogether like the way he said that, but didn't realize exactly why until much later.

We parted, scarcely the best of friends. He saw me as the arch-villain. I saw him as a non-ally, that most unpredictable species of friend. I should have remembered that.

For an hour I sat in a pew in the Gesuati church,

poring over a replacement map of the lagoon and
laboriously working out possibilities by the light of the
candles on the second altar.

When the boatman came for me at eight o'clock I was
mapless and dozing fitfully at one of the café tables on the
waterfront, and pretending not to notice the lovely white
yacht *Eveline* moored two hundred yards away, which I'd
last seen rocking in the cold wind of an East Anglian
estuary.

The drill was frighteningly familiar: searched, hooded
and exchange boats here and there. Drift. Turn, drift
again. Motor on a short while, cut engines, move on.
Finally, bump and ashore with more than one pair of
hands pushing me along and the same old inertness of
those taps on my elbows. No funny ducking jokes,
though, ending with me brained on some low overhang.
And no Carlo. Well. Maybe it was his night off, I thought
as they took me down the steps and doors clanged shut
behind.

Third in, this time. Luciano was already hard at it up
there on his high desk, giving me a friendly specky
twinkle. Giovanni wasn't there yet, but Domenico was
slogging away. A new bloke was painting across in the
opposite corner, on panel as far as I could tell at a
distance. No Tonio, either. Placido, motioning me to the
stonemason's screens.

'Start immediately, Lovejoy,' Luciano called.

'Got my wages sorted out?' I shed my jacket and waded
in with the ventilator on above the stone block.

Now I was more or less used to the place and didn't
have Giovanni breathing down my neck I had the chance
to suss the workshop out as I worked.

Definite thump-thump-thump noises passed close to
the brickwork three times during the first four hours or
so. Very near a lagoon channel for biggish boats?

'Most of these things,' I observed to old Luciano when I stopped for a bite after a good couple of hours, 'are paintings. Why's that, pal?' We were now up to twenty, others having arrived one at a time under escort.

'Decisions, Lovejoy.' A shrug which accidentally displaced a mound of his manuscripts. I let them fall. His quill work was good on the Gregorian chant, but the forged paper wouldn't pass as original in a Finsbury pub. He climbed down, grunting, to retrieve them.

'Same old tale, eh? When're we going to do Venice's bronze horses?'

He smiled at that. Not pleasantly, sadly and almost wistfully. I couldn't understand it. Upset, I wandered about, having a bite of pizza and a swig from my bottle. I became more than interested at our team of slaving troglodytes. You could put us into two main groups, stone fakers and painting fakers. I was doing another capital from the Ducal Palace, that heart-rending cycle of love, life and death in tiny scenarios, while a surly unesponsive bloke under another extractor hood was doing a copy of that altar bas-relief from the church of San Trovaso. They simply call the anonymous Renaissance genius Il Maestro di San Trovaso, and a lovely piece of marble work the original is, too. A metal faker was putting the finishing touches to a bronze candelabrum — God knows where he'd slogged over the initial stages; hell of a dust and heat. It had more than a look of the Santa Maria della Salute's piece by Bresciano, though when you think of it, their conditions in 1570 were probably much worse than ours.

The others were painters. There was a rather shifty geezer doing Jac Tintoretto's *Last Supper*, another San Trovaso piece, and I saw Titian's *Descent of the Holy Ghost* in its early stages of fakedom being done at frightening speed by the pimpliest bloke I'd ever clapped eyes on. Long-haired and young, but bloody good. I was delighted, because Titian's original in the Salute has been all but massacred by lunatic restoration. Yes, I definitely approved of Pimple's labours.

It was enjoyable, like having your very own mediæval artist's shop. I was annoyed when one of the overseeing goons came over and warned me I'd idled long enough.

'I know,' I said wearily. 'Get to work.'

The ships which thumped so very close to that brick wall weren't tiny *vaporetti*. They were big double-deckers. And 'island', they'd said. A third clue was the freedom with which they moved and talked between our landing-point and the steps leading down into our underground factory. Which meant uninhabited. Fourth: those taps and scrapes on my elbows, as I was marched to my night work, spoke of an overgrown place, perhaps some once cultivated island which was now abandoned.

As I slogged on the capital, copying from the plaster cast, I mentally cancelled out the far northern part of the lagoon and the more westerly bits. Big ships avoid shallows, and I'd discovered the hard way that those areas were covered in *valli* fishfarms and crisscrossed by perimeter nets.

That left the Lido runs, the island channels like to Burano and Torcello, and the southern bit to Chioggia. I'd never been south, but it must be a longish trip. Now, you don't need to stop and feint to conceal direction on a long boat trip, because you can turn ever so casually over a distance. Therefore delete Chioggia and the south. The Lido is always thronged with beach-hunting sun-grilled skin-peelers. So it was among the islands.

Delete the cemetery island of San Michele—too near, too visited, too much underground to leave room for this vast factory. And cross out the island where Bryon (with a little bit of help from his friends) dashed off his Armenian dictionary, because the resident Armenian priests

wouldn't appreciate our particular brand of artistry.
Delete, too, Saint Francis of the Desert. The legendary
friendliness of the eleven resident priests would convert us
load of crooks by sheer dogged holiness. No quiet
deserted overgrown paths in Murano, because of their
obsessional glassmaking taking every inch of space. Ditto
for Burano, that incredibly pretty 'island of the rainbow
barque', where each house is a brilliant spectacle of
colour and its leaning campanile shows that gravity's all
balls. Torcello? Well, maybe, but tourists and fishermen
and its few inhabitants and that posh *locanda* where
inquisitive visitors can stay . . . No to Torcello.

There were undisguised recesses in our brickwork wall.
Seats, where monks could perch and read their office for
the day. Adding two and two, as I ground out the
maiden's dress in stone, it came down to one island in one
exact spot. I began whistling, to everybody's annoyance.
They all shouted to shut up and get to work. I did,
remembering what the deserted island of San Giacomo in
the Marshes looked like from the boat. I'd seen it with
Cosima as we'd sailed past on the steamer, of course, but
in Venice appearances are entirely for concealment.
Cosima's Law.

Now I had everything, or so I thought. Explanation of
the scam. Knowledge. I even knew who was on whose
side. Now the fur could fly. I worked on more carelessly
than usual, because there were only a few hours left to a
showdown. My showdown, with Signora Norman. As long
as I winkled her away from that viperous Tonio for a few
minutes . . .

'What're you doing?' Giovanni asked me.

'What do you think?' I said rudely, wielding the electric
drill. 'Stone's too soft. It has to be hoisted.' The wretch
called Luciano across just the same. I greeted him with
scorn. 'Please, teacher. May I erect a ribbed hoist, to
double the speed of this idle burke? There's a strong

crosspiece among the heaps of waste materials over there. It'll take an hour, and save us days rolling these bloody stones all over the factory floor. If we've over two dozen to make . . .'

The old man looked at me, then at Giovanni. 'Do you really need one?'

'Answers on a postcard,' I prompted, not pausing, doing a couple of shallow holes in the mortar. 'Get up off your bum and fetch me some of that chain.'

'It would be easier,' my mate said reluctantly to Luciano. 'I'd have put one up before, but I've not really had time.'

That made several of us give a derisory snort. Old Luciano plodded off back to his court-hand script. The guards relaxed. The painters painted. And I went inside my head: now if a wall measures four bricks wide, plus mortar of one inch between bricks, then . . .

'Shut up whistling, Lovejoy,' Luciano called.

'Sorry, sorry,' I called back to everybody. 'Won't happen again, lads.'

That was a dead certainty, for the lot of us.

CHAPTER 24

'Luciano.' I stepped out of the alley.

The old man halted in the patchy darkness which Venice has patented. 'Lovejoy? Is that you?'

The Calle dei Frati leads off the Zattere waterfront. There's always a lot going on at the Maritime Station end. The advantage is that the Zattere is straight. You can see all down the fondamenta paving. Precious few boats at that ungodly hour, though. Twice I'd been disappointed waiting for Luciano, and once I'd startled a lady who was sneaking ashore from a muted water-taxi near the great

Gesuati church. We'd both recoiled in alarm, then snuck on our respective ways. Live and let live. I was pleased that somebody at least was keeping the exotic carnival days alive.

I asked Luciano, 'Are they watching us?'

'At this hour?' That amused him. 'You overestimate their dedication. Once they hand over to the day shift . . .' He stopped and tutted at his carelessness.

So each transfer between boats was a two-way swap. One forger going on duty, one off, the factory continuous.

'And compulsory silence to make sure nobody slips up, eh? What's the punishment, Luciano?'

'For indiscretion?' The old man glanced apprehensively across the Giudecca Canal. An early thousand-tonner was shuffling eastwards towards the Adriatic. 'Nobody knows.'

'Except Carlo, eh?' I restrained him with a hand. 'Where is Carlo, Luciano?'

For the first time he actually seemed tired. His old body sagged. 'Don't do it, Lovejoy. You're young and silly. I'm older, wiser. Money's too powerful. It has given us our orders. It will wreak a terrible vengeance on those who oppose its wishes.'

'Don't be a bloody fool. Money's nothing except its own myth.' There must be something in the air of Venice that makes everybody talk like reading Shakespeare. 'The forgery factory's a send-up, *non è vero?*'

'Lovejoy.' The poor old bloke sounded knackered, standing in the waterfront gloom. '*Do as you're ordered*. Work. Take the money. Do like the rest.'

'I came to warn you, old man. Get out. It's a matter of hours.'

'What can one man do, especially a stupid one like you?' He patted my arm, dabbed his rheumy eyes with a hankie. 'Go home. Sleep. Come to work. That's the way to live.'

'Like you do?' Look.' I snatched his hand and turned it palm up. 'The best manuscript hand I've ever seen. And you work for a nutter like Tonio? You let people get executed and still do nothing?'

Gently he took his gnarled hand back. 'We can only do nothing. Not even run.'

'But it's evil, absurd.'

He actually chuckled. 'It was evil and absurd that a whoring alcoholic horse-thief could rule Russia. But Rasputin happened.'

He walked away, stooping with the grounded gaze of the elderly.

I called after him, 'You've got till ten o'clock, Luciano,' but received no answer. To think, I had my breakfast in a nosh bar. Day was up and boats were really on the move as I reappeared about an hour later feeling quite good. Sad that Luciano hadn't heeded my warning, but at least I'd tried.

The *Eveline* had been moored nearby the previous night. Gone now, but she hadn't been an illusion, though I sensed she represented some sort of threat I hadn't yet reasoned out. At 9.15 a.m. I was inquiring at the *Magistrato alle Acque*, local ruler of the waves since 1501. Carlo was right about the high water, and so was Mr Pinder. Two such flood tides happened annually in the 1880s; there were seven a year by 1930; sixteen frighteners by 1955, and now forty annual dunkings. Long ago the *acqua alta* barely wet the pavement. Now, it could waterlog your belly-button however tall you stood. I learned too of Venice's six round-the-clock water-watchers, and the emergency phone number for tide forecasts: 706-344. I would use it.

I thanked them, and went out memorizing the number and feeling ill.

*

'Signora got the kettle on, Placido?' I halted obediently because he had his vast mitt on my chest. 'She told me ten o'clock, Placido, so don't blame me if you get your cards.'

He hesitated at that, and I walked into the palazzo and on up the stairs. It's odd how convictions alter things. I don't just mean attitudes, or the way people respond. Once you're committed, a curious order takes over as if all is suddenly well once a battle's begun. No indecisions, doubts. Berserk conflict is tranquillity, utter peace of mind and soul. And if the body suffers it's cheap at the price.

It was coffee time in the grand salon. Signora Norman in startling orange, with silver jewellery and a brilliant lipstick. She had me gaping. You have to hand it to these older women. Tonio was unbelievable in clumsy-looking satin gear that was probably the height of fashion. I had the odd idea they were waiting for guests.

'Have I spoiled things? I won't take long.'

Tonio moved his face, smiling his opaque smile. '*Cara*, we simply can't let this peasant continue—'

'The white yacht means Caterina's hit town, I suppose?' I went to the window and looked down at the gondola ferry, already busy across the Grand Canal.

Tonio rose. His expression was exactly that of those newspaper cartoons which have empty circles drawn for eyes. I quickly went and sat by Signora Norman. I'd have to stick fairly close to the truth to survive.

I said kindly, 'There's something wrong with your forgeries, chuckie.'

'Isn't there always?' She was being unexpectedly entertained, so was all smiles.

'He wants Luciano's job,' Tonio interrupted. 'A chiseller. On the make.'

'Luciano said he's good,' the signora reprimanded. 'Continue, Lovejoy.'

I said to her, ignoring him, 'Name any forgery your factory's doing this minute, missus.'

'Paintings.'

'Right.' I drew breath, ready to judge the effect of all this on Tonio. 'Most are doing them wrong, love. Wrong canvas, wrong paints. Wrong brushwork. A kid could spot they're duff.'

'Are *you* so expert, Lovejoy?' Tonio was in his pigeon-toed stance now. His expression became almost human with delighted anticipation. 'Better than all our fakers?'

'You know how long it took us to recruit the teams?' The signora's smile was gone. She got her cigarette in action. I edged away from her smoke and her fury as she surged on. 'Two whole years! And a fortune. The best artists, goldsmiths. The world's greatest woodcarvers, manuscript fakers, stonemasons. From every country in Europe—'

'There's only one worth a groat, from what I've seen,' I interrupted. 'Your scam's clever, love. But it's cack-handed.' I had to turn away from her blinding face. 'Look. You age a canvas *before* you paint it. With a high-intensity ultraviolet light and a thermostatically controlled inspissator you can do wonders to a modern canvas. Yet not one canvas out there has been aged. That Domenico has no idea of brushwork. And he's using some acrylic paints, for God's sake.' In outrage I began ticking off the faults. 'Nobody's even got a smoke-gun for age-colouring new varnish on your fake oils. The woodcarving's done in American pine, a clear give-away—'

'You've not seen any pine carvers,' Placido put in.

'It stinks the frigging place out,' I said contemptuously. 'And that San Trovaso altar bas-relief's supposed to be marble, not light-weight crap made up of laterite dust, Polyfilla powder and polyurethane varnish. Fakers gave that trick up decades ago. And why no watermarks on the paper? It takes a skilled antique paper faker about ten minutes to knock up a class watermark.' I nudged the signora offensively. 'You're so proud of inventing Italian traditions about cocktails, Signora. Watermarks really *are* a local tradition. Right from the thirteenth century Italy was streets ahead. The Arabs, Japanese, Chinese, none of them could do a class watermark till modern times. And they gave me York stone, far too light, to fake the Ducal Palace's carved capitals. Want me to go on?'

'But we proved it, Tonio. Our reproductions are faultless.' She sounded puzzled. In a minute she'd move to worse anger as my news sank in. I rose apologetically, ready with my explanation.

'I know we did, *cara*. That's why Lovejoy's a fraud.' Tonio was practically quivering with eagerness. Placido carefully put the door to and turned to face me. War.

'You mean that auction? Your Carpaccio painting?' I smiled, but my knees were beginning to wobble so I rose and walked to the window. Tonio nearly fell about at that, thinking I was sussing out an escape route by a Douglas Fairbanks leap. How wrong he was. Even the thought of all that risk and energy made me palpitate.

'Why, yes.'

'Didn't Tonio or Caterina tell you? That the wooden stretchers weren't properly plugged?' I lied. Actually, they'd been reasonable. 'That the canvas was obviously modern?' It had actually been well aged. 'And the varnish could have done with a little more nicotine discolouration, especially over the—'

'Lies!'

The doorbell rang, halting Tonio. It rang, rang, rang. A furious knocking on the door accompanied it, non-stop. My relief-sweat broke out. I almost fell down. For a million panic-stricken heartbeats I thought the *traghetto* ferry men had simply taken my money and welshed. She could learn the horrible details now.

'Is it lies about the murders, Tonio?'

'What murders?' The signora's cigarette smoke was vertical.

'Two antique dealers. They also spotted the flaws. Malleson, Cramphorn.' In the din from the door I kept my eyes on Tonio but was speaking to the signora. By a lucky fluke I found myself standing behind the settee. A born coward.

'He's making it all up, Lavinia,' Tonio said.

'Am I? Signora. Phone any East Anglia newspaper.'

She put a hand to her temple, trying to concentrate. 'That *noise* . . .'

'It's the fire, police and canal ambulance out there,' I explained cheerfully. 'I bribed the gondoliers to phone and give this address.'

'Get rid of them. Both of you.' The signora rose and crossed to the window. The palazzo's door into the *campo* was not visible from inside the room. I'd checked. 'Explain that it was some stupid tourist's hoax.'

Sadism reluctantly postponed, Tonio and Placido left me with the signora. I let them get half way downstairs before I spoke.

'Actually it's only the *traghetto* blokes. I bribed them to make a hullabaloo.'

She had to smile despite the new worries I'd given her. 'You're a pest, Lovejoy. You know that?'

'Not without trying, Lavinia.'

'And all this about the two murdered dealers and the fakes. Yet more annoying tales?'

'Come to my apartment at noon, Lavinia. I'll tell you what's really happening to your scam. And who's out to ruin you.' I gave her Cosima's address.

Her eyes were shining. 'I may not trust you.'

'Don't bring Tonio or Placido. Nor anybody else. I don't trust you either.'

The downstairs racket was lessening. Time to go. I

crossed the room, shutting her in behind me and turning away from the landing which overlooked the noisy hallway. It had to be left turn, and down past the dumb-waiter. That had given me the clue to where the kitchen was, directly below somewhere, and inevitably the back staircase which accompanied it. Which meant access to the low arches of the palazzo's canal exit I'd inspected from the nicked gondola that other night.

Incredibly, a stout oldish bird was amiably cutting stuff in the kitchen as if the world was normal, when I passed. She was caterwauling a song accompanying a radio. One more floor down, and I was through a dampish doorway into the sleaziest, longest and wettest cellar you ever saw. Talk about damp. I looked through a grille which emitted a feeble yellow.

He was sitting on a small camp stool beside a bed, his face averted from the grille set in the door. It was bolted on the corridor side. A patrician's dungeon, practically inaccessible and frighteningly private.

'Luciano? It's me. Lovejoy.'

He didn't even move. There was a small table lamp. He didn't look as if he'd been knocked about, but I was peering in at an abject picture of utter defeat.

'I'm undoing the bolts, mate.'

There were three. I tried the door and it opened, but by then I was so frightened at the vague thuds transmitting themselves through the palazzo's structure that I scarpered quickly along the passage and unbolted the end door. It had an old tumble lock. No key, but anybody with a wire in his turn-up can unlock it as fast as with the right key.

Beyond, that narrow set of steps and broad daylight on the canal. The barred portcullis-type gateway between me and freedom was still down, only inches from the surface of the water. It meant swimming, ducking under the portcullis and emerging into the open canal in full sight of anybody on the nearby bridge.

I waded down the steps until the grotty water was up to my middle. I drew a deep breath and plunged.

CHAPTER 25

It was predictable. Within two hours I was dry, free and anonymous as ever. Looking at it now, my public re-emergence from the canal's dark grot was a scream. Of course, anything's hilarious as long as it isn't yourself slipping on that comical banana peel, but on this occasion I needed to play the clown. I clambered out of the canal into an assembly of a few tourists and the stray Venetian, talking nineteen to the dozen. Two laughing Germans even took my photo. In the pandemonium I gave different versions — fell in photographing the bridge, tumbled in after a few drinks, etc. Rueful and grinning, I sloshed my way to the Giardinetti where I sat in the garden and watched folk queue for their loo tickets. Lots of cats and bonny trees — and me, drying out. Odd, but once you're seated you tend to vanish even if you're extraordinary. Stand up, and people are all attention.

At a different tailor's I bought a T-shirt and had them bag my stuff for carrying. Because I now had no need to hide from Cesare and the other water-taxi men, I walked quite openly to the Zaccaria and caught a waterbus.

The Australian butterfly painter, dreamer Gerry, was on board in the standing-room-only middle bit.

'Wotcher. Still at it, eh?' He looked rather heavily daubed and was carrying his gear, to everybody else's discomfort.

'Lovejoy! Where did you get to? Poor Cosima! We searched for you, you know.'

'Oh, all over with now. Cosima's great, off to

convalescence,' I reassured him, at which he sho
relief. No questions after my health, mean sod

'Keith's playing with one of those dredger eng
Murano. He'll be sorry he missed you. Are you
supper?'

We chatted all the way. They had sha
somewhere near the station, after returning fro
('Queer light for painting in Padua, and no
Gerry gave me their address. We said so-long
undying determination to meet for a drink, the
do. Honestly, I was pleased at having met a
neutral for once, and kept thinking of Keith's f
for engines. An artist is a poor sort of ally, bu
with a dredger is a different matter.

At Cosima's tiny apartment I had a bath,
defilthed, and was flitting anxiously about th
calli when midday struck.

Ten minutes later, with me all but demer
depressing convictions, a gondola tapped its h
on the nearby canal and a woman's heel-clic
through the *sottoportego* archway. Alone, I wa
silhouette take colour as Signora Norman eme
the shadow. The gondolier pushed away,
warning 'Ioooo' at the sharp corner. The gor
looked genuinely fresh from its three-weekly tar
was probably innocent, not some cunning pri
ballasted out with an armoured division. I stoo
in the little *campo*.

'Hello, Signora. This way.'

She was amused because I peered in every
'You're like a little boy playing Indians.
frightened I'd bring Tonio?'

Derision's a woman's chief weapon, probably
always works. 'Deep locked cellars are fine for
and Luciano. Not for me.'

'Tonio was furious with me for letting you go

'I'll bet. Erm, excuse me, please.' Red-faced, I fumbled
with my wire and let us both in. 'Sorry about the
shambles, but I haven't had a minute lately.'

'Night work, I suppose,' she said evenly. Women
entering somebody else's home look about with peculiar
intensity. 'Is this *it?*'

'It's nice,' I shot back, irritated. 'No dungeons.'

'You mean Luciano?' She walked about, swishing her
finger along surfaces and distastefully rubbing the dust
away. They always make you feel to blame for everything.
'Tonio explained that Luciano came with some tale of
you making trouble. Placido had him wait downstairs—'

'Like they did Carlo?'

'Who on earth's Carlo?'

'Never mind.' She was probably not in on Tonio's
detailed arrangements—like life and death. 'Erm, would
you care for a drink, signora?' I had this little tray with
two glasses and a bottle of cheap wine. It was decked out
with a few small carnations in a cup, though I'm normally
on the flowers' side.

'How kind.' She sat in a wicker chair, clearly still
slumming. Suspicious she was taking the mickey, I waited
for the guffaw at my floral poshness but it never came. I
was glad of that, and poured the wine with only the odd
shred of floating cork.

'Who is she, Lovejoy?'

'Eh?'

'The woman so conveniently absent.'

You have to admire a woman like that. Never been
here before, and instantly she spots that its a woman's
flat. Clever. It's a female knack.

'Oh. A friend. She's not here now.'

'She forgot to leave you her key.'

'Careless,' I agreed, working out how to start. 'But
you've been a bit careless too, lately.'

Actually her presence was worrying. There was none of

that naturalness which Cosima brought, that inner shining. Older, with a brittle quality which somehow overlay her wealth. She knew she was beautiful, which intensified her as if her movements announced: I have power, you peasant—bring me more. Uneasily I remembered that it was in a nearby palazzo that poor old philosopher Bruno was betrayed to the Inquisition—by his patron, of course, in true Venetian tradition. You have to watch friends.

My remark had touched some nerve. 'I'm never careless.'

'Indiscriminate's careless.' I gave her a filled glass. 'Your scam must have seemed as foolproof as Mr Pinder's.'

She looked into wine. 'There's only *one* plan, Lovejoy.'

'No, love. On the one hand there's your dad's plan—forgeries galore, replace Venice's fabulous stuff as you go along. All,' and I couldn't help smiling, 'for the very best motives, preserving the treasures for when Venice sinks. Then there's *your* plan. Very different. Your plan requires teams of expert movie people to make advertising videos of the fakes and the nicked antiques, right? In a score of different languages for marketing in different countries.'

'I'm simply carrying out Babbo's orders—'

'Not you, love. Not once you'd shacked up with Tonio. Was it his idea to defraud your dad's syndicate, and keep the originals? Or yours?'

She smiled beatifically. 'Mine. I have a safe house in Tuscany.' She did that breast-tilting shrug I was coming to know and love. 'They're morons in Tuscany, but what choice has one?'

'And instead of taking them to the refuge Mr Pinder's syndicate had organized you'll send the counterfeits? Naughty girl.'

She took a swing at me, blazing. 'Don't you lay that

tone on me, Lovejoy.' I only just escaped another clout as she spat out, 'Or your word *counterfeit*. Everything's counterfeit, or didn't you know? Belgium exports counterfeit heart pacemakers, for Christ's sake. France counterfeits wine. Italy exports counterfeit car brakes, even counterfeit medical drugs. Britain exports counterfeit jeans. America's mass-produced counterfeit African tribal designs for ages—the Yoruba, Kuba and Senufo have never got a bent cent in royalties. Taiwan counterfeits spares for Boeing jets, Cartier watches, every damned thing.' She was breathless, heaving with fury. 'Want me to go on?'

'And you'll have hundreds and hundreds of originals?'

'Only some originals, Lovejoy,' she pouted. 'The best ones.'

She sounded so indignant I had to laugh. After a startled second she laughed with me. That really set me off. We sat there like fools, falling about, wine spilling so much she squawked and held her glass away to save her skirt, and that made us howl all the more.

I roared till my ribs hurt and I lay spreadeagled at the sight of the lovely bird, helpless with her eyes streaming and her luscious shape skewiff in the chair. Just when we'd start subsiding, one or other of us would gasp, 'Only *some* originals,' to set us off wheezing and choking with laughter.

Gawd knows what Cosima's neighbours thought.

As it turned out, Cosima's neighbours kept their thoughts to themselves. If they heard anything at all they showed no sign, not even later when the little bed thumped the wall under the stress we inflicted on it, Lavinia desperately shushing us by shoving her hand, still erotically gloved, between the headboard and the wall but to no avail. Her ungainly attempt set us laughing again so much it nearly made us ill. Sooner or later I'd have to make a list of the enemy, complete with reasons, but for the moment Lavinia's softness was all over me and I'd other things on my mind.

Eventually after love we slept, Lavinia giving occasional moans as the laughter's ache returned now and then. Just before I fell into oblivion, I tried hard to work out why the hell she didn't know the real truth, but with my head warping her soft belly and my sweat drenching our sticky slumber I hadn't a chance. It's an odd fact that oblivion is better shared. I remember thinking how this truth in itself was a problem. What I wanted for the next two days was no friends and no lovers, and with luck I'd manage to pull off my own private scam. Instead, I leap into bed with the naked — you can't count gloves — boss enemy and develop this weird feeling that she and I are on the same side after all. Typical.

'I thought real Venetians didn't use gondolas.'

'Only in extreme necessity. They're a diminishing breed.'

We were at the canal by the arch. The approaching gondolier couldn't believe his luck at getting a fare. I tried not to remember that Lavinia held Tonio's arm exactly like she was holding mine.

'Do I report for work tonight?'

'Certainly not, darling. It's suspended for two days.'

'Any reason?' I tried to sound thick, but I knew the *acqua alta* was coming.

'Don't bother your head, darling. I'll be here with you tomorrow, after breakfast. You'll receive further orders then.' She descended grandly and took her place. 'Your flower is artificial,' she reproved the man severely. Gondolas have a little gilded vase fixed near the prow. Its carnation was plastic.

'Apologies, signora,' the gondolier bleated.

'Genuine is infinitely preferable,' she said primly. The gondolier gave a puzzled glance at my snort of incredulity, and even Lavinia looked round in surprise. She caught sight of my expression and got the joke.

Her laughter echoed along the chasm of the narrow canal and reverberated under the pretty bridge until the gondola was out of sight. I remained there, smiling reflectively, in case she had second thoughts. When I was dead certain she'd gone I streaked off over the bridge and down the narrow *calle* in a hell of a hurry. I needed Cesare urgently. And Keith. And Caterina. And I was due at my own private funeral by midnight.

When you need friends, where are they? Or even enemies. Cesare was nowhere, the bum. Two solid hours it took me, zooming exhausted around the Riva, searching. I asked Ivan the Terrible, who only laughed. I spent a fortune on water-taxis and gondolas. I even crossed hopefully to the Giudecca, and funds were becoming dangerously low.

Eventually, would you believe, I found him half-sloshed in that same bar down the Garibaldi laying down the law about a football match to two old geezers doing mental battle about who'd buy the next round. He was practically pickled and glared blearily up at me when I accosted him.

'Cesare!' I made sure I looked elated and breathless. 'Congratulations. Come quickly, mate—'

'Eh?' He peered, and chuckled. 'Oh, Lovejoy.'

'Help me!' Pulling him to his feet wasn't easy. The old blokes blinked while I tapped Cesare's face. 'You drunken sod. We've got tenth prize in the Irish Lottery! Come *now!* Where's your boat? The money—' At the magic word, the Venetian catalyst, three elderly blokes and the young barman had Cesare up and out in a trice.

'It's down the Garibaldi, signore. This way.'

Another geriatric propelled me along at a sprint. Everybody fired questions about the money, the lottery, the money, as we tore through the market to where Cesare's water-taxi rocked in a small *bacino*. I told my eager helpers Cesare and I had equal shares.

'Lucky I caught sight of our names on the board,' I gasped, flopping into the boat. 'Don't know how much, but . . .' Willing hands cast us off amid shouts. Cesare's drunken attempts at the controls were too much for the spectators who were frantic at the thought of escaping gelt. Two of the bar blokes got us going and reversed fast to the intersection so I could turn.

I yelled thanks above the roar and was off, with Cesare giving a boxer's triumphant handclasp and falling over. The crowd babbled satisfyingly on the *rio*.

'Lovejoy,' Cesare cried in a drunk's thick voice. 'Where's my ticket? I've not lost it, have I?'

'There is no ticket, stupid burke.' Boats go faster than they seem. It was hell to control, trying to rear up out of the water. I had to put her down to walking pace. A hand clamped on my shoulder.

'*You* got my ticket, Lovejoy?'

'No,' I said wearily. I'd have to go along with him until he sobered. 'A lady's keeping it for you.'

'Where? Where?'

'I'm not exactly sure. In the *Eveline*, a big white yacht. It *was* on the Zattere . . .'

Drunk as a newt, he determinedly took the controls then. I was glad and sat back. I didn't want time to be too much of a problem. After we found Caterina I'd need every second.

Boat people are funny. Drunk or sober, they can manage very well thank you. Like antique dealers, really, though on the whole we're ignorant of our pursuit whereas boatmen know all about fathoms and other nauticals.

Exactly two hours later, after umpteen shouted discussions with other boats and a long run down the lagoon, we found the *Eveline* wharved among smaller leisure fry in Chioggia.

Beginning of the end, you might say, I thought as we stood off and looked at the great two-masted yacht from the lagoon. For whom I wasn't quite sure, but it was coming, almost within reach.

CHAPTER 26

'Chioggia's the *enemy* port,' I once heard a Venetian explain, nastily referring to some long-vanished barney at the bottom end of Venice's lagoon. It's very different. Venice is as unplanned as tangled wool. Chioggia by comparison is mathematical, its canals practically straight and the bridges predictable. The mediaeval Chioggians knew their trigonometry.

Cesare had sobered by the time we hauled into port. He of the bloodshot eye and bleary gaze no longer believed the tale of my invented lottery. During our dash southwards he'd sussed that I was still labouring in some criminal vineyard. That put him in a foul mood. I was really pleased about that. It meant Cosima was being as distant with him as she'd been with me. Served him right, surly sod. Cosima had judged him to a nicety, even if it was odd how little she trusted me. He hovered us off the wharf while I gazed at the lovely vessel and schemed.

'Park down the canal, okay? Be in that café.'

'Moor,' he groused. 'Cars park. Boats moor. Any more orders, Lovejoy?'

'It's all in Cosima's interests,' I explained sharply.

'It had better be, Lovejoy. What *are* you up to?'

'Look, mate. If you won't help . . .' I stamped ashore and marched along the narrow *fondamenta*. Why the hell people aren't more trusting I'll never know. Just because I'd nicked his girl, ruined his happiness, tricked him about a lottery, wasted his day and conned him into assisting my criminal enterprise was no reason to get narked. I ask you. Where's trust gone?

Here in Chioggia the *Eveline* assumed a wholly disproportionate grandeur, a cathedral visiting a shanty town. Stooping with reverence, I walked its ridged gangway and knocked politely. Ship doors always look misshapen to me but I suppose shipbuilders know what they're doing.

The cabin was hangar-sized after Cesare's titchy boat. I'd never seen such floating opulence. Modern gunge, apart from an expensive small Malayan dancer carved riskily from stained meroh wood, but all of it costly and therefore full of messages to the world's poor. Malaysian meroh wood's usually reserved for the planks from which those Red Sea dhows are still built, so it took a particularly skilled ancient carver to tackle that length of grain —

'Tonio! Darling!' Feet clattered and Caterina practically tumbled into the cabin. She'd been washing her hair and was wet and turbanned. And astonished, and then furious. Her female mind instantly blamed me, because she was the one who'd misunderstood.

'Well, not quite darling. Only me.' Even messy she was beautiful.

She hated me, as usual. 'What are *you* doing here?'

I had to make something up, now I suddenly knew everything. 'Erm, is Mr Pinder with you, please?'

Her lip didn't quite curl. 'He stayed home, like the little piggy in the nursery rhyme.' She towelled her hair, thus casually stating that appearances didn't matter for the likes of Lovejoy. 'Grandad's too old to come out much any more. I want to know why you're here, Lovejoy.'

'I came with a message for anybody who . . . represents Mr Pinder's interests.'

That spun her, stopped the towelling. It put naked alarm into her eyes. The fear was clearly for Tonio.

I thought, Well, see if I care; and said, 'I've been working for Mr Pinder's scam, night shift. I called round at . . . Signora Norman's palazzo.' To hide my near-mistake—I'd nearly said Lavinia—I crossed the cabin and peered at the wharf. 'You see, Caterina, I think your grandad's being fobbed off with inferior stuff. Deliberately. I told your mother that.'

'What did she say?' Still frightened. The picture was becoming clearer. Hard-hearted vicious nympho Lavinia was looking purer by the minute.

'She didn't believe me. Slung me out.'

She smiled then without fear, resumed towelling her head. 'So you came to tell me.'

'Naturally,' I lied, now just wanting to get the hell out. 'I can give you proof.'

'You would.' She stood before a mirror, fluffing her wet rats-tail hair off her nape. 'Has it ever occurred to you, Lovejoy, that you're an arrogant pig? You always right, everybody else always wrong?'

'Be at the island about midnight,' I said through a throat suddenly gone thick. First time I'd told any enemy I knew where it was. 'It'll be empty then. Tonight's our night off. I can show you what I mean about the antiques.'

'Why me?'

'Nobody else I can trust, is there? But come alone.' Dangerous to look into her mirrored eyes, in case she spotted that I'd guessed her sudden new plan, so I moved towards the cabin steps. 'It wouldn't be any use telephoning Mr Pinder. He wouldn't believe me. And I've not enough money to stay here any longer. Your mum's lot hasn't paid me yet.' I spoke the last bit with honest bitterness, which pitched everything safely at a proper level.

'I might come.' Her mind was going like a racing pigeon. Tonio had a real ally.

'Want me to call here for you?'

'No,' she said quickly. 'Somebody can boat me over—if I do come.'

'Right. I'll have everything ready. You'll see.' I made the steps to the outside world.

After a quick check to confirm that Cesare's boat was really and honestly moored outside the canal café where I'd said I'd meet. him, I trotted off in the opposite direction. Now back to Venice, leaving him stranded and completely out of the picture. About time Cesare'd done something right for once.

Gerry and Keith were in a fine old sulk when I got to their place. They'd rented a garret straight out of *La Bohème*, not quite as tidy. It was only then, seeing them arguing, that the penny dropped, and Cosima's faint blush whenever they came up in conversation tipped off my stupid mind. I looked at the two fuming Aussies thinking, Well, well. The row was something about painting.

'It was a perfectly *innocent* remark, Gerry.' Keith pushed me to a chair while Gerry broke out the wine. Neither said hello. I said wotcher, and sat there feeling an interloper.

'No remark's innocent! Is it, Lovejoy?' Gerry demanded, white as a sheet and glaring at his mate.

'Erm,' I quavered. I was in crossfires of my own.

'That's right! Side with *him*.' Gerry fetched a glass, pointedly leaving Keith's on the tatty sideboard.

'I wasn't,' I said quickly. 'Honest.'

Keith's turn to go all frosty. 'Oh? So *I'm* in the wrong! Is that it?'

I began to get a headache. 'Honestly. I don't even know what it's all about—'

Gerry went all dramatic. '*He* said I should paint

engines instead of butterflies. Would you stand for *that* poisonous remark, Lovejoy?'

'I said nothing of the *kind*, dear—'

'You *did!* I distinctly *heard* you.'

Christ. People say they're worse than women, don't they?

'Keith can't have meant it like that, Gerry,' I said in an inspired moment.

'Then how *did* he mean it?'

'Erm, probably, erm, that your talent should, well, conquer new fields . . .'

'Lovejoy's right, Gerry. You *know* you're better than you think.'

Gerry was mollified. 'Am I?'

' 'Course you are,' Keith said. 'Plain as silly old day.'

'Really? Honestly?'

Keith rushed the bottle over to us, and it was end of World War III, thank God. We drank to Gerry's new career as engine artist and chatted amiably about the merits of oils and egg-tempera. Gerry was impressed, once we got talking, because I knew how to transfer Old Master oil paintings to new canvases. We all finished up slightly merry, which suited me because I was keeping a frantic eye on the wine and the time and working out how to get round to the all-important question of doom.

'I'm so glad we met up again,' I confessed eventually. 'Cosima's glad, too.'

They were pleased. 'She is?' Keith popped another bottle. 'Nice little thing. Wrong clothes, of course, and scandalously thin feet for wearing cage heels. Be sure to tell her that having no dress sense isn't her fault.'

'I like her, too,' Gerry added. 'You've made an absolutely marvelloso choice, Lovejoy. Remember, you don't actually have to *look* at her dreadful blouses. Somebody said she cooks, though women can't. Can she do kibbeh?'

'Think so,' I guessed hopefully. Sounded like swimming.

'We *must* try them.' Gerry gave a beatific smile. I'd have to warn Cosima to be on her best culinary form that night. Nobody gets criticized like the cook at the best of times.

'It's a date,' I said. 'Not too soon, though. I've an engine problem.' So much for tact.

'Engine?' Keith unglazed. 'What engine?'

'Somebody I know wants to, erm, borrow a powerful boat.' I scraped together a little circumspection. 'Any idea where I, er, he could get one?'

'Of *course*!' Gerry nudged Keith into a reply.

'How fast does it have to go, Lovejoy?'

'Not speed. Strength. Like those stone-lifters.'

'A working dredger?' Keith really lit up. His subject.

'Something like that, I suppose.'

'Funny. I've just been giving two of those a good going-over,' Keith said.

'Astonishing coincidence,' I agreed gravely.

Gerry refilled Keith's glass, giggling. 'Know what I think? I think naughty old Lovejoy didn't come just to see us. He was only after our dredgers.'

Keith was looking wary, mistrustful swine. 'Hire, Lovejoy? Borrow? Or . . . ?'

I cleared my throat and peered into my empty glass but Gerry stood there holding the bottle. Both were watching me, exchanging glances. No good mucking about.

'This friend of mine was wondering where he could, well, get on to one that's, well, moored. Just interest. No, er, need for anybody to spot him. Like the two near the Sacca Serenella, in Murano.'

'See what I mean, Keith?' Gerry relented with the plonk. 'Watch him.'

Keith nodded, still suspicious. 'They're blocking the wall near the Canal of the Angels. Istrian limestone.'

'Look, Keith. How strong are they? Pulling.'

'Depends what you—your friend, I mean—wants to pull. Suppose this glass here is a pile of pine, like they use . . .'

He was off, frowning with concentration, moving crockery and matches about the coffee table and muttering lunatic technology. I settled back with relief. These amateur enthusiasts are great. No, really. I mean it. Daft as brushes, every single one, and boring as algebra, but great. All I wanted to know was if there was a night watchman and how to work the damned thing.

'Paying attention, Lovejoy dear?'

I looked up into Gerry's sardonic gaze. 'Of course,' I said, at my most innocent. 'I'm really quite interested in engines.'

'Don't you mean your *friend* is?'

'Erm, sure. My friend.'

Gerry tapped Keith's wrist. 'If you lend Lovejoy one of those filthy machines, dear, make him promise to put it back, won't you?' He smiled roguishly. 'We don't want the police calling here spoiling our breakfast.' Keith fell about at that. Some private joke.

Yet it was an important point. Keith must be well known as the keen amateur who had been dissecting the bloody dredgers, and police jump to nasty conclusions.

Keith abandoned his gear ratios. 'Would tomorrow do, Lovejoy? Your, ah, friend could come over with me. The foreman's a sweet bloke.'

'My friend hasn't much time,' I said. 'It'd have to be tonight.'

Keith ended the long pause by saying, 'You—he—can't see much of the engine in the dark, Lovejoy.'

'He'll manage.'

'There's an *acqua alta*.'

Suddenly apprehensive, Gerry sat beside Keith. 'The sirens will go soon, during the night. The radio said.'

'Dredgers don't work on, in a high water.' Keith was asking a question.

'But one could, right? And nobody'd see.'

Gerry suddenly said, 'Don't ask Keith to go with you, Lovejoy.'

'Go where?' I demanded indignantly. 'Look, Gerry. Have I said anything about Keith going anywhere? Well? Have I?'

Gerry had a hand on Keith's arm. He'd gone white. 'Send Lovejoy away, hen. For his own sake. He's a bad dig.'

I said disgustedly, 'Keith. Just tell me how to move one of the damned things, and I'll do the best I can.'

Keith tried, 'Don't get upset, Lovejoy. Gerry only meant—'

Hamming away, I kept it up, all brave and quiet and hurt. 'Honestly, there's just no trust anywhere nowadays. I didn't come here to drag you into my troubles. Tell me quick. Is there a guard, and how do I switch the bloody thing on?'

Over Gerry's protestations Keith began to explain, gradually submerging in his subject. Gerry glared all sorts of despair at me but I ignored the silly nerk. I wish I'd been cerebrating, because things might have turned out different, but all I could think was, If Keith won't nick a dredger and bring it to the island dead on time then I'd have to do it myself. None of it was my fault. God alone knows why people keep blaming me.

Listening to Keith, I took notes.

CHAPTER 27

The No. 5 vaporetto emitted its departing roar and left me standing on the rocking boat-stage in the night. God, I felt forlorn. I had a stupid urge to shout after it, try a flying leap as it churned away. Daft for a grown man, but those vague Venetian mists can give anybody the spooks. The canals and bridges have a weak bulb or two bragging haloes but they don't seem to deliver the light where it's actually needed, and the occasional distant chug of an engine and the warning 'Ioooo' of the gondolier make it spookier.

The Madonna dell' Orto church square was empty. I made sure by strolling round, pretending the aimlessness of the tourist to an old lady who creaked into the gold-glowing church doorway for a quick spiritual high. Venice was retiring for the night. The canal was a street of black oil, what I could see of it. Above, scudding clouds soaked in moon kept me rain-guessing. It wasn't my scene, especially when I got near the funeral place.

I needed to steal a funeral barge, and they were placidly moored facing the church. The trouble is, there's no real school for thieves, is there? How do you suss out a canal in a night mist? Twice I walked across the bridge which marked the end of the canal, and peered hopelessly out into the dark blanket covering the lagoon, imagining I saw the distant lights of the cemetery island of San Michele. The Sacca della Misericordia turned out to be a big rectangular stretch of water facing north-west, the way I wanted to travel. It was as handy an exit as ever I was to find now I was having to do every bloody thing alone as usual. I walked back towards the church, keeping close to the wall of the doorways and touching drainpipes, not wanting to vanish with a splash.

Nowadays even posh antique dealers, like most other criminals, use those little disposable Keeler pen-torches, and I carried two. The light just about made it to the wall. I climbed over and dangled cautiously from the church bridge. The bridge's own single bulb was practically useless. A good stabbing night, when you came to think of it. Uneasily trying not to think at all, I replaced my pen and swung to and fro from my hands till I was sure of the momentum, and let go. I hit the foredeck of the funeral gondola with a hell of a loud thump, nearly braining myself on one of its little gold decorative lions. But I'd made it. I clung and looked about.

From canal level the bridge looked impossibly far out of reach. Visibility was pretty bad, worse than on the canal bank. I could see the wall of the funeral building, of course, the winch, the double doorway. The bridge's feeble bulb. The narrow pavement opposite, and vaguely the oblique gold blur of the church's doorway. A single lit window in one of the terraced houses across the canal. That was that. Above, the moon showed but too irregularly to be much help.

I clambered along the gondola. Behind it, a larger boat was moored, and beyond that the indistinct darker mass of a third. It looked as if I'd collected a funeral gondola and two funeral barges. A fleet.

A funeral gondola is rowed by sad gondoliers, but a funeral barge is a wide motorized thing, maybe thirty or so feet long. It has a kind of well where you stand to drive between two glass-enclosed cabins. There are tidy little white lacey curtains lending elegance to these cabins. Uneasier still, I shone my torch to see I wasn't accompanied by any terrestrial beings before making sure the starter motor could easily be fired by slitting the insulation in the same old way. I'd have to trust it was fuelled up. The Volvo-Penta service station, about a hundred yards down and on the right, would presumably have its own night-watchman to guard petrol supplies. I undid the ropes, swearing because they'd got wet somehow, and pushed off.

It was only then that I noticed how high the water was. I barely scraped under the bridge, poling away with the nicked pole. The water had risen. Not only that. It was moving. Mostly canal water just hangs about. One push on a pole and your craft careers along until something stops it. Not now. I was struggling just to gain headway. I even heard a gurgle as water eddied past, coming in from the lagoon to lift the canal even higher. The barge moved with sedate grandeur bumping into the wall of the Palazzo Mastelli with a nasty hollow sound which frightened me to death and re-echoed for a million noisy years.

It's only about a hundred yards from the church to the Sacca, but it felt like a circumnavigation. I was reduced to giving two desperate long pushes, shipping the pole and trying to keep the barge going forward by manhandling her along the canal wall. That worked once or twice, but I was scared of rousing people. Even the most tranquil Venetian would be alarmed at the sight of a stranger's claws emerging from a mist-bound funeral barge to scrabble at his shuttered windows.

I knew the stone bridge had arrived when I bonked my forehead and got a mouthful. The barge just made it beneath, at the expense of a cracked glass pane or two as it scraped under the arch, but by then I was too worked up to care. I was late, and I still had to start the wretched boat and get across to the island.

Visibility across the Sacca was worse, if anything. The Volvo-Penta fuel depot's light was barely visible. No lights showed out in the opaque blackness of the lagoon. Christ, but it felt spooky. I'd assumed lights, direction easily found, maybe that ironic moon being some use. Me in control. Instead, I was floating blind and becoming terrified of letting go of nice solid stone. Once out there it'd be hit or miss. I tied the barge to the bridge's balustrade and had a crack at the starter motor. You won't believe this, but the engine was going a full minute before I realized it. The boat was shuddering slightly and gently butting the bridge's arch while I like a fool kept on trying to start it. Unbelievably quiet. It was a wonder I hadn't electrocuted myself.

For a split second I dithered. Then Caterina and her tame psychopath came to mind. And the fortune in fakes they were going to double-steal. Plus some originals. All those desirables going to undeserving nerks was a tragedy. I discovered I'd cast off without thinking.

Okay, I thought. Sod it. In for a penny, in for a pound. I turned the tiny wheel. My great one-speed barge trundled out into the void. I hoped there was water out there.

Caterina kept coming into my mind. She had everything—looks, youth, wealth, intelligence, that commanding manner which proved true breeding. Normally I'd have been grovelling near her ankles. But here I was, risking life and limb in a pathetic attempt to do her down. Surely it wasn't because of Cosima? Or was I subconsciously so hooked on Lavinia after today's carrying-on that I was talking myself into saving her skin at the expense of Tonio's? It was all too much for my addled brain. I concentrated on not knowing where I was instead.

The moon stayed where it was, thank God. Even when it was cloud-obscured I could get an idea of its direction by the glow. That mist was really odd, dense patches which suddenly thinned or ended, leaving my silent runner quivering its nose towards a thick blob of the stuff.

It made the lagoon surface change, too, into a pasty kind of translucent oil. Until then I'd assumed I knew everything about fog.

This was rotten stuff all right. Worse, a siren went, almost frightening me out of my skin. Presumably the high water was on its way, and here was me still a million miles — well, nearly four — peering anxiously at the bright fog-glow which indicated the Fondamenta Nuove where the big Lido steamers lay. Counting to a quick hundred to allow for getting past the monastery (it's a barracks now, sign of these ugly times) I swung left and knew myself heading for San Michele.

Venice's marine engineers aren't daft. It would be cheaper and simpler to put these lights on floating buoys or shorter posts, but you'd lose them in this dense lagoon mist. They've worked it all out. As long as you know where the last one was, and the next one should be, you can keep going fairly accurately by staring upwards and slightly wall-eyed until the mist begins to glow on your retina. That's how you follow the chain of lighted blobs across the dark water. It's quite an art.

The channel forks past Murano where the St James Marshes start. Right, a baffling course to the sea through stretches of marshy islets. Left, more or less direct between two lines of marker lights towards Mazzorbo and Torcello. I knew from my terrified checks of the marker lamps that, in the vast open expanse between Murano and the islets, the lanes of double lights ended. They became single, and finally the smaller channels had none at all. Where they continued, though, they would show to the right. That gave me a file to move along.

The island didn't actually surprise me much, though even an unsurprising island can scare you a bit when it moves swiftly out of a pitch-dark fog. I remember yelping, flinging the barge into a dangerous turn and cutting the engine. Speed lost, sweat wiped from my streaming face, and I was shakily in control again, able to take a mental line from the moonshine and the one mark-light still visible. Somehow I must have come up on the channel side of the island rather than the western aspect because I thought — or imagined, in my fear — I'd glimpsed a less dark rectangle set in brick. Possibly the relief of the Madonna which tourists competed to photograph as the steamers pounded past. The pale stone patch had looked disturbingly near the water.

Apprehensive, now with more to worry about than merely getting lost on a foggy night of the dreaded monster tides, I put the barge at a silent glide along the southern approach.

San Giacomo's a low island. Soldiers occupied part of it until 1964. The nearby Madonna del Monte had a munitions factory, but I'd guessed from what I could recall of seeing the gaunt derelict building that it was just too obvious for old Pinder's scheme. From some parts of the lagoon you can practically see nothing else. The San Giacomo's a different thing altogether, and I could remember the rough vegetation overgrowing the few low red-tiled buildings, as seen from the boat to Torcello. The island's unused landing-point was the stepway beneath the Madonna relief. Round the side might be a grottier but often-used landing-stage which my feet might just recognize.

Once you leave the main channel, you're lost. No lights. Heart in my mouth, I set the funeral barge creeping at right-angles to my original direction. Bravery shouldn't feel like terror, yet in my experience it always does. I was so sure I was being heroic. The island is more or less rectangular, so I knew the barge was nosing through the fog a matter of mere yards off the shore. Scared as always, I fancied just then that I heard a soft thud from out there in the misty blackness, but froze until I was certain no boat was approaching. The question was when to turn inwards and meet the island to find the landing-stage. Seven times my prow, with its golden two-winged ball and little lions, nuzzled to a stop against a solid dark island. Seven times I slipped her in neutral and crawled forward to push her off before resuming the journey. The eighth time I found nothing but a level step all awash, and a low brick-supported archway with tendrils and small clattering pods dangling in the opening.

That was a measure of the appalling height the tide had risen. As far as I could recall, they had made me climb steps. Now they were all awash. All height is relative. Everybody knows that. But any increase is bad news when you're looking for some underground factory.

Some things were on my side: my barge was black and quiet, and Tonio wouldn't come with lights blazing. He'd come with stealth like me, the smarmy bastard, determined to rely on unfairness in a fight. That meant my boat might remain undetected if I tied her close inshore further along. This I did, moving by grope till I found a rickety post about fifty feet from the submerged landing-stage. Caterina might come alone, in which case it was a waste—only partial, but still waste. But like all women, she could have done the natural feminine thing and lied in her teeth.

The island was silent. The path felt right. I risked the Keeler torch, crouching to peer at the ground and trying to guess directions. Even the vegetation felt right. It was great. The watch I'd borrowed from Gerry—at least they'd lent me that, I thought bitterly—showed one hour to Caterina's arrival. For Caterina read Tonio.

Being alone on a derelict island isn't good for one's nerves. For a lily-livered no-good like me it's terrifying. The place through which I was creeping was obviously some kind of derelict vegetable garden, with stupid shoots trailing about and the path crumbling. A couple of times

I came close to brick walling, one with broken or shuttered windows. Either monks or military. Originally, when blindfolded, I'd counted my paces. I wasn't to know there'd be no need. The path led only to one place.

The doorway was steel, rivets driven in at its sides and its two padlocks reinforced by a welded steel plate. The purist would have been disappointed at these feeble precautions. I was relieved and delighted. Of course, there was normally our full-time night shift of industrious fakers busy in the subterranean forgery factory, and two or more murderous men watching over all. It was only on such a night as this that guards would seem superfluous.

Nothing looks more daunting than a padlock, and nothing's easier. If you've got one on your garden shed, try picking it with a thick hairpin. Some come simple, like this first one. Five seconds. The second had some combination rollers I'd never seen before, so I sawed it through with my hacksaw — always carry the smallest and cheapest, incidentally. The door gave, beautifully oiled.

Funny feeling, seeing a familiar corridor for the first time. We'd all been blindfolded, of course, but I wasn't prepared for how narrow the corridors were. I put the door to, and followed my little torch. Finding a handrail just where I knew it always was, by the steps, was somehow astonishing. There were no other obstacles, no alarms, no angry shouts. Two careful minutes, and I entered the subterranean factory. I was in possession. Exactly as I'd planned.

A quick look round. Everything just as left, fakes in various stages of completion, each faker's position showing his own particular level of tidiness. All predictable and well. My wall-plate had not been disturbed, thank God. I slung my jacket and started work.

CHAPTER 28

A couple of tallow lanterns did for light. Domenico, hamfisted as ever, aged his handiwork by tallow smoke. Only the Cantonese still try that kid's trick nowadays, which shows you the level of my fellow fakers' expertise. Duckeggs.

In our stonemasonry corner I'd drilled a steel plate, head-height and as wide as a man can stretch, nothing more than some old shoring batten left by the military. Now it was pinned into the thick wall by four long steel bolts. From its face projected three metal pegs. Ostensibly it was a simple reinforced lifting device. To me it was one gigantic cork. If anything pulled at it from outside, a hell of a gap would appear in the cellar wall, and maybe the wall would go with it.

Nothing like fear to make you crack on speed. I used a cold chisel to bang out the bricks, levering with a crowbar and flinging the debris anywhere like someone demented. One brick to either side, top and bottom. Then another between. And another. When I could reach my arm round behind the big steel batten, I was satisfied. Then I set to weakening the wall still further, slamming the chisel into mortar, peppering my face with brick fragments.

There came that ugly moment when the mortar in one of my new recesses grew damp and started seeping water. I drew off with a terrified yelp. Like a fool, I even began cramming bricks back to stop it before I realized my stupidity and made myself pause to think straight.

Every faker of Old Masters carries packets of childrens' balloons, to hold his pigments. They're a godsend. They can be tied at the neck. They're waterproof, airproof. They're cheap, lightweight. They don't crack or shatter, so buy a bumper pack and you can match the balloons with the pigment each contains. The cleverer the forger, the neater he is. I easily blew up a whole bag of Domenico's to about a quarter of their capacity so quick I went dizzy. By now I was going like the clappers and reeled a bit as I tied the balloons to a string, a long multicoloured chain. The string I fastened to a strong cord, and the cord to the metal chain. I fixed its free end to a metal peg on my plate.

Now for the nasty bit. I'd no idea where the water level normally came to on the outside. All I knew was it would be hellish high out there now. Shaking scared at the possibilities, I procured one of the polythene tubes from Luciano's rolls of painting canvas. They're about four feet long, and wide enough to take the chain. The balloon string went into it easily, trailing the rope and chain. There'd be a hell of a squirt from the water out there, so I collected great bags of clay from the sculptors' enclave across the factory floor, and made sure it was handy. Then, all ready, I slammed my chisel into the seeping mortar and tore the half brick out.

The water shot me off my perch like a popgun going off. The horrid filthy stuff cascaded into the cellar with such force I was slithering screaming across the floor, scrabbling for a hold to stop myself. I was lucky not to have been brained. Panicking at the near-destruction I'd cause, I avoided the violent rush and climbed up underneath it to see what I'd done.

My hole into the lagoon was about as big as my palm. Enough for the tube. The water which had clouted me so savagely was merely a thin spout, as if from a hose. Not much, but it leapt over my shoulder and hit the cellar floor about half way across. I lifted the tube and got drenched shoving the damned thing into the waterspout, driving it in. Naturally the chain and my balloon rope was washed out so I had to do the whole thing again.

That's where my time went. It must have taken all of half
an hour to fix it in place, the seeps sealed with clay and
the edges of the tube held with nailed battens. I was a
wreck. The clay packed the tube, so no seepage from
that.

Out there on the surface of the lagoon, beyond the
cellar wall, there now bobbed a string of multicoloured
balloons. Easy enough for anybody to find. I could have
done with a kip, but drove myself to make certain my
chain was securely fixed to the steel plate. Once that went
it'd need more than Lovejoy with a handful of clay to stop
the water flooding and sweeping in, rising . . .

'Agh.' I'd yelped, scaring myself even worse, but only
for a split second — it took me just that long to grab my
jacket, blow out the tallows and dash out of that now-
vulnerable cellar, with its puddles of water and mini-
workshops crowded along its walls like huddles of untidy
market stalls. Even so, leaving that mass of fakes and
forgeries there, some hopeless, others not really too bad,
was a pang, but I've always found that terror's a better
prime mover than petrol ever was.

Odd, but I felt clean in my funeral boat as I did the rest
of the job. Even though I knew that time had gone faster
than my plans wanted, I was somehow content. Almost
confident. I found the balloon string by creeping the
barge along the building's lagoon wall and dangling over
the side with my Keeler torch practically on the water.

Still in that extraordinary mood of euphoric contentment when it seems nothing can possibly go wrong
and everything's going right, I cut the engine and gently
hauled the balloon string aboard. The chain came into
my hand. I hauled as much aboard as would come.
About eight feet, until the chain stopped with a jerk and I
knew it was holding taut on my steel plate in my
weakened wall. I cut the balloon string and rope and
airily chucked them overboard. Let some seaborne sleuth

work that one out when they were found bobbing mysteriously on the briny. More cavalier still, I let the little stern anchor go overboard and used its shackle to fasten the chain to the barge's stern. Now my barge would stay there for sure. No worrying nautical complexities to worry about.

But where was Keith? And the dredger?

Phase X of my plan had depended almost entirely on Keith nicking a dredger and bringing it over to the island. Fix chain to dredger, drive off and out comes the steel plate bringing half the cellar wall with it. Cellar flooded, and the subterranean factory would be submerged forever in a torrent of lagoon. That was the idea. Do Tonio in the eye and leave old Mr Pinder's scam untouched, if not vastly improved. If it wasn't for Keith, the idle sod. He was probably paralytic drunk back in Venice by now. I'd have to nick the dredger myself now, once I found some way of fixing the chain in some prominent way. Then I'd use the dredger's engine to pull the plug, and home to report to old Pinder and reap a richly earned reward. Pity about my stone carving, but I didn't mind too much because I'd signed *Lovejoy fecit* with the date to entertain any future archæologist who came diving through the nuclear fallout in years to come . . .

A dull boom sounded. Long, long pause while I waited and tried not to worry about it. An echo from one of those wailing sirens which sounded so mournfully out in the black night? That boom. *It was in the building.* I thought, Christ! Just when I'd been feeling all confident.

Cut and run? Every neurone snapped into action sending tingling messages of escape. I even found myself fiddling with the controls. Then I thought. Caterina. Okay, so she hated me and loved Tonio. So she was double-crossing stepmother Lavinia who made me laugh and promised me much. And so she possibly knew that

Tonio was a psychopath, possibly even knew he had done for Mr Malleson and old Crampie. But the cellar was a deathtrap. And what if she honestly had turned up, on her own in good faith, like I'd said? I thought, Oh hell. Just my luck. From perfect confidence I was plunged back into my usual dither, all because of some stupid noise. I'm pathetic, I told myself, pulling on the chain so the barge bumped against the brickwork and I could climb into the entrance above the plaque. My brain felt back-combed. I was completely befuddled, all reasoning gone. Don't think I'd fallen for Caterina. I hadn't. I'm not that daft. Just because a bird has everything and can't stand the sight of a bloke doesn't mean he can't take a hint. And so what, if she has a boyfriend who did for Mr Malleson?

The trouble was I hadn't come in this way. I'd sneaked in on the other side of the island. The steps were deeply awash and my feet sloshed nastily in my shoes, making silence difficult. The wretched lagoon was slurping greedily ever higher, bloody thing. As if I'd not enough to worry about.

Cursing everything, I fumbled round the wall, inching as if on a ledge. I actually might have been, for all I knew or could see. There was comfort in the notion that I could always find my way back to my funeral barge by simply following the wall until I hit.

A vague golden glow showed brightly to my right and I squelched a pace back. A light. It moved an instant, then was gone. I'd been in the entrance to the factory, not realizing I'd got that far, and the light had been flicked on briefly, as if from a torch. *Somebody was in there.* And that somebody was being damned quiet. I'd used the same trick myself with my Keeler, partly covering its light with the fingers and putting light ahead for an instant at a time.

I was almost on the point of deciding to scarper when I heard a low murmur. A man's voice. And a low laugh.

Another murmur, receding. They were moving along the corridor and down into my—their—cellar. Still I hesitated, scared, but the logic was inescapable. I knew they were in there. They didn't know I was outside. And I knew for certain there was no other exit except the corridor and this external door. *I had them.*

Exulting, I slipped my shoes and socks off, felt round me, and put them beside the door. No need to risk my mini-torch now. The glow down the corridor leading to the underground factory came more frequently, now they felt more certain they were unobserved. *Was* it plural still? I slid after them, palpating surfaces for stairs, handrails, any landmark at all as I went. They were in the cellar now with no attempt at concealment.

'He's tried to make a lifter. See? On the wall.' Placido? Or . . .

'What for?' Now that *was* Caterina's voice.

They were inspecting my handiwork.

A laugh. 'Hoping to lift all this to the floor above. Poor fool. The high water has defeated more than him.' Another laugh. At me, of course. Not Tonio's voice, though.

'Where is he?'

'On his way. No need to worry.'

'Come here.'

Then silence. The torch came on, stilled. No movement. Had they sensed me?

Out in the corridor near the metal door I listened in a fever. Caterina and a bloke, that's for sure. But why the stillness? And they'd gone very, very quiet. Maybe I should just cut my losses and get the hell out, leaving them to it. A faint regular sound, like a distant tapping, struck my ear. Worried, I glanced back along the corridor but it seemed to be coming from inside the cellar where Caterina was. And a—what?—a distant but steady beat of noise. As if of a rhythmic exhalation, even a grunting.

I peered round the door like a kid in a comic.

Cesare and Caterina were together down there, oblivious. In the torchlight their copulating shadows moved metachronally, explaining the rhythmic beats. Caterina's legs were splayed to take a grip of Cesare. Her arms clasped him. Her mouth was on his as he beat into her on the long central table where the artists and sculptors argued continuously over space to put their materials. Cesare. And—in—Caterina. Not Placido. Not Tonio. Or all the lot of them?

For an instant a voyeur's curiosity delayed me, almost fatally. I'd no idea clothes looked so ridiculous when couples were taken by storm, in the act as it were. I'd assumed they only got into a mess afterwards somehow. But there was a gun on the table near Cesare's hand and I saw sense.

'Sorry,' I said, as the door slammed and I dropped the great metal stave to lock it. I meant the sudden noise.

'It's Lovejoy!' came audibly from Caterina a moment later. I moved a few steps away up the corridor in case he shot that damned thing.

'Yeah, me!' I called. 'I see why you were so glad to know where Cosima's convalescing, Cesare.'

He laughed, actually laughed. 'Placido's on a little Sicilian trip, Lovejoy. Don't think she'll make a complete recovery.'

'When did you take Caterina's shilling, you pig?' I blazed. 'Right from the start or only recently?'

'What you'd sneer at as patrimony we know as duty, Lovejoy.' He wasn't at all discomfited. 'You'll learn soon enough that others have the same honour.'

'Caterina!' I yelled, to shut the bum up. 'Did you know Tonio was going to do Malleson and Crampie?'

'Oh dear no!' she trilled, all little-girl.

Even as Cesare roared with laughter I thought: Surely she can't be joking? Not about people getting killed.

'Are you sure?'

'I'd never have let him go back and keep on hitting him that way, Lovejoy!' And she too laughed.

I turned and left them to get on with it, sickened.

'Thank you for locking me in with a lovely lady, Lovejoy!' Cesare's shout was just audible as I reached the gloom, fog and obscurity. My natural habitat.

Maybe my distress made me careless. Maybe I walked straight ahead for a few dazed steps. I honestly thought I turned the correct way coming from the exit door, but after a few steps I stopped and tried to backtrack. It was hopeless. I finished up crouched down feeling for the edges of the path. No good. I was lost.

Stupidity's an art. It seemed best to me, at that daft moment, to crouch down and pad round in small circles feeling as I went. Logically, move in increasing-sized circles, and you sooner or later touch on the place you've lost, right? Well, it's logical if you go in precise circles. Do an oval or a spiral and you're more lost.

The last thing I wanted to do now was use my Keeler torch, in case Tonio was already here. Cesare had sounded too confident. And all that shouting. I fell down, over a mound of soft earth among the vegetation.

Feeling more carefully, I tried to work it out. Somebody had been digging. Recently. A patch maybe big enough to bury a sizeable load of antiques? My hand touched an instrument. I lifted it. A hand-hoe. Something left by a monk, or the recent digger? It would be at least one way of getting back at them all, if I were to nick whatever it was they'd hidden. Possibly their most precious fake or antique. I decided to risk it and scrabbled at one end of the mound. Maybe six feet by three feet, possibly a good-sized original statue that wouldn't hurt from the water now ploshing about my ankles and seeping into the hole I was scuffing. An obstacle. I'd found something. Grinning evilly and whispering to myself, I put out my hand and felt. Definitely features. A face. Definitely configurations of . . . a face. Pliable. Soft. Waxen softness of eyelids. A fucking *face*. Whiskers . . . I screamed, screamed, and clawed babbling and screaming away from Carlo's face and ran crashing into every bloody thing and anything, flinging myself demented and still screaming through bushes with the aid of the hand-hoe and splashing through the encroaching water, leaving that ghoulish grave behind me in its solitary nightmare. Shivering and retching, I ran blind, the wavering blur of my Keeler light which I'd somehow got out doing more to make the fog opaque than show me the way.

A pane of glass cracked underfoot. A tendril lapped round my neck and I howled, terror-stricken. A building hit me. I reeled away, tried to find those precious bricks again, couldn't, and ran and ran. A tree, its roots awash in rising waters, shot out of the fog and dazed me as we collided. I screamed and wailed, reeling. Somebody told me to stand still and put my hands up. I screamed in terror and tried to run.

A hand grabbed my shoulder. I saw this figure. He looked immense, looming out of the fog like a Disney giant. I struck out with both hands, felt my hoe send a shock up my arm and struck again and again in the darkness because my light had gone. I ran, flinging the hoe into the space where the figure had stood. And ran until the water was up to my knees, and there was only stillness and the water. There was no direction, nowhere else to go. I was a ruin, breathing and coughing like a spent horse and weeping and whining at the whole frigging mess, hands on my knees and the black water rising.

God knows how long I stood there before I did the only

sensible thing I'd done since I came to Venice. I put my
head back and bawled, '*Help!*'

And blessedly, out of the wet night, quite close, came
Keith's voice delightedly yelling, 'Lovejoy! That you,
blue? Keep shouting, mate! We're on you!'

And lights began to glow as I bawled and bawled.

CHAPTER 29

We worms of this world can't look heroes. I tried my best
to seem noble while Tonio died on the dredger where
Keith and his two burly mates had finally managed to
carry him.

I could hardly look. He was covered in blood where my
hoe had dug into his neck, his cheek, his temple. It was
Gerry, astonishingly along, who did what could be done
for him. In the brilliant light of the great dredger's cabin
everything was ghastly. Blood and mud everywhere. But
even in all this, Caterina had to get away.

'Caterina knew about you killing Mr Malleson and
Crampie,' I said. 'She told me.' It came out like an
accusation. I'd meant to sound kind. 'You had to do
Malleson. Mr Pinder had hired him to recover that
Carpaccio fake. He'd guessed about you and Caterina,
hadn't he? And your plan to cheat Lavinia as well as his
syndicate.'

He smiled, oddly friendly for the first time. 'She was
there, Lovejoy,' he explained. His voice seemed oddly
chatty, no hard feelings.

'Where?' I said blankly.

'She's left-handed. Ask the witnesses.' His neck ran
brown blood. Gerry thrust me aside and did something
with a folded white square that instantly bloomed bright
scarlet.

'What's he saying?' one of Keith's burly dredger pals said irritably.

'I'm not,' Tonio informed us all in quite a conversational tone, and died in silence.

'Not what?' the dredger bloke demanded. He was annoyed with practically everything. I wondered what it all had to do with him.

'Not left-handed. He was telling us.'

'What the hell!' the man said. 'He died?'

'Poor, poor thing!' Gerry was in tears, kneeling beside Tonio on the cabin floor. 'If he hadn't been so hacked about . . .'

Christ, I thought, faint. It would have been *me* otherwise. Tonio had a frigging gun with him. No wonder Cesare and Caterina had laughed. Chains rattled outside.

Keith consoled, 'Don't cry, Gerry dear. Please.' A call sounded from the outside man and his mate yanked a lever and put the wheel over, probably turning us or something. Tonio's body rocked a bit.

Hopeless. Me nearly demented, frightened out of my senses on an island being flooded by the highest tide ever recorded, blinded in a fog, stumbling on buried corpses all over the frigging universe, attacked by an armed psychopath, and Keith tells Gerry please don't sob. I felt sick.

'Listen, you burke,' I said to Keith. 'Why the hell were you so late?'

'The fog. We were watching the island, but—'

'Watching?' I said, furious. The chains rattled. The outside bloke shouted in a slow shout. 'In *this*? I said eleven o'clock.'

The dredger's motor gunned. The cabin gave one shake as we began to move, and a sudden jerk. The driver swore.

'We couldn't come any earlier,' Keith said, apologetic. 'We had to call at the Rio dei Greci for permission.'

'Eh?' I began wondering if Keith was off his nut. There's nothing down there except the water police depot.

'Oh, Lovejoy!' Gerry sobbed. 'I *said* don't come out here tonight!'

'I'm so sorry, dear,' Keith consoled Gerry. I looked at the steersman for enlightenment, but he was preoccupied with something outside in his fog-blind searchlights. The big dredger lifted an inch, maybe the tide turning.

'What's he on about?' I asked Keith, suddenly uneasy.

Keith gazed fondly at his mate and explained, 'He's so tender-hearted. He feels things so, Lovejoy. And you're under arrest.'

'Eh? Me?'

'You.'

'Here,' I said queasily. 'You can't do that. Can he?' I added to the steersman.

He finally took notice of me, as he swung the wheel frantically. '*Si*, signore,' he said bluntly. 'And so can I.'

'Oh, Lovejoy,' Gerry wailed. 'I *said*.'

And he had. Don't go, he'd said to Keith. All the time he was pleading with his pal not to betray me.

'And your interest in these dredgers . . . ?'

'We kept the island under surveillance from the dredgers. They're the only vessels always left out on the lagoon. Come hell or *acqua alta*.'

'You a cop too?'

'Art squad. We both are.'

'We knew something's been going on, Lovejoy,' Keith explained, his arm consolingly round his pal. 'A bit amateur, really. None of the regular art thieves would be so careless. We never even find a trace of the London-Amsterdam teams. They're still the greatest thieves.'

'So you've been watching us all?'

'Fakes were appearing all over Venice. Stumbled on them by chance. We had an idea it was Tonio and maybe his grand signora—'

Tonio. Caterina. I tore out of the cabin to stand helplessly in the grotty fog-bound air. And saw the funeral barge trundling along astern from a towing chain.

'What's that?' I yelled to the burly man at the rail.

'Only the funeral barge you stole,' he said reprovingly. 'We were lucky to find it. It had fetched up against the wall—'

'Did you untie it?' I could hardly speak the words. 'I chained it to . . . to . . .'

'Thought there was a bit of a pull.' He shrugged. 'But what's an anchor worth on a night like this?' No wonder the wheelman had been struggling to control the dredger. He was wondering what had made it temporarily difficult to get moving. Oh Jesus.

They turned the dredger back when I managed to convince them. All we found was a caved-in building just submerged by a tide that had laid almost the whole island awash. No trace of a living soul. Caterina and Cesare were buried, under the ruins, and under the tide.

My idea had been to release them in daylight, select the best fakes, and exit laughing as I pulled the plug, destroying all trace of my filching. All I'd done was do for everybody else.

CHAPTER 30

The villa was set off the road a hundred yards or more. It looked pretty, absolutely colourful and charming. A tennis court, a swimming pool. A splendid orangery in true Victorian style. A delectable little enclave of vines climbing up ornate trees. And a walled kitchen garden.

'This it?' I actually felt pale. The car journey from

Mestre hadn't made it any more pleasant, sandwiched between Keith and Gerry, those two eccentric expatriate members of the Antiques Fraud Squad.

'This is it, Lovejoy,' Keith confirmed, poisonously cheerful.

'*Bellissima, non è vero?*' The police sergeant who had accompanied us was delighted it looked so fetching, as if he was trying to sell me the damned place.

'*Si, signore,*' I said courteously.

'So many amenities!'

'All securely netted, wired, walled.' It was a prison.

The sergeant looked despondent. 'So much money in antiques.'

'It's that rose-coloured wallpaper,' Gerry whispered to Keith. 'I'm just not sure.'

We walked in. The gate was wrought-iron, head tall, and gave a telling double click to shut.

'Before you case the joint, Lovejoy,' Keith informed me in proudly dated slang, 'your duties are to be available at eight-thirty each morning.'

'Where's the trial?'

'No trial, Lovejoy.'

I presumed he meant to give evidence. 'See the lawyers?'

'Not that either. You're going to do an honest day's work, Lovejoy. Every single day.'

That shook me badly. 'Look, Keith, mate. If you can pull a few strings . . .'

'No way, old sport.'

'It's to do with antiques, Lovejoy.' Gerry ushered us all into the living-room and waited hopefully for praise. I gave his decor a surly nod. His face brightened as if I'd exulted. 'Keith's done a deal with the police.'

The villa seemed full of crummy modern gunge. 'Signora Norman's villa is just over the hill,' Keith explained.

'A very beautiful, attractive lady,' the police sergeant put in huskily.

'You go there every day to examine the four caches of assorted antiques and fakes which the signora had distributed all over North Italy. They will be brought under escort . . .'

Scheming bitch. She'd told me one houseful. Still, Lavinia wasn't bad company, even after all this.

'And I will divvie them?'

'Too right, Lovejoy. The signora also came to agreement with us.'

'Come and see the kitchen!' Gerry cried excitedly. I trailed dejectedly after.

'How do you know I won't cheat?'

'A video film record will be made of every single antique. By a special film unit. We arranged it with Miss Nancy Waterson.'

'She too is a very beautiful, attractive lady.' The police sergeant's voice was huskier.

'True,' Keith said, staring into the distance while I tried to look ecstatic at Gerry's kitchen design. 'We chose her because Signora Norman once engaged them for making her private advertising movies showing what stolen antiques she expected to have on sale.'

'And, erm, where'll Nancy be, erm, based?'

'Oh, around,' Keith said.

'And I want no criticism from her about the bathroom tiles,' Gerry warned. 'I sweated *blood* over those. Come and see.'

We trooped after him. He extolled the hallway and the special windows on the way.

'Great,' I echoed morosely into the bathroom.

'*Not* avocado, note,' Gerry said proudly. 'I *hate* that colour.'

'And how long's this arrangement to last?'

'Six months in the first instance, Lovejoy. Renewable.'

'That's a sentence.' I was sussing out the grounds. I

was trapped in a bloody fortress.

'True.' Keith nodded to Gerry, pleased. 'I think he likes it, Gerry.'

'Do you think so, dear?'

'And Signorina Cosima,' Keith added as he plodded after Gerry who had squeakily decided we were to inspect the bedrooms next. 'She'll be here.'

'*Eh?*'

'A very beautiful, attractive lady,' from the sergeant in a husky moan.

'Well—' Keith shrugged—'we have to keep an eye on you both. Why not together? After all, you were . . .'

'And we do approve of her,' Gerry reminded us all. 'Not like that bossy cow who's just arrived.'

I was getting a headache. 'Erm. Look, lads. That makes, er, four.'

'You asked us to cable her,' Gerry said through pursed lips. 'When you wanted all those lawyers and thought you were going to gaol.'

'Connie? Here?'

'In Venice. She can visit you each evening.'

'A very beautiful, attractive . . .' the sergeant moaned.

Forty miles. Bloody hell. Lavinia over the hill, thinking me hers alone. Nancy nearby with a camera she would doubtless brain me with. And Cosima here in the villa frying up spaghetti pasties. With Connie who'd strangle me for just glancing at any of the others.

'Now the garden!' Gerry trilled, eyeing me keenly. 'This way! You're falling for it, aren't you, Lovejoy?'

Dear God. I'd not survive a day. How the hell do I *get* in these bloody messes? My heart was banging at the battles to come.

'What a good idea!' I cried, following Gerry. 'Yes. Let's see what sort of plants you selected!'

Gerry went ahead, anxiously watching my face as he listed the wretched fronds in the ground. I alternately frowned and beamed to keep Gerry on edge, and we walked along the perimeter path.

Between fleeting changes of expression my eyes roamed the surrounding countryside. A road ran along the nearby slope, and a path led up from the edge about two furlongs from the villa's tennis court.

'And these fuchsias, Lovejoy.'

'Lovely, Gerry.'

'I *knew* you *would* love them!' Gerry cried, calling the splendid news to Keith, who was watching me with narrowed eyes. The sergeant was lost in secret raptures.

'And over by the pool?' I prompted.

'Yes, well, lace-cap hydrangeas have such a riot of blues I almost went out of my tiny little mind . . .'

'A beautiful blue,' I said, pausing. 'Chrysanthemums?' If I could nick an antique piecemeal, and conceal it bit by bit near this perimeter fence, I might be able to get over the wire one dark night, and lam up that path — but there was a police patrolman having a smoke on his motor-bike up there. Hell fire.

'Pansies, Lovejoy,' Keith explained sardonically, suspicious swine.

I smiled. 'I just had to stop. My favourites.'

'*Are* they, Lovejoy?' Gerry gushed. 'Oh, thank *heavens* we decided to put some in that border!'

'They grow well, don't they, Lovejoy?' Keith was still watching me.

'Great.'

'Especially since the wire fence carries an electric current.'

Gerry saw my face. 'Positively *no* harm to your flowers, Lovejoy dear. We've been into all that.' Gerry gave Keith a sharp glance. 'Don't you start worrying Lovejoy, Keithie, there's a dear.'

'A car!' The police sergeant brightened. A red Acclaim was bowling over the hill, the way we'd come.

'Two.' A second car hove in sight.

'Your friends, Lovejoy,' Keith said. 'Here they come. All your little helpers.'

'Er, great,' I said in panic, thinking, Now if I could nick a tin-opener from the kitchen, I could maybe use it to fuse that frigging wire fence while the cop is mesmerized by the birds . . .

'We'll be off, then.' Keith and Gerry moved.

'Erm, look, erm,' I tried. 'Any chance of a deal . . . ?'

'Aren't you going to go down and say hello?' Keith said innocently.

'Not yet. I'll stay here a minute.' Maybe Earth would collide with Saturn or something.

Gerry's eyes filled. 'With his pansies! Oh, how sweet!'

I could have trampled the bloody things. In a desperate sweat I was working out: Now if I got Cosima or maybe Connie to sunbathe one day, then while the cops were mesmerized I could nick one of the antiques and cut the current and steal out . . .

'And the patrol police are on four sides, Lovejoy,' Keith called from the gate. 'Give them a wave now and then. To show you're still here. 'Byeee.'

I could almost swear the bastard was still suspicious of me. Why is there no trust in the world any more? Why is it that we trustworthy honest folk always come a cropper and everybody else gets away scot free? There's something wrong somewhere.

A car pulled up and a motor cut.

'Lovejoy! Darling!'

'Hello, love.' Smiling, I quickly developed a limp and went to embrace Cosima while the second car came nearer and nearer. She looked well and beautiful. 'Look,' I whispered to her. 'Can I go and lie down, sweetheart? And be left strictly alone? Only, I've had an absolutely terrible time since I saved your life in that lagoon . . .'

THE END